Published by Accent Press Ltd 2018
Octavo House
West Bute Street
Cardiff
CF10 5LJ

www.accentpress.co.uk

ISBN 9781786155344
eISBN 9781786155337

Printed and bound in Great Britain by Clays Ltd,
Elcograf S.p.A

Published by Vision Press Ltd 2018
Peacock Books
Wrightington ...

© ...

The right of ... to be identified as the
author of this work has been asserted by ... in accordance
with the Copyright, Designs and Patents Act
1988.

... All rights reserved. No part of this publication may be
reproduced, stored in a retrieval system, or transmitted in
any form or by any means, electronic, mechanical, photocopying,
recording or otherwise, without the prior permission of ...

ISBN ...

Printed and bound ...

Before we Fall

Grace Lowrie

C016631455

For Mum,
I miss you every day.

The desire of the moth for the star,
Of the night for the morrow,
The devotion to something afar
From the sphere of our sorrow.

– Percy Bysshe Shelley

Chapter One

I didn't cry when the doctor gave me the news. I didn't gasp or swear – I certainly didn't faint dramatically as I got up to leave – I'm not one to make a fuss. As I left the hospital I smiled at a man who held the door for me on my way out. I suppose I was in shock. It was April the first – April Fools' Day – and the joke was on me.

It was Wednesday evening. I caught the bus back to town so that I could attend my weekly ballet class – whether it was tap, salsa, belly or even pole dancing (I had tried them all), dancing was the one thing that always made me feel better and I could definitely do with the distraction today. Sitting in my favourite window seat in the back corner, I watched the familiar streets of Wildham appear. The trees were bursting with fresh green leaves despite the chill in the air, and a recent shower made the hedges, grass verges and benches sparkle as the sun peeked out near the horizon. The town I'd grown up in looked as safe and homely as ever. The birds sang in the trees and the residents quietly went about their business as the bus rolled by the garden centre and the White Bear pub on our way towards the cobbled town centre. Everything looked the same, but inside I was different – changed forever.

'One of my sitters has really dropped me in it,' Marguerite said as we sat side by side pulling on our ballet slippers in the changing room. 'Bloody Craig was supposed to be covering a six-month placement, but his boyfriend surprised him with a holiday and he's dropped out last minute! There's no way I can get anyone else for a long-term placement at such short notice, and until I do I'll have to go there myself every day, just to pick up the post, water the plants and feed the bloody fish!' Marguerite and I had been best friends since nursery school. She was bright, bossy and opinionated; the sort of person who instinctively knew what to do, what to say, and what to wear in any given situation. Without her friendship I'd be lost. And yet, for the first time I had real news to share, and I hadn't told her. Telling Marguerite would make it real. She would leap into action, seize control and take charge; she would be on the side of the doctors – the experts – of course she would. But that wasn't what I wanted. I saw what chemotherapy did to my grandmother – watched it destroy her slowly and painfully, day by day; crushing the light out of her until she had no life left…

'I'll do it,' I said, surprising myself.

'It's not as if I haven't got enough on my plate what with all the new clients we've taken on recently…' Marguerite continued, standing up and scraping her chestnut curls into a bun at the back of her head with a stretchy hair band, '…and Craig was one of our best – I can't believe he's done this to me.'

'I'll do it,' I repeated, adjusting the elastic around my foot and flexing my toes.

'What?' Marguerite stared at me, hands on hips, one eyebrow up. Even at 5'4", there was something very intimidating about her.

'I'll take the placement; I'll house-sit for six months.'

2

'Oh bless you, Cally,' her eyebrow lowered and she went back to fixing her hair 'that's very sweet but the flat isn't here in Wildham, it's in central London.'

'I realise that, but I fancy a change of scenery.'

'But... no... what about your job? It would cost you a fortune to commute back and forth every day, not to mention all the extra travelling time. The company pays for my season rail ticket, but they can't afford to cover the travel expenses of a sitter – that's why we only recruit locally.'

'Actually I was thinking of leaving my job – taking a break from that, too.'

'What?!' Both eyebrows were up now. 'Why?'

I shrugged. 'It's boring – you know that – working in a call centre was never my dream career.'

'I know but... what's going on?' She perched beside me, clutching my arm in concern. 'Is everything OK between you and Liam?'

'Yes, Liam's fine – same as always – this isn't about him.'

'What is it then?'

'I just want to get away for a bit – try something different – I've always fancied writing a book; maybe this is the perfect opportunity.'

Marguerite cocked her head to one side. 'What are you running away from?'

'I'm not,' I lied. I had never lied to Marguerite before. It was stomach-churningly easy. I pushed the feeling aside. 'Look, you need someone to house-sit in London for six months and I want to get away from here for a bit –

3

problem solved.' She knew for sure I was hiding something, but she was also desperate.

'It doesn't pay all that well…'

'That's OK; I'll figure something out – maybe get a part-time job.'

'And the property isn't one of the plushest on our books – it's a two-bed flat at the top of an office building – so the area's practically deserted at night…'

'Sounds ideal for writing – nice and quiet.'

'Oh my god, are you really sure about this?' A cautious smile of relief spreading across her face. 'Do you want to talk it over with Liam first?'

'No. My mind is made up.'

'OK – I'll have to take you over there, talk you through everything, and there'll be some paperwork to sign… when do you think you could start?' It was almost Easter and the thought of spending the four-day weekend trapped at home with my boyfriend and my diagnosis seemed like a prison sentence.

'How about I meet you there tomorrow morning?'

'Really? That would be marvellous.' The muffled sound of ballet slippers tapping against floorboards indicated the start of the class, and I followed Marguerite into the large mirrored studio. As I took up a position facing my reflection I couldn't help noticing how normal I looked – entirely familiar and unremarkable. And yet the girl staring back at me was a stranger now. 'I'm shocked by your spontaneity, Cally – I'd never have guessed you had it in you!'

'No, me neither,' I muttered under my breath, averting my gaze.

I was weary by the time I let myself into the small terraced house I shared with Liam. After our warm-up we'd practised complex pirouette and allegro enchaînments until we were sore, but at least Marguerite was kept too busy to interrogate me further about my sudden change in plans. I'd never kept anything from my best friend before, and if she pushed too hard, I knew I would cave and tell her everything.

'Alright, Love? Good class?' Liam called from the living room as I hung up my coat. I stuck my head round the door to find him sat in his favourite armchair, as usual, watching the TV news. Visually my boyfriend was a giant – a hulking great six-and-a-half-foot tall, broad-shouldered, furrow-browed rugby player, who physically filled the tasteful interior of our rented home with muscle, heavy footsteps, and the earthy scent of wet grass. And yet he was the gentlest, sweetest, most considerate man you could ever hope to meet. He worked locally as a gardener with his brother, Lester, and lived quietly – keeping his thoughts to himself. He was handsome in a natural, outdoorsy sort of way, with short dirty-blonde hair and warm brown eyes, and he was steadfastly loyal.

'Yes thanks.'

He glanced up and smiled at me, the fondness in his expression was habitual, but no less genuine for all that. 'Good. Your dinner's in the oven.'

'Thanks,' I said, swallowing back a surge of guilt and ducking back into the hallway.

'Salmon and new potatoes,' he called after me.

'Sounds lovely,' I replied, my voice wavering slightly. In the kitchen I fetched a glass of water and stood at the sink gazing out across the neat back yard to the shadowy trees beyond. My waiting dinner smelled delicious, but I had no appetite.

There was no denying that I was lucky to have a kind, considerate boyfriend who loved me and cooked for me. And I loved him too, of course. We'd been together a long time – nearly six years – and our life together was comfortable, familiar, settled. Like being asleep. That was how it felt now. I hadn't really noticed before, but since this morning it had become glaringly obvious – I'd been sleepwalking through my life, tiptoeing so as not to rock the boat or ruffle any feathers. Thirty years old and my whole life was nothing more than a montage of quiet compromises. But no more. Liam didn't deserve to have his heart broken, but I had to do this; get away; for me. I didn't have time to worry about his feelings or let him down gently – if he knew the truth he'd never let me go. I ate as much of my dinner as I could and then kissed Liam goodnight as we retired to bed.

But there was no way I could sleep.

As Liam slumbered beside me, I was wide awake and alive with possibilities as if for the first time. I made a list in my head of all the places I wanted to visit. To start with it comprised of random, far-flung exotic places abroad, but as the night wore on, my sensible, practical nature took over. By morning I'd narrowed down the list to a few financially-achievable destinations within the M25.

While Liam rose, showered, and loaded his van with gardening tools, I stayed in bed and made a 'to do' list. I'd always been good at lists. At work all our calls were planned, scripted, bullet pointed and organised into flow charts – providing step by step procedures for all phone call eventualities. I'd always found it reassuring. I waited until I heard Liam drive away before reaching for my phone, my stomach filled with butterflies. In a calm voice I rang my boss and told him that I quit, effective immediately, and despite his understandable disbelief and irritation, I managed to end the call, and my career, with remarkable ease.

Pulling on my safe blue jeans, a grey marl T-shirt and a beige jumper that wouldn't show the dirt, it occurred to me that I despised my clothes. They were sensible, practical, and ordinary – deliberately chosen so that I would go unnoticed and blend into the background. With a rush of gusto I emptied the entire contents of my wardrobe out onto the bedroom carpet and stuffed everything into bin-bags. I held back a spare outfit, a night shirt and some underwear, enough clothes to tide me over, and then set off for the charity shop around the corner. It was raining outside and it took three trips, but it was exhilarating to know that the collection of ugly clothes was no longer mine.

On the way back I stopped at the bank and stared at my current account balance on the ATM screen. There were ample funds available, but I couldn't bring myself to withdraw them – it was one thing to leave Liam, and another to leave him short of money – the thought of him struggling financially was too much to bear. With the account still complete with standing orders and direct debits to cover my half of the rent and bills for another two months, I switched over to my savings account and emptied it completely. Exiting the bank with a bag full of cash was surreal – as if I'd robbed it – and felt faintly preposterous. But it was necessary; using my debit and credit cards would only make it easy for Liam to track me down once my statements arrived through the door. And if he found me he would try to persuade me to return home with him. I'd no doubt fall back in to the easy comfort of his arms readily. No, if I was going to do this, I needed to give it my best shot. Mentally I made a note to also have my post redirected, so that Liam wouldn't see any letters from the hospital.

Back at the house I packed the cash and my remaining few clothes into a wheeled suitcase along with a few toiletries, my passport, my mobile, my laptop, my eBook-reader and all the relevant chargers. After a few seconds deliberation I added a framed photograph of my parents at their home in Spain and an action shot of Liam playing rugby before zipping the case closed. Bessie was too big to go in my case, so I popped her in a separate carrier bag, aware that I was being sentimental, but unable to leave her behind. Childhood stuffed bunny rabbit aside, it seemed I owned few material possessions that I couldn't live without.

The notepad magnetically stuck to the fridge drew my eye and filled me with dread. It had provided the space for hundreds of brief communications between us over the years, most of them fairly innocuous – 'I'll get milk' or 'your Mum called'. But some of them, particularly in the early days, were sweet and loving – 'back around 10pm, miss you already x'. Right now, all it held was the beginning of a shopping list in the bottom corner, and the power to destroy our relationship forever.

I'd spent half the night trying to compose a Dear John in my mind; something that adequately conveyed all that I wanted to say without divulging my reason for leaving. But that was the one thing he'd want to know – the why. I was tempted to leave no word at all, but that was worse. Too cruel. I had to write something. I picked up a pen, absently chewing the end before attacking the paper with hasty, clichéd phrases:

I'm sorry but it's over. I can't stay. Please don't try to find me.

It's not your fault, it's nothing you've done, it's just over, I'm sorry.

Goodbye, Cally.

My eyes filled with tears as I read it back. There was so much missing. I wanted to thank him for being so good to me; for protecting and caring for me, but 'thank you' sounded trite and impersonal in my head. I yearned to point out that he didn't deserve to be treated this way, but that was hypocritical. I longed to add that I'd always care and wouldn't forget about him, because it was true, but I couldn't give him hope. I would not be coming back.

I left through the front door, locked it, and then dropped the keys through the letterbox. They landed on the mat with a dull thump. It started to rain again and I squared my shoulders and pulled my raincoat tighter around me as I walked away.

Chapter Two

'Come on, Bay, man up,' I told myself.

I could do this. I *would* do this. I had to. It was time to go. Closing my eyes I steadied myself, sucked down a breath, and pushed the bar to open the fire exit. But it was stuck. Fuck.

Incredulous, I opened my eyes. Un-fucking-believable. After a whole year of psyching myself up I was finally ready to do this, and now I couldn't get the fucking door open. Just as well it wasn't a real emergency. Jiggling the handle I wrenched at it a few more times and then kicked angrily at the door frame with the sole of my bare foot for good measure. It probably hurt but I was too coked up to feel it. And anyway, pain was all relative. I pushed again at the emergency release bar, and at last it gave way, the door swinging open and pushing back a year's worth of accumulated leaves, debris and dirt. Stooping, I shifted a concrete block to wedge the fire exit open, and then sagged against the door; pressing my forehead to the smooth surface. The fresh air whipped around me, chilling my clammy skin and making my balls contract.

A panorama of lights speckled the canvas of the city in all directions – a proliferation of lit windows, traffic lights, street lamps, neon signs, spotlights and touristy illuminations, straddling both sides of the slithering black river. I focused on the music spilling out of the flat below, carrying me forwards; the haunting melody riding the swell of the wind; the call of her sweet voice luring me closer to the concrete edge of the roof. Wedging my naked toes up against it I gazed down into the inky black void below. She was down there in the darkness waiting for me. Three years had passed, but she wasn't going away. She was only growing more impatient; more insistent. This time I would do it. I owed her that. Stepping up onto the low walled edge I carefully positioned my feet, holding my arms out to the sides for balance, like a tightrope walker. I closed my eyes feeling the wind buffeting against my body, hearing the buzz, hum and wail of the city below. All I had to do was fall forwards; relinquish my fear and let go of my miserable existence, once and for all.

My heart pounded in my chest, my ears ached with the timbre of her voice, my eyes glazed with uninvited tears, and my muscles clenched taut and trembling. You can do this.

Just. Fucking. Let. Go.

Chapter Three

'Cally!' Marguerite cried, waving as she strode towards me, her heels slapping on the wet pavement. 'Sorry I'm late; signal failure at Baker Street; you'll have to get used to things like that while you're living here.' She smiled as she squeezed me in a one-armed hug and air-kissed my cheeks. Her other arm supported a large purple leather handbag and a manila file full of papers. 'So this is it!' She said glancing up at TMC Tower – a sleek, glass-fronted office building – before rummaging in her bag for a set of keys. 'You found it OK?'

'Yes, thanks,' I said, finding my voice. We were in the heart of London – the financial district. Revolving doors fed into a spacious, light-filled lobby complete with a reception desk, a chrome seating area and a bank of elevators beyond. The building was modest by skyscraper standards, reaching only twelve storeys in height (I'd counted) but I could see lights and movement behind the tinted windows on the floors above, and business was in full swing. I felt conspicuously scruffy in my jeans and trainers as professional-looking men and women swept past us in their suits. 'What sort of work do they do here?'

'Oh, I'm not too sure, finance of some kind I think? But there's a separate entrance and lift for you to use at the side. Come on.' I followed Marguerite to a discreet door, set within larger solid double gates, to one side of the building. 'There are just two flats and you're in number two. This is your mailbox, and this is your buzzer,' she said, indicating the panel on the wall where 'S. Curtis' was written in neat black script. The label for flat number one was curiously blank, but before I could comment Marguerite was rushing on. 'There's a little camera and a microphone so you can see and talk to whoever's calling and then you can press a button to admit them from inside. I'll show you when we get up there.' By entering a code into the keypad she unlocked the door and then we stepped into a passageway beyond, which was open to the sky but hemmed in by the tall buildings on either side. 'There are security lights all along here so it's perfectly safe and you can dispose of your rubbish in the bins at the end, but you don't have to worry about putting them out; that's all taken care of.'

'There are trees back there!' I said, surprised. They looked lush, green and incongruous against the harsh urban surroundings.

'Oh yes, there's a garden, didn't I tell you? It's rather overgrown I'm afraid – mostly trees – and it's shared with the other flat but I don't think it gets used much.' Marguerite, clearly in a hurry, led me into a waiting lift and we were swept smoothly up to the twelfth floor.

Once Marguerite unlocked the door to the flat I barely registered the empty landing, the burglar alarm or the entry system. Dropping my bags in the hallway I stepped inside, gazing in awe through the huge plate-glass windows which provided a drizzly but breath-taking view east across London's rooftops. Identifying The Gherkin off to the right, I was tempted to pinch myself. And the interior of the apartment was no less amazing. It was vast and mainly open-plan with bare brick walls, parquet floors and high ceilings, and furnished with quirky character. The kitchen was tiled with glossy turquoise splashbacks while the lounge area was furnished with vivid violet velvet sofas and a shaggy lime-green rug. The two areas were separated by a huge fish tank and a breakfast bar with tall, vintage diner-style stools. A collection of large multi-coloured retro American signs adorned the walls above a wide, clear Perspex dining table with six matching chairs. The signs advertised everything from gas stations and lobsters, to hot dogs and superheroes. A selection of house-plants hung from the ceiling in seventies-style macramé baskets. They dangled at various heights in front of the windows, and as I watched their leaves quiver with the draft from the open front door, I realised I'd have to water them. Maybe even trim them. For the next six months these were my plants. I'd never been anywhere remotely like this, and it was going to be my home for the next *six months*.

Marguerite opened a succession of doors to reveal two spacious bedrooms, a candy pink bathroom and a storage cupboard, all the while venting a stream of information regarding fuses, timer switches, cleaning days and fish food.

'Sorry, Marguerite,' I interrupted, trying to tune into her words. 'What was that about the fish?'

'Don't worry it's all written down in the Sitter Information File,' she waved a heavy-looking binder at me and slapped it down on the breakfast bar. 'I just need you to sign the contract and the insurance docs for me.' She produced a ballpoint pen from her bag and clicked the end. I took it from her and signed my full name, Calluna Drey, without really reading anything – I'd known Marguerite long enough to trust her completely. 'Thank you so much for doing this, Cally, you're a life saver,' she said scooping her things up and handing me a set of keys. 'As I said, everything you need to know should be in the file, but if there's anything you're not sure about you can always call me, day or night.'

'Thank you.'

'Now, is there anything else before I go?' she was already on her way to the door, checking the slim silver watch on her wrist.

'Actually, there is one thing.' She paused and rotated on her heels to face me with a smile of expectation. 'Can I ask a huge favour? I don't want anyone to know where I am – not Liam, not my parents, not any of our friends – no-one.' Marguerite's pencil-thin eyebrows lifted towards her hairline. 'I know it's a strange request, and I promise there's nothing to worry about, really. It's just that I want a complete break, you know, without distractions…'

Sadness crept into my friend's eyes. 'You've left him.'

'Yes.'

'He must be gutted.'

I didn't reply. I didn't want to think about it. She glanced at her watch again.

'OK,' she said with a sigh. 'It's not going to be easy – I'll probably see him around all the time, in the pub, at matches…'

'I know, I'm sorry.'

She stared at me for a moment. 'My loyalty has always been to you first – you know that.'

'Thank you,' I said with relief. 'I won't always have my mobile switched on but you can leave a message or ring me on the landline here.'

'OK,' she said reaching out and pulling me into another one-armed hug. 'If you get bored or lonely just call me and we'll go out for cocktails or something.'

'Sounds great,' I said, with more conviction than I felt.

I waited until the lift had carried Marguerite away before wheeling my suitcase inside, closing the door behind me and turning to face my new life with a long, slow exhale.

Chapter Four

I gradually became aware of a persistent buzzing which grew louder and more irritating as I slowly gained consciousness. Eventually the screaming pain in my head, the stiffness in my limbs, and the urge to vomit conspired with the buzzing to force my eyes open. Squinting in the bright daylight I groaned aloud as the familiar contours of my flat assembled into focus. Fuck. I was still alive. I'd bottled it again. Fucking coward.

The persistent buzzing was someone down at the front door trying to get my attention. I wished they'd stop. Gingerly I dragged myself up into a seated position from where I'd been curled on the floor beneath an open window. With great effort I reached up one hand and pushed the reinforced glass shut behind me. It slid home with a hard, audible click of finality, punctuating my abject failure to escape yet again. Whoever was pressing the entry buzzer was now stabbing out an infuriating little tune. 'Fuck off!' I yelled ineffectually across the room, clutching my head in my hands. How long had I been out? The digital clock by my bed read 09:05 but was it still Thursday or had I been out longer; missing a day or two like last time? My gaze alighted on an open bottle of vodka a couple of feet away and I reached out and grabbed it with stiff fingers. There were only a few mouthfuls left, but I downed it quickly, savouring the burn as it made its way down my throat and hit my churning stomach.

By the time I'd made it to my feet and staggered across the room I was ready to kill whoever was downstairs still pressing the damn buzzer.

'WHAT?' I roared into the handset.

'Bay, at last, I was about to call the police.'

'Fuck off, Felix.'

'Charming. I'm just gonna keep buzzing until you let me in…'

Sighing, I punched the door release button with the side of my fist and stumbled towards the bathroom. While Felix made his way up to my door, I managed to knock back some prescription painkillers with more vodka from the freezer, pull on a sweatshirt and recover a slightly squashed fag from behind my ear.

'Jesus, Bay, you look like death.' The irony of his comment was not lost on me, but I was too irritable to laugh. Lighting up I walked silently back to the centre of the room while he closed the door behind him. 'Shit it's freezing in here. Why's it so cold? Has your heating broken down?' I didn't respond. 'At least the air's fresher – makes a change from the usual fog of tobacco smoke in here.'

'What do you want, Felix?' I said, collapsing onto my bed and taking a long drag.

'Bay, your feet are blue, put some socks on for god's sake.'

'Felix…' I growled in warning.

'OK, OK,' he held up a hand in surrender as he righted a chair and sat down to face me. 'You know why I'm here.' He furtively surveyed the jumble of canvases of various shapes and sizes that littered the room, most of them faced the wall, turned away from prying eyes. 'I'm holding that exhibition over on the other side of the river in the summer and you said you'd have some finished pieces for me by now. I need to have some idea of what I'm going to be displaying if I'm going to curate and market the show properly.'

I took another drag and blew smoke rings out above my head.

'Bay, tell me you've got something for me. I can't make you money unless you give me something to sell.'

Sighing heavily, I bent to drop the remains of my fag into a half-empty coke can on the floor and shoved my hands into my hair – it really needed cutting. As annoying as Felix was, he was my agent and a friend; a good friend; he didn't deserve all the shit I subjected him to. 'Yeah I've got something for you.' I rose to my feet and he followed me into my storeroom. 'That doesn't mean they're any good, though,' I added, self-doubt brewing in my mind.

'Just let me be the judge of that,' Felix said as I dragged dust-sheets away from a selection of canvases stacked in a rack along one wall. I stood back and observed as Felix carefully spread the series of oil paintings out around the room, silently considering and scrutinising each one in turn. I told myself I didn't care if he liked them or not; whether he thought they were good enough for his exhibition, or commercially saleable, or complete and utter shit. But deep down, I did care. What little life I had left was poured into those paintings; my very soul was spread within the pigment, carried in each brush-stroke and sealed in every scrape of the knife. I didn't paint because I wanted to. For me, painting was a compulsion; an addiction, as surely as drinking, smoking, and getting high was. I would still paint if no-one else ever saw them. But being able to send paintings out into the world – knowing that they existed somewhere beyond here, beyond me – *that* mattered, even though I'd never admit it.

'Extraordinary,' Felix muttered to himself.

'Extraordinarily bad?'

'No, Bay, these are fantastic – seriously. Slightly disturbing as usual, but no less brilliant for all that. Most people don't want anything this depressing on their walls – you know that – but there's a niche market for your work now. You're developing something of a cult following...'

I snorted with derision and returned to the main room, uncomfortable with Felix's praise now that he'd restored my fragile ego. He stayed behind, taking photos and making notes on his phone while I rolled a spliff and checked the contents of the fridge for something edible. Thankfully the flat was warming up again and the painkillers were beginning to kick in. Now all I wanted to do was crawl into my pit and sleep – it was disconcerting waking up in the morning instead of late afternoon.

Felix was grinning from ear to ear when he re-emerged. 'Thanks, Bay, you've made my day. I can really relax and enjoy my weekend now.' Weekend? Was it Friday already? I took a bite of cold pizza from the limp slice in my hand and then hastily spat it back out again. It didn't taste right. Felix grimaced in response. 'I know I've said this before, but you know you need help, right?' I

21

rinsed my mouth out with mouthwash from a bottle by the microwave and spat into the kitchen sink. Why it was there, instead of in the bathroom, was anyone's guess. Had I been drinking it? 'I mean, you should really check yourself into a clinic, or at least see a therapist or something,' he pressed.

'Isn't it time you were going?'

Felix sighed and shook his head in defeat. 'OK mate.' I followed him to the door. 'Listen; will you email me a list of titles so I can start working on the promo material? Nearer the time I'll send someone round to transport them over to the gallery.'

I nodded, distracted by the sight of a large plastic carrier bag on the landing. A pair of long brown furry ears where sticking out the top. 'What the hell's that?'

'I don't know, nothing to do with me,' Felix said, lifting a large stuffed bunny by one ear, so that its glassy eyes peered out at me. 'Maybe it's the Easter Bunny?'

'Easter Bunny?'

'Yeah,' Felix shrugged, dropping it back in the bag. 'It's Good Friday after all.'

'Oh.' I'd been unconscious for over twenty-four hours.

'Maybe it belongs to your neighbour?' Felix said stepping into the lift.

'Maybe,' I said doubtfully, raising a hand in farewell as the lift closed and whisked my agent away. Admittedly my neighbour, Sidney, was a little camp, but he was in his late forties and drove a BMW; a fluffy bunny didn't seem his style. I vaguely recalled him telling me he was going abroad for a while, but I was stoned at the time and couldn't remember any specifics. As I shut the door and

sloped off to bed I shivered, hoping the mysterious bunny
was not going to lurk on the landing for long.

Chapter Five

I didn't get up until mid-afternoon on Easter Monday, having stayed up all night eating popcorn, chocolate mini-eggs and ice-cream in front of Mr Curtis's epic surround-sound TV. It was peculiar living in the home of a complete stranger. His personal effects were presumably tidily stashed in the locked bedroom cupboard – there were no family photographs lying around, no notepads, no letters, no books – no clues from which I could glean more about him. Not that I was one to snoop, but I was curious, and found myself trying to guess at his first name, age, occupation and looks. The only thing I knew with any certainty was that Mr Curtis was the sort of man who has a pre-paid movie package. I had comfortably vegetated all weekend – sitting and soaking up virtually any film I fancied. It was pure indulgence, but one that I could no longer afford.

By leaving Wildham I'd taken a big risk – one that I justified to myself repeatedly – after all, it was my life and I was young, fit and healthy – in all respects but one – surely as long as I ate well and maintained an active lifestyle the worst of any symptoms would be kept at bay. But leaving my old life behind was only the first step towards transforming it, and the clock was ticking.

Having fed the fish and poured myself a bowl of cereal, and very careful not to confuse the two, I gazed out at the massive grey buildings across the street and the jumbled sprawl of London beyond. It was far removed from the safe, leafy world of Wildham. But I refused to be intimidated. I had a book to write and I wanted to make the most of my time in the capital – do a bit of sightseeing, visit art galleries, explore markets – not to mention I had a whole new wardrobe to buy. But that was going to cost money, so my first priority ought to be finding a job.

I'd always been a wallflower, an introvert, and I'd always been OK with that; content to observe from the sidelines and go unnoticed. But not anymore. Now I wanted to be seen. For once in my life I wanted to shine, sparkle and burn brightly… before it was too late. And my hopes for that rested in the hands of the only famous person I'd ever met; rising actress and all-round star, Jasmine Reed. Setting my afternoon breakfast aside, I grabbed my mobile and switched it on. Immediately it erupted with sound, the screen flashing with voice mails, text messages and missed-call notifications, mostly from Liam. But I couldn't read them. Ignoring them all I located Jasmine's number, jotted it down and quickly switched my mobile off again. Taking a steadying breath I picked up the Bakelite receiver of Mr Curtis's 1960s rotary-style phone, cleared my throat, reminded myself I was a new person, and bravely dialled.

'Hello?'

'Hi, Jasmine, you may not remember me, my name's Cally, I'm a friend of James Southwood – we met at his birthday party a couple of years ago…?'

'And…?'

'It's just that I'm a dancer and you told me if I was ever looking for work that I should give you a ring; you said you might be able to help…'

'Did I?' She sighed. 'Look, Kelly is it?'

'Cally.'

'Whatever, look, I was probably drunk when I said that; I can't get you a job just like that.'

'Oh, no of course not,' I mumbled, a tremor of embarrassment creeping into my voice.

'Taxi!' Jasmine yelled, making me jump and pull the handset away from my ear. I listened as she climbed into a cab and gave the name of a posh-sounding venue to the driver. 'Are you still there, Kelly?'

'Yes.'

'Do you know The Electric Fox on Lexington?'

'No, but I'm sure I could find it…'

'All I can suggest is that you go there and ask Pavel, the owner, for a job. Tell him I sent you and if he likes you, you might get lucky.'

'Wow, OK, thank you, Jasmine – I really appreciate it.'

'No worries, take care—' She'd hung up before I could say goodbye, the drone of the dial tone echoing in my head as I dropped the retro handset back into its cradle.

For several minutes I stared out the window as I ran the conversation back in my mind. She hadn't been as friendly as I remembered, but then she was a busy, famous celebrity and I was lucky she'd spoken to me at all. And she'd given me a lead – a real life opportunity to fulfil my secret dream of being a paid, professional dancer! I flipped my laptop open and chewed my lip while it warmed up. The Electric Fox… was that a dance troupe? A theatre company? Or the name of a performance venue…?

My shoulders slumped as the information popped up on Google. I should have known. What did I really expect? Show business was one of the hardest industries to get into and I was a nobody. I clicked through to the relevant website and jotted down the address. I owed it to myself to at least go along, check it out and give it my best shot. After all, what, aside from my dignity, did I have to lose?

I arrived at the club half an hour before opening, just as the rain was stopping. I squinted up at the neon flash of the sign, bright and exciting against the grey of London, and made my way round to the side entrance where two large muscle-bound bouncers were holding the door open for two women. Taking a deep breath I reminded myself I wasn't Calluna anymore; I was Luna; I could do this; I *wanted* to do this. And if I didn't enjoy it I could always leave.

Despite the inscrutable expression on his face, one of the doormen reminded me of Liam – he had a similar haircut and prominent brow – which was oddly reassuring. I approached him with a smile.

'Hi, would it be possible to see Pavel?' In my peripheral vision I could see the other man looking me over with suspicion, but I kept my eyes on the stolid-looking guy before me.

'You looking for work?' His voice was a low grumble.

'Yes, I'm a friend of Jasmine Reed's,' I said calmly.

He nodded thoughtfully. 'You might be in luck; someone just quit.'

'Great!' I said brightly.

He sighed. 'Give me a minute.'

As he disappeared inside I was left standing with the other bouncer who ignored me but leered openly at all the other woman who passed into the building. It was a huge relief when the other man finally reappeared and signalled for me to follow him, with a tip of his head.

The interior of the club was much larger, lighter and less seedy than I'd been expecting, with a long mirrored bar, a lavish raised stage, and a series of polished metal poles dotted throughout the remaining space. Each pole was mounted on a round, elevated plinth and surrounded by a cluster of cosy-looking seating. For all my false bravado, the sight of those podiums almost crippled me with fear. I was a long way from Wildham.

Pavel was a round man of short stature, with a shiny bald patch and a neatly-trimmed goatee. He was perched on the edge of a plinth and flanked by two tall, Amazonian women; a redhead and a tanned blonde.

'So, Jasmine sent you?' he said.

'Yes.'

'She's a good girl, Jasmine. She has gone far but she has not forgotten where she began.' Pavel had a Russian accent and shrewd eyes and I smiled non-committally at this fresh insight into Jasmine's beginnings. 'So, you want a job.'

'Yes.'

'What can you do?'

'I can dance.'

'You work in a club before?'

'No, but I have trained in ballet and contemporary and commercial dance.'

'Ballet!' He chuckled. 'You work the pole?'

'I know the basics, yes,' I said, ignoring the double entendre that had raised a snigger from the redhead.

'Show me.'

'Now?'

'Change first – Zena will show you.' He turned away, effectively dismissing me, and the blonde stepped forward with a tight smile. She was older than me, and intimidating, her generous curves strapped inside a leather corset and skinny jeans. I hurried after her swinging hips as she sashayed towards a door marked private.

The changing room was cluttered but clean-looking, with long dressing tables, orderly rails of costumes and clothes, and women in various states of undress. Zena wordlessly hung my raincoat and jumper on a peg and I bent down to pull off my shoes and socks. She was called away to the bar for several minutes and I took the opportunity to do a few warm up stretches.

'You're not going out there like that, are you?' Zena said on her return.

I glanced down at my T-shirt and leggings. 'I don't have anything else.'

'Sweet Jesus,' she muttered under her breath. 'Here, put these on.' She thrust a studded black leather bra with matching hot pants at me and my mouth dropped open. 'Honey, we need to see your assets – tits and arse – that's what this job's about. If you're not prepared to flaunt it, you might as well leave now.'

I took the clothes from her and changed quickly, aware that I was blushing furiously but trying hard to ignore all the eyes on me.

'Try these, they're fives,' Zena said handing me a pair of black stilettos.

'Can't I just go barefoot?'

She shook her head. 'Your legs will look much better in these, believe me.' Despite her brusque demeanour I was grateful to this woman for taking pity on me and squeezed my feet into the shoes without further comment. 'Hold still.' Zena clamped my jaw in one hand and, with well-practised efficiency, applied black eye-liner and mascara to my eyes, powder to my nose, and blood red lipstick to my mouth.

A shiver of exhilaration passed through me as I turned to a mirror and saw 'Luna' for the first time. 'I can do this,' I said under my breath.

'Right,' Zena said, placing her hands on my shoulders and staring into my reflection. 'The most important piece of advice I can give you is to be bold. You can pull off just about anything with enough confidence.'

'OK,' I said. 'Thank you so much.' Zena nodded once in acknowledgement before steering me out into the club as if I was just the latest in a long line of willing fools.

The lights had dimmed and a DJ was playing music over loud speakers from a booth in the corner. He winked at me as I passed and I smiled back, pleased that it was Erykah Badu's 'Next Lifetime', a tune I was familiar with. Telling myself it was merely a performance, just like any other, I stepped up to the pole nearest to Pavel, who was in conversation with several other people at the bar, and began to dance. I blocked out everyone around me, concentrated on my body and let the music be my guide; blending practised moves together with a liberal smattering of improvisation as I threw myself around the pole.

After a couple of songs, Pavel approached and signalled for me to stop. The room was filling with people – more girls gyrating around poles, and men in suits who sat drinking, while a woman on the stage, dressed as a schoolgirl, performed an elaborate striptease, complete with classroom props. Breathless, I sank down to a crouch on my aching feet, allowing Pavel to shout in my ear.

'What's your name, darling?'

'Luna.'

'Ah, like the moon.'

'Yes.'

'So. You survive tonight, and the job is yours.'

'Really?' I grinned, genuinely thrilled.

'This is good club; respectable club for nice girls. You work hard and we will look after you – understand?'

'Thank you, Pavel.'

'Take a break; five minutes.' He held a small, soft palm out to help me down and I spotted a couple of fivers lying on the podium. I offered them to my new boss but he smiled and shook his head as he folded the cash and tucked it neatly in the waistband of my hot-pants. 'Save it 'til the end, then come see me, Luna.' My head buzzed with satisfaction as I made my way back to the dressing room with a spring in my aching instep.

It was gone 2 a.m. by the time a taxi delivered me back to my swanky flat; tired, sore, and hungry. Once inside I peeled off the clothes I'd thrown on for the journey home, kicked off my trainers, readjusted my borrowed leather bra and limped into the kitchen area. Having loaded bread into the toaster I collapsed onto the sofa while I waited for it to cook. What a night! Most of what I'd earned in tips I'd had to pay to Pavel by way of a House Fee – that was how it worked – but he had offered me three shifts a week, starting in just a week's time. Zena, the House Mum, had given me a whole load of House Rules and a comprehensive Code of Conduct to read through, but it all looked fairly straightforward. Despite never having stepped into a strip club before, I was confident that once I got into the swing of things I could earn myself good money. Especially once I'd worked up the courage to go completely naked. Tonight, I'd kept my borrowed outfit on and focused on the dancing, but that was how you earned the real tips – nudity and plenty of eye contact. Seeing the other girls perform made me realise I needed serious practise, if I was going to be successful. Closing my eyes I wearily flexed my blistered, aching feet. My new persona 'Luna' was also in need of proper attire, including decent size six, four inch high heels...

I woke with a start, leaping up in terror at the ear-splitting scream of an alarm, the smell of burning and the sight of smoke pouring from the kitchen.

The toast!

I rushed over and gingerly hooked the scorched bread out with the end of a fork, inadvertently risking electrocution, before remembering to switch the appliance off at the wall.

'Shut up, shut up, shut up,' I yelped, swatting ineffectually at the small, flashing ceiling alarm with a tea towel.

'Sidney? Are you there?' A man shouted through the front door, hammering on it with his fist.

'Shit,' I muttered under my breath, running to the door with my hands over my ears. 'Sorry! Sorry!' I yelled, yanking the door open. 'There's no fire; I just burnt some toast!' The alarm stopped abruptly so that my final word was shouted ridiculously loudly at the guy before me. He was tall, dark, and wild-looking; his hair sticking up in tufts, enhancing the stormy expression on his face. 'Sorry,' I whispered into the ringing silence. It was a shock finding myself in such close proximity to a strange man, having kept a careful distance from them all night. And this man was particularly intimidating – I guessed he was slightly older than me; the flecks of silver at his temples giving him a wolfish look. I briefly registered dark, paint-splattered clothing, extensively tattooed muscles, a pierced eyebrow and intense eyes, which narrowed as they slid all over me.

'Who the hell are you?' he said. He reeked of turps or white spirit and held a bristly paintbrush in one grubby hand. His glowering frame filled the doorway like a malignant shadow and I instinctively took a step backwards into the relative safety of my smoky flat.

'I'm Cally.'

'Cally…?'

'Calluna… Calluna Drey. I'm house-sitting for Mr Curtis while he's away.' I stammered.

'House-sitting? Well, Cally, you're obviously doing a *splendid* job.' His eyes mocked me.

'I just burnt some toast...' I said, folding my arms, '...and I've apologised—'

'When's Sidney back?'

'In six months. Sorry but, you are...?'

'Why are you making toast at two in the morning?'

'I'm hungry,' I snapped. 'Not that it's any of your business. Why are you *painting* at two in the morning?'

His eyes darkened, adding to my unease. 'I live next door – own the whole building in fact – so if you could try to refrain from burning it down...' He stepped backwards onto the landing.

'Fine. I'll do my best,' I said, pushing the door shut with an irate bang. What a rude, arrogant, patronising arsehole! No-one had ever spoken to me like that before – not in person, anyway. Sure, I'd dealt with my fair share of disgruntled customers on the phone at the call centre, but they weren't usually angry with me personally. Where I came from, people were polite and courteous to people they met for the first time, especially neighbours. And the way I'd snapped back at him... that wasn't like me at all – normally I avoided confrontation at all costs. But he wouldn't even tell me his name. Jerk.

I stalked into the bedroom, still riled up and trembling with adrenalin, and then cringed as I caught sight of myself in the mirror; still scantily clad in leather underwear; my hair a bird's nest of tangles and my eye make-up smudged with sweat; giving me panda eyes. Ugh. How humiliating. That settled it; I would do everything in my power to avoid my only neighbour. If I *never* saw him again, it would be too soon.

Chapter Six

What the fuck was that! What did Sidney think he was doing inviting a complete stranger to come and live in my building without even telling me? Why hadn't he just asked *me* to feed his fucking fish? Actually... probably because I'd kill them off – not intentionally of course, but I wasn't the most reliable of people. But still. Fuck. A woman – a beautiful woman who blushed when flustered, owned a ridiculously big stuffed bunny, and dressed like a hooker! What the hell was she doing up in the middle of the night? The night was my territory; I didn't want to share it. I'd been so careful about selecting a tenant for the flat next door – someone quiet and tidy, someone who went out to work all day and slept all night and didn't throw wild parties. Sidney was almost as much of a loner as me. She'd better not start throwing parties or I would throw her out. End of story.

'Calluna Drey...' her name rolled around my tongue as if I was tasting something new and exotic and I fought the urge to repeat it over and over again. The way she had looked at me, warily, as if I was a rotten smell best avoided, was nothing new. I recognised her type; snotty, privileged and judgemental. She was right to be wary; I was bad news. But who was *she* to judge *me*, dressed like *that*! She had invaded my own private hell, up on the top floor, completely without warning and she wasn't welcome. It was unnerving knowing she was just on the other side of the wall. I already couldn't stand her. I would avoid her like the Black Death.

Returning to the canvas I was working on, I dabbed my paintbrush into a dollop of wet paint and scrutinised my efforts so far, but my concentration had been shot to hell. Those long, shapely legs... that slight gap between her front two teeth which made her look so innocent... those eyes; those startling, cobalt blue eyes. And the way she'd said "I'm hungry"; the way she'd looked at me as she said those two words, had made me instantly hard – rock hard. Fuck it. Angrily launching the brush across the room like a javelin I watched as it daubed a crimson smear on the opposite wall before clattering to the floor. I wouldn't be getting any more work done tonight. Grabbing my tobacco tin I stalked to the kitchen to fix myself a strong drink.

Chapter Seven

Once my feet had recovered I went shopping for a new wardrobe. It had been years since I'd been clothes shopping alone – I'd always been dragged along by Marguerite, who prided herself on her fashion sense and considered each purchase an investment in her own success. This time I didn't want, or dare ask for, my best friend's input, but I tried to channel her self-confidence.

Zena's application of red lipstick to my lips had made me feel like a completely different person; it wasn't a mask, but it had still given me an enormous sense of freedom; freedom to be whomever I chose to be. I took that lipstick as my inspiration and ran with it, purchasing an array of lingerie in a range of scarlets and blood reds. Lace Basques and silk bras with matching knickers – nothing I bought was studded leather, but I was confident these garments were erotic enough to have the desired effect. They certainly made me feel sexier than I ever had before. Trying them on I marvelled at my own reflection with growing excitement. Marguerite, Liam, my parents, all would be horrified at the sight of me like this, but that thought only made me more determined.

Next I stopped at a shoe shop where I purchased several pairs of strappy heels in black, red, and gold. And I didn't stop there.

Once I had my dancing outfits organised I was free to style my new daytime self. Throwing caution, and my savings, to the wind, I bought beautifully feminine dresses, skirts, cardigans and scarves, all in crimson hues; accessorising them with soft leather handbags, belts, shoes and boots. It was the vibrant shades of red I favoured; for making me feel most alive, striking and womanly. My tired, once-white, cotton underwear were replaced with simple black pieces, to differentiate from my dance wear. They were still sexy, but for my eyes only.

Less than a fortnight into my London stay, and I already had a job and a new wardrobe sorted out, but I still needed somewhere to practise my routines. Back at the flat I was standing by the window, eating stuffed olives with my fingers straight from the jar, when inspiration hit. The rain had stopped, it had just gone half past five, and the surrounding buildings were emptying of workers for the day. It was time to investigate the garden

The barrage of greenery took my breath away as I exited the lift on the ground floor and rounded the corner. This part of London was mainly comprised of offices in a smart blend of styles, from traditional to modern, with a smattering of eateries and coffee shops at ground level. Space was at a premium, and aside from the odd formal pocket of corporate landscaping, the public Royal Parks, and the private railing-enclosed squares in the west, real gardens were rare.

This secluded walled oasis had clearly been around for a long time, because it held several mature trees, including a gnarled old oak tree, an impressive copper beech and a mixture of smaller contorted fruit trees. The lawn beneath the trees petered out into thistles and nettles at the base of the high brick walls, giving the space the atmosphere of an orchard rather than a garden. The trees nearest to the surrounding buildings had been coppiced in recent years, presumably to restrict their growth and allow more light in, but the trees near the centre provided a green umbrella of privacy, protecting the garden from the several storeys that otherwise overlooked from above. The sounds of the city were muffled by the foliage and as I closed my eyes and breathed in the fresh scent of leaves and bark, I felt comforted – as if I was back in Wildham, in the woods behind the house. How had a shabby, under-used garden such as this withstood the pressure of development? And how had someone as young and obnoxious as my jerk of a neighbour ended up owning such a place?

Weak sunlight filtered down through the trees, along with occasional wet drips of rain, as I stepped through the damp grass. It was bare in patches and mossy in others, springy beneath my flat shoes. I stopped at a small tree that stood alone in a clearing, separate from the rest. It was maybe a wild cherry; younger and upright, with a slender trunk and smooth, shiny bark. Cupping the trunk in my palm, I walked right around it, gazing up into the canopy of delicate white blossom. The girth fit my hand perfectly, and though the bark wasn't smooth enough to slide up and down on, I figured I'd still be able to practice some swings and jumps, provided the tree was sturdy enough. Taking an experimental leap around it, I let the trunk take my weight, and it held firm with barely a quiver. I couldn't help laughing in delight – it was if it had been planted especially for me. Kicking off my wet shoes I proceeded to pole-dance around the tree, practising my routine to music only I could hear; a light confetti of snow-white petals, drifting to the grass around me.

Chapter Eight

In the moment of silence between one track ending and the next beginning, I heard the whirr of the lift rising. Curious, I dropped my sketchbook and pencil and sauntered over to the door. Through the peephole I had a clear view of the lift doors as they parted, depositing Cally onto the landing. She looked entirely different to when we'd met three nights ago. Her hooker outfit had been replaced with a stylish rose-coloured summer dress, a cropped cardigan and burnt umber leather boots. As she moved I caught a tantalising glimpse of pale, bare skin behind her knees. The other night I'd believed her hair to be jet black like mine, but the late afternoon light streaming through the landing window, revealed it to be shot through with fine strands of Indian red. It hung straight down, silky smooth, elegantly framing her face. Her lips were painted to match her dress, but tightly pressed together as she deliberately avoided looking in the direction of my door. Quickly and quietly she let herself into the neighbouring flat and was gone, but I stared at the vacant space she left behind for several long minutes afterwards. Was this what I'd become now? A creepy loser who spied on the girl next door whenever she happened to pass by? Was my life really that empty?

Eventually, just as I was about to move away, Cally's door re-opened and I was rewarded with the sight of her stepping back out onto the landing. She'd changed into leggings and a red shirt which only just covered her bottom, and I tried not to notice her perfect proportions; the demure curves of her tight calves and toned thighs. Standing in the lift, waiting for the doors to close, she raised her eyes to the ceiling and pulled her hair back into a ponytail, exposing finely pointed elbows and an elegant neck. It crossed my mind that she might be going out for a run, but the flimsy, slipper-like shoes on her feet didn't look fit for purpose. Abruptly the doors closed, stealing her from view, and I let out a breath. One thing was for sure; I was not going to stand here like a dick waiting for her to return.

Stomping across my flat I cracked open a window, extracted a fag from behind my ear and my lighter from inside my pocket and lit up. It was gone five thirty and lights were going off in the surrounding buildings as business closed down for the day. I hadn't been up long, but the sun would be setting in a couple of hours and a solitary night spent painting stretched ahead. A movement in the garden below caught my attention and I leaned out of the window to get a better look. What the hell? It was Cally – I could see flashes of red as she moved about below the memorial tree, which was in full flower. What was she doing down there? As I watched I saw glimpses of a bare foot every now and then; her toes pointed. Was she dancing…?

Great. She was a fucking fruit loop. I knew she'd be trouble. If she damaged that tree she'd regret it. Flicking my fag butt out into the air, I slid the window shut and turned my music up so that thrash metal guitars filled the room. Was it too early in the evening to do a line of coke?

Chapter Nine

I smiled at the lone man I was dancing for, trying to catch his eye to encourage more tips, but his expression was so glazed over that I wasn't convinced he was seeing me at all. I got the impression he was a 'legs man' and had adapted my routine accordingly, with extra prominent leg stretches as I moved around the pole. He wore a crumpled suit, but no tie, his jacket hanging open to reveal a generous beer belly. He looked unhappy, and although he was neither attractive nor friendly, I hoped I was at least distracting him from his troubles as I danced.

Without warning, the man suddenly lurched forwards in his seat and grabbed me round the ankle. Losing my balance I clung to the pole for support, letting out a startled cry that was lost in the loud music. As I tried to wrench my leg free of his grasp, he only gripped me tighter, and I watched in horrified fascination as he began to lower his wet mouth to my shin. I'll admit I was sorely tempted to kick him in the face, but at that moment Leroy, the bouncer who reminded me of Liam, appeared behind him, wrapped a meaty bicep around the punter's neck and yanked him away from me in one burly move. To my relief my leg was released immediately and I stumbled backwards, instinctively putting the podium between us.

'No touching, mate, you know the rules, you've been warned before – let's go,' Leroy said, his low voice lending threat to his words. The punter leered at me, but

44

made no attempt to struggle as Leroy hauled him away to the exit.

'You OK, Luna?' Zena asked beside me.

'Yes, fine.' I straightened up, pleased that my voice sounded steady. I'd been warned by the other girls that I would experience harassment at some point, and as incidents went, this did not constitute a bad one. The speed and efficiency with which Leroy had come to my aid was reassuring. Even so, the sudden, uninvited contact had been a shock, and that was hard to hide.

Zena eyed me speculatively. 'You might as well finish up for the night; it's not busy and we're closing soon.'

I smiled gratefully. 'OK, if you're sure... thanks.' I wasn't about to let my new-found confidence be shaken by one idiot, but I'd spent a busy day sightseeing before starting my shift and now I was keen to get home and crawl into bed.

It was only once I reached my front door, at quarter to four in the morning, that I realised I didn't have my keys. Panic set in as I frantically searched my handbag and my pockets again and again. Had I forgotten to take them with me this morning? Or had I left them at the club? Or dropped them somewhere? Had they been stolen...?

I couldn't go back to the club; it would be locked up by now, and ringing Marguerite at this time in the morning would be unfair, especially since I'd been missing her phone calls and ignoring her messages. Calling out an emergency locksmith would cost a fortune, and what if my keys were simply waiting for me on the other side of the door? I had only two options as far as I could see – sit here on the landing until morning, or ask my obnoxious neighbour for help.

I could tell he was still up, amazingly, given the hour. I could hear music emanating from behind his door. He'd said he owned the whole building. I wasn't sure if that was really true or pure arrogance on his part, but either way he might have a spare key I could borrow. Recollections of the way he'd spoken to me swept through my mind.

Maybe I'd just wait until morning…

I groaned aloud. Come on Cally, this is the new confident you. So what if he's rude and nasty? It'll be over quickly – you can do this.

I knocked loudly and then chewed my lip as I waited several long seconds for a response.

He was scowling when he opened the door; all dark eyes, frown lines and shadows, but said nothing.

'I'm sorry to disturb you,' I stammered. 'But I've locked myself out…' He smelled of tobacco and raw masculinity; his sleeveless black vest showcasing broad, muscular shoulders smothered in tattoos. I fought to keep my gaze on his face as he stared back at me, but he didn't speak. 'I… I don't suppose you have a spare key I could borrow?'

The tension in his expression eased slightly and he folded his arms, resting his lean torso casually against the door frame. 'Do you really get paid for this service?'

'What service?'

'House-sitting.'

'Oh.' My face heated at his implication that I was making a hash of it. 'Actually it's my first time; I'm just filling in for a friend and it doesn't pay as well as you might think…' Why was I explaining myself? 'Look, do you have a spare key or not?'

He sighed and glanced down and I inadvertently followed his gaze over his dark, paint-flecked combats to his naked feet. I found myself thinking they were attractive, despite also being splashed with paint. 'I think I've got one somewhere; give me a minute.'

He turned and disappeared out of sight, leaving me standing in the open doorway. It was chilly on the landing and I was conscious of all the heat escaping from within, so after a moment's hesitation I stepped inside, pushing the door behind me. This flat was a world away from the one next door. For a start it was about double the size, dimly lit and virtually devoid of furniture. A large, unmade bed sat right in the centre of the industrial-sized space like an island, surrounded by stacks of books and a scattering of used crockery. I wondered what it must feel like to sleep in such a cavernous place.

All along one wall, large windows where hidden behind blackout blinds, concealing what must be a spectacular view west across the city. Off to one side the kitchen area looked to be made of solid concrete and was similarly cluttered with dirty dishes and an extraordinary number of bottles of booze. The odd wooden chair, table or trolley was dotted about; each one chaotically loaded with paints, brushes and other artist's paraphernalia. At the edges of the vast room, leaning against the bare brick walls, as if washed up by a tide, were hundreds of stretched canvases ranging in size from several metres across, to just one. Most of them faced away, their messages hidden from view.

My eyes were inevitably drawn to where two bright, free-standing spotlights were trained on a large canvas fixed to the wall. I hadn't intended to venture further into the flat uninvited; I was lured in through sheer curiosity, and only realised once I was close enough to see that the painting was wet. I recognised the music playing through wall-mounted loud-speakers as Linkin Park, but I could still hear my neighbour cursing as he rooted about in one of the bedrooms. He'd be angry when he found me snooping, but the painting before me had captured my attention so thoroughly that I couldn't turn away.

It was intensely beautiful and abstract in style, though certain elements within it were easily recognisable. The primary subject was a group of trees, depicted so realistically – the texture of the bark and the dappled, eerie green light illustrated so masterfully – that they almost reached out of the canvas towards me. In places the trunks and branches were streaked with ribbon-like drips of crimson, as if the trees themselves were weeping blood. But there was the suggestion of a figure there, too; the traces of a young woman, wearing white, hidden amongst the trees. She was by no means substantial – there was a hint of a slender elbow, the outline of her neck, the spread of delicate fingers – and I could only see her out of the corner of my eye. But she was there.

My skin prickled with goosebumps despite the room being stiflingly warm around me. Feeling light-headed I unbuttoned my coat. As I shrugged out of it, I stepped nearer to the canvas, careful to avoid the wet splashes of paint on the parquet floor.

'It's not finished,' said a low voice close behind me, making me jump. I turned to find my neighbour towering over me, his dark eyes glowing with something I couldn't read – mischief maybe. I was thrown by his sudden proximity and by the fact that he didn't look angry. Despite the hard planes of his face, the silver barbell in his eyebrow and the scruffy stubble at his jaw, he was actually rather handsome, and that awareness unsettled me even more. 'What do you think?'

My thin, cotton dress felt inexplicably tight around my ribs and I stared at him for a moment, my blood pulsing loudly in my ears as I attempted to unscramble my thoughts. 'I... it's... unnerving.' *Unnerving*? Of all the adjectives I could have used; amazing, beautiful, mesmerising, haunting even, why had my brain thrown that up? Probably because *he* unnerved me.

His dark brows lifted slightly in surprise and I rushed to correct my mistake.

'I mean in a good way; it's beautiful and so realistic in places; the way you've captured the feel of the trees; it's almost...' His gaze had dropped to my mouth as I rambled and I found myself drawn to his in return – his lips looked unexpectedly soft and pink.

'Almost what?'

Damn. I had forgotten what I was saying. Dragging my eyes away from his I turned back to the painting. 'You never told me your name.'

He sighed and padded over to the kitchen area and I clocked the perfect shape of his bum as he strode away.

'Bay,' he said grudgingly, rinsing a couple of tumblers in the kitchen sink.

Encouraged, I moved towards him, keeping the kitchen counter between us. 'Bay? Is that short for something?'

'Bailey, but everyone calls me Bay.' He poured himself a generous measure of vodka and then hovered over a second glass, looking at me with an eyebrow raised in unspoken offer.

'Yeah, why not,' I said, lowering my coat to a clean-looking patch of floor, relieved that Bay was being civil to me at last.

He pushed the glass across the cluttered counter towards me and immediately took a swallow of his own drink. All the paint residue embedded around his fingernails made his hands looked filthy.

'Don't you have any mixers? Coke? Lemonade…?' He glared at me before opening the fridge, pulling out a carton of orange juice and holding it up for me to see. 'Perfect, thank you,' I said, made to feel like a difficult guest as he sloshed some into my glass.

The drink was refreshing and welcome, though it burned on its way down. It was surreal standing in a stranger's apartment drinking vodka in the middle of the night; completely out of character for me and therefore, oddly satisfying. And I didn't feel as if I was in any danger – my reluctant host was unlike anyone else I'd ever met, and moody as hell, but I didn't think he would hurt me. After all, anyone who could paint so beautifully couldn't be all bad…

'You're not a hooker are you?' he said.

Chapter Ten

'You're not a hooker are you?' I regretted the words as soon as they were out of my mouth. I hadn't meant it that way – in my head it was a rhetorical question; a conclusion I'd reached; a statement – but Cally looked like I'd slapped her. She downed the rest of her drink in one and pushed the empty tumbler back onto the counter.

'Did you find a spare key or not? Because I'd like to get out of here and leave you in peace.' She glared at me; her spectacular blue eyes stunning me into silence.

Reaching into my pocket I pulled out the modest set of keys I'd found.

'Great, thank you,' she said tightly, holding out her palm. It was bright pink and covered in blisters, a couple of which had recently burst and looked sore.

'What happened to your hand?'

She glanced down at her raw palm as if she had forgotten the state it was in. She sighed. 'If you must know I'm a pole dancer,' she admitted at last.

'You're a stripper?'

'I prefer exotic dancer, but yes,' her voice was defiant, she held my gaze.

'Is that what you were doing down in the garden the other day? Pole dancing around a tree?'

She blushed then, which was surprising considering she had just confessed to removing her clothes for strangers for money. She shifted uncomfortably, a curtain of silky hair falling to hide one side of her face.

51

'Yes, I needed somewhere to practise and that tree happens to be the perfect size. But don't worry; I haven't damaged it in any way. If anything, it has damaged me,' she gently stretched out her sore palm.

The sight of her pain bothered me. I moved around the counter towards her, re-pocketing the keys and taking her hand in my own. She started slightly at the unexpected contact, but I lifted her other hand and tilted both of her palms towards the light, so that I could inspect the damage. The feel of her soft skin sent a pleasant sensation coursing up my arms but I studiously ignored it. 'These need washing and dressing or they're going to get infected.'

She went to withdraw her hands, but I didn't want to give her up yet, and I tightened my grip.

'If you let go of me, I can do that,' she said. I was close enough to smell the sweet orange juice on her breath and see the endearing gap between her front teeth. Her hands trembled slightly in mine and I wondered if she was afraid of me.

'Has Sidney got proper bandages?'

'I don't know.'

As I waited, silently, the anger slowly dissipated from her eyes and her hands relaxed in mine. Wordlessly I released one and led her to the bathroom by the other.

Cally didn't complain or even so much as wince as I carefully washed and dried her hands and applied sterile dressings to both palms. Neither did she comment on the jagged hole above the sink, which was once a mirror, and I was grateful for that.

'Do you always work at night?' she said.

'Yes.'

'Don't you need natural light to paint?'

'No.'

'And you really own the whole building?'

'Yes.' Deliberately turning my back on her I packed the first aid kit away. I knew I was being a dick, but I resented her intrusion in my life. My self-imposed solitude – the time and space to work without interference or distraction – was everything to me, and her continued interruptions couldn't be tolerated or encouraged.

And yet... she fascinated me. She had an elegant, almost regal way of holding herself, and a classical, enigmatic beauty; dark features, dark hair and a contrasting milky-white skin. There was a softness, a shyness about her which was completely at odds with her job as a stripper. I couldn't work her out. But asking her any questions would only invite more about me in return; questions I was not prepared to answer.

She was biting her lip in frustration as I turned back to her, or maybe in an attempt to hold back more words. I took the spare keys from my pocket and placed them carefully in her bandaged hand.

'Thank you,' she said, resigned.

I walked her to the door.

'I'll try not to bother you again,' she said quietly.

I nodded and she disappeared next door without another word.

Chapter Eleven

It was Friday night in the capital, in one of the most happening clubs in the world, and my colleagues and I were queens of the dance floor. Destiny (I didn't know her real name) winked at me as yet another guy danced up close behind me, his hands on my hips. Rolling my eyes I firmly pushed the stranger's hands away and sidestepped to reclaim my personal space without looking back. I wasn't here because I wanted to pull, or because I particularly wanted to dance – my job provided enough opportunity for that – I was here to make friends.

I'd convinced myself to join the girls from The Electric Fox on a night out in a blatant attempt to ingratiate myself with them. Most of the other strippers were friendly up to a point, but I was the new girl and I sensed a general level of distrust amongst them, not least because I'd still not been brave enough to strip naked in front of the punters.

Admittedly, clubbing felt a little like a busman's holiday, but on the plus side our dancing skills made us popular, and I'd not had to buy a drink all night. Such was the potent combined effect of our group on the men present. I was pleasantly drunk as I danced, the cocktails in my bloodstream enhancing the party atmosphere and effectively numbing my aching feet.

It was silly, really – this need to make friends – I shouldn't need them. I'd achieved what I'd originally set out to do – left everyone behind, changed my life beyond all recognition, become a new person. Within days of being in London I'd crossed several long-held ambitions off my list: visiting the Royal Opera House, the London Eye, Kew Gardens and the Butterfly House at the National History Museum. But I hadn't expected that experiencing all those things alone would feel so hollow.

I was proud of myself for earning money by dancing; it was an ambition I never expected to fulfil, even if I wasn't yet exploiting my full potential. And now my days were free of obligation; imbued with quiet solitude in which to write.

Except that I wasn't writing – had not written a single word, in fact; good, bad or otherwise. I couldn't seem to get started. What should I write about? Nothing about my life was worth recording autobiographically, and I hadn't yet had a decent idea for a fictional novel or even a short story.

It didn't help that I was spending most of my daylight hours asleep. Somehow I'd slipped into a nocturnal habit. Returning home from work in the early hours of the morning I was too wired to sleep and would waste time watching movies, or baking biscuits. Then, just as the rest of the world was starting their working day, I would crash out, only waking again in time to get ready for another shift. My antisocial schedule had become so routine that it endured even on the nights I wasn't working. And I was starting to feel cut off from the rest of the world; marooned in the top of a tower.

But making friends wasn't proving easy. In clubs such as these, the music was too loud to permit anything other than non-verbal dialogue, and most people were too drunk to conduct a decent conversation anyway. I missed Marguerite terribly – missed her buoyant chatter, no-nonsense attitude and heartfelt hugs – but I was reluctant to call her. I told myself I didn't return her calls because of our conflicting schedules, and because she was still in contact with Liam. But honestly I just couldn't speak to her knowing I was hiding things from her – I was afraid I'd spill everything, give up London and crawl home with my tail between my legs. Instead I sent her apologetic text messages riddled with lame excuses and placating smiley emojis. The last person I'd had a real conversation with (if you could even call it that) was my truculent neighbour, Bay.

More than two weeks had passed since he'd bandaged my hands for me. My palms had healed nicely into calluses and, to my great relief, I'd found my own set of keys inside the flat, but had chickened out of returning the spares to Bay in person, leaving them in his mailbox instead. True to my word I'd stayed away from him. But he seemed to invade my thoughts every day.

He was an enigma; a bad-tempered but oddly-compelling guy, who owned an office block, right in the heart of London, and spent his nights painting eerily beautiful pictures. He treated me with obvious disdain – when he wasn't being sarcastic, he was downright insulting – and yet, he had tended to my hands with such care...

I had taken that opportunity to check out his tattoos; what I could see of them without making it obvious, anyway. Trees seemed to be a theme for Bay because a black forest of skeleton branches stretched their way up from his left wrist to above his elbow as if straining towards the light. Above, adorning his left shoulder, sat a full, grey moon, complete with shadows and craters. This in turn was incorporated into an intricate monochrome pattern of skulls; most of which I hadn't been able to see properly. And on his opposite shoulder sat a large, delicately-detailed moth, with what looked like another skull on its back. Death, it seemed, was also a theme.

Clearly Bay was hurting inside – a tortured soul – his excessive drinking alone pointed to that, if nothing else, and in the days since then I'd decided he was best avoided. But I was bored of dwelling on my own mistakes and mortality, and as obnoxious as Bay was, my guilty conscience nagged at me for turning my back on someone so clearly in pain. It was tempting to pry into his problems rather than ponder my own.

'Get a life, Cally,' I muttered under my breath, shaking my head in exasperation. Throwing my arms up in the air with fresh abandon I kept dancing as one of my favourite tunes, Joe Goddard's 'Gabriel', flooded the air.

Chapter Twelve

Chain-smoking cigarettes I waited until almost midnight before letting myself into the flat next door. I knew full well that what I was doing was wrong, but I couldn't help myself. In my mind I justified it by reminding myself that I owned the freehold; that Sidney only paid for the lease; and Cally, not even that. And I had a right to know who was residing in my building, who was living next door to me and sharing my wall. But in truth I was breaking and entering – snooping, plain and simple.

Over a fortnight had passed since I'd spoken to Cally. I'd seen her a few times through the peephole in my door as she came and went. I'd figured out her shift pattern and that's how I could be confident she was out at work now. But it wasn't enough; I wanted to know more.

The inside of the flat looked much as it usually did; not trashed or re-arranged; it wasn't even messy. At a glance everything looked as clean, neat and tidy as Sidney kept it; there weren't even any dirty dishes lying in the sink. As I moved further into the main room I noted that all his potted plants were flourishing and the fish tank looked immaculate – the water clear and the fish well-fed. Not that I could tell a well-fed fish from a hungry one, but it was a reasonable assumption given all other signs. I rapped my knuckles on the glass making them scatter.

'You had a lucky escape, guys – if you'd been left in my care you'd all be flushed down the toilet by now.' The fish ignored me.

Turning my attention to the laptop sitting on the dining table I flipped it open, but it was password protected, and after a couple of obvious attempts I gave up, closing the lid again and making my way to the bedrooms.

Cally had chosen to sleep in Sidney's spare room over the master, despite its smaller proportions. The large stuffed bunny from the landing sat squarely in the middle of the bed, one ear held aloft and glass eyes staring, as if inviting me to speak. But I wasn't off my face enough to do that, despite having recently addressed a tank full of tropical fish.

Two framed photographs on the dresser caught my eye and I picked them up to take a closer look. One was of a retirement-age, middle-class couple, sitting outside a villa somewhere Mediterranean and sunny. I could detect something of Cally's features in the two faces when I squinted and assumed they were her parents, though I couldn't be sure. The other photo showed a burly rugby player, clutching a muddy ball to his chest, mid match. He had a scowl of concentration on his face, his mouth-guard bared, and was about to be tackled from several directions; his body twisted in mid-flight. Was this her brother or her boyfriend? Was this the type of guy Cally went for? Physically large and sporty? It was hard to surmise anything of his personality from such an image, but he had a sensible haircut and no visible tattoos…

But why should it matter to me? Whoever he was, he was on the dresser next to her parents rather than over by the bed – that had to be a good sign, surely?

The fitted wardrobe looked like it had been stocked by two different women. In one side hung a neat range of elegantly feminine clothes – mainly dresses and mainly in shades of cadmium red, carmine, crimson and vermilion. This fitted the classy Cally that I'd observed coming and going over the past month. But on the other side hung a daring array of scarlet lingerie – all skimpy lace, soft satin and criss-crossed ribbon. It was this side of Cally that confounded and intrigued me. No matter how long I spent thinking about it, and I'd clocked up a good many hours by now, I couldn't reconcile Cally's prim-and-proper demeanour with stripping. I'd seen enough exotic dancers in my time to recognise their empty eyes, resigned expressions and mechanical movements – that just wasn't Cally. Part of the puzzle was missing and it was driving me nuts.

Like a true creep I rifled through her underwear drawer. Disappointingly it consisted of nothing more than simple sets of black bras and matching panties that were nowhere near as exotic as her stripping gear, and yet the mere sight of them got me hard. What was wrong with me? I considered stealing a pair of her knickers, but even I wasn't *that* creepy.

Entering the bathroom I was further aroused by the scent of Cally's toiletries. The clarity of the images they evoked in my mind surprised me: her hair falling in a curtain across one side of her face, the delicate veins beneath the skin of her wrist, the twitch of her mouth when I swore at her…

Despairing at my own insanity and disgusted with myself, I made my way back to the front door, switching off lights as I went. There were no answers for me here. Cally seemed to have few personal possessions, none of which explained why I was so interested in someone I didn't even like.

A small pile of unopened post caught my eye as I was about to leave. It had been redirected from an address in Wildham; a small commuter town north of London. I had no idea what could have prompted Cally's move to the city, but something inside me was strangely pleased to note that Calluna Drey was officially a 'Miss'.

Returning to my flat, I headed straight to the kitchen, poured myself a stiff drink and speed-dialled my dealer. Sinking to new depths of depravity and becoming a virtual stalker definitely called for something stronger to see me through the night.

Chapter Thirteen

The Electric Fox ladies partied hard. It was gone eight o'clock on Saturday morning by the time I stumbled out of a cab in front of the office building I'd come to accept as my home. I was shattered – there was no way I would be able to go clubbing with any regularity.

A cute young delivery driver with a mop of blonde hair and a look of resignation was leaning into the buzzer at the door, a boxed parcel on the pavement at his feet. His face lifted at my approach, his down-turned mouth rising into an attractive smile.

'You going up to flat one by any chance?'

'No, sorry, I'm flat two; but I can take it up if you'd like?'

'Great, thanks! Do you mind signing for it? Can I take your name?'

The courier surreptitiously looked me up and down as I signed his hand-held device. It was obvious I'd been out all night, but his gaze was flattering rather than sleazy, and prevented me from feeling like a dirty stop-out. I smiled gratefully at him as he walked away with a cheerful wave.

The parcel, from an art supply company and addressed to Mr B. Madderson, was not heavy, and now that I had a legitimate excuse, I was strangely excited at the prospect of seeing Bay again. Slipping off my heels I journeyed up in the lift barefoot, idly wondering if he would be out, or simply asleep. But as the doors slid open on the top floor I realised both assumptions were wrong. Absurdly loud and angry music roared from behind Bay's front door, the bass vibrating right through my chest as if I was back in the club. My first instinct was to dump the parcel on the floor outside his door for him to trip over. But on second thought, there was no way I could sleep with such a racket going on, and Bay's blatant disregard for my eardrums made me irritable.

I waited until a break between songs before rapping loudly on his door. As the next tune started up, just as aggressively as the last, I thought he hadn't heard me and I was about to leave the parcel when the door swung open and I was engulfed in noise and smoke.

Bay looked awful – like he hadn't washed, shaved, slept, or eaten in days. His skin looked deathly pale and shiny with sweat, his dilated pupils were black holes within shadowy sockets as he glowered at me.

'What do you want?' His voice was lost in the heavy metal, but I read his lips easily enough. Temporarily speechless, I gaped at him, but before I could recover a woman with bright purple hair and a short black skirt pushed passed us on her way to the lift. Despite heavy make-up, various metal studs in her ears, nose and mouth, and a pair of bulky leather boots, she was pretty. But the smug smile on her face matched her just-fucked hair and only increased my irritation.

Was she his girlfriend? Did it matter? Why should I care?

As the lift carried her away I returned my attention to Bay, but he shuddered and lurched off towards the bathroom.

Left alone in his open doorway once again, I dumped my handbag, my heels, and his parcel inside the door, slammed it shut and then stalked over to where a docked iPhone sat on a shelf alongside a battered-looking Mac Book. Abruptly I dialled the volume down from deafening to a murmur, and in the invading quiet I could clearly hear Bay vomiting.

Sighing, and allowing my anger to dissipate, I glanced around the vast, dimly-lit room, now even messier than I'd last seen it. The queen-sized bed in the centre of the room was in complete disarray, and there were more empty liquor bottles gathered on every surface. I should leave. Bay was ill. It was almost certainly self-inflicted – too much booze, too many drugs, or a combination of both – but even if it wasn't, he wouldn't appreciate me hanging about to witness his suffering.

On my way back to the door a new canvas caught my attention – it was attached to the wall in a bright spotlight, vibrant with energy and potential – but as I deviated towards it I stubbed my toes on an ashtray that was seemingly carved out of granite and lurking like an iceberg in the shadows. Hopping about, I cursed my stupid neighbour under my breath. Right, that was it, I was getting out of here; this guy was nothing but trouble.

As the pain in my injured digits subsided, I carefully limped to the front door, determined to leave my neighbour to his miserable retching. But then I heard a sickening thump followed by a silence that made my scalp prickle. On instinct, but against my better judgement, I picked my way over to the bathroom where I found Bay slumped in a heap on the floor.

Wrinkling my nose against the smell, I knelt beside him on the cold tiles, patting his clammy cheek and calling his name. To my great relief he groaned, confirming that he wasn't dead.

'Bay, get up, come on.' Reaching up I turned on the tap in the sink and flicked cold water at his face until he scowled and blinked, grumbling with irritation.

'I'm fine, go away.'

'You're not fine – what have you taken?'

'Nothing; just something I ate,' he muttered unconvincingly, bracing one paint-stained hand on my thigh and the other on the side of the bath as he sat up.

'Can I get you something? A glass of water? Or I could make coffee…?'

He shook his head but the action obviously hurt, and he stopped abruptly, taking his head in his hands. 'Just leave me.'

Despite Bay's attitude, body odour, and general unpleasantness, I was reluctant to leave him alone in such a sorry state; my conscience wouldn't allow it. Being back in his bathroom reminded me of the care he had taken of my sore hands and, if nothing else, shouldn't I return that favour? 'Tell me how I can help first.'

He groaned again. 'Switch the shower on; let it run cold.'

I did as he requested, trying not to look as he leaned forwards and dragged his soiled T-shirt off over his head. To my amazement, a beautiful and disturbing rendering of the Grim Reaper was revealed, inked right down the centre of his back. The tattoo made me vibrate with anger. Why would anyone taunt death like that? Tempt fate, when life was so damn short already? Biting my lip I let Bay lean heavily against me as he struggled to his feet. With the unhooking of a button he let his paint-splattered combat trousers drop to the floor and I took a startled step back away from him – he wore no underwear – but he grabbed hold of my arm again to steady himself as he stepped into the shower. He gasped as the cold water hit him, his head falling back and his eyes closing.

In the face of Bay's unexpected nakedness, my mouth went completely dry. I tried not to gawk as my eyes drank in every detail of his long, lean, tightly muscled body; so different to Liam's; harder, meaner, no softness to spare. And, despite the onslaught of cold water, Bay's tackle was impressive enough to explain, if not excuse, some of his arrogant swagger. The icy spray rebounded off his body, plastering my hair to my skin and trickling down inside my dress while I worked to get over the sight of him and mentally pull myself together.

After several minutes Bay began to shiver. Reaching past him without a word, I adjusted the temperature until the water provided a comforting heat. His eyes still shut, he collapsed back against the tiled wall, bent his knees and slid down until he was sitting on the floor. With my arm still anchored in his grasp, I sank to a crouch beside him, resigned to being soaked right through.

At last he released his grip, opened his eyes and looked at me. 'I made you wet,' he said with a smirk.

As heat rose to my cheeks I frowned at him, embarrassed and annoyed at myself for reacting. 'Nothing I can't handle.'

'You didn't have to stay.'

'I know.'

'Why did you, then?'

I stood up to leave.

'Wait, don't, I didn't mean it like that; I'm an arsehole.'

'Yes, you are.'

Bay smiled. It was like sudden sunshine through black cloud;. I took a large towel from where it was slung haphazardly over a rail, dabbed my face and chest and then dumped it on the edge of the bath where Bay would be able to reach it.

'I'm going to make coffee, do you want one?'

'Yeah, OK,' he said, his smile gone again.

By the time I'd found two chipped mugs, washed them up and made coffee, Bay had re-emerged. He still looked pasty and unshaven but he'd washed himself, cleaned his hair and brushed his teeth, so he smelled much better – surprisingly appealing in fact. Dressed in a fresh shirt and boxers, he held a faded black Alice In Chains T-shirt aloft in his hand.

'Here, put this on, it's clean; I don't want you catching cold on my account.'

I hesitated. It made more sense to nip next door and change into something of my own, but he was offering the garment up like an olive branch so I accepted it. Out of prudish habit I considered going to the bathroom to change, but it seemed silly given my job, so without looking at Bay, I slipped off my wet dress and pulled his shirt over my damp underwear. It was large on me - almost as long as my dress had been - but cosy and dry. Bay walked over to his bed, roughly straightened out the cover and flopped down onto it face first with a groan. Following him, I set his coffee down on a stack of dog-eared paperback books – they appeared to be gritty crime novels – and then, at a loss for anywhere else to sit, I perched on the edge of his bed, sipping from my cup.

He convulsed with a moan, awkwardly wrapping his arms around his stomach.

'Why do you let yourself get into such a state?' I said.

'If you're gonna have a go, you can fuck off.'

I clenched my teeth. 'Are you at least going to try to drink some coffee?'

Sighing, he sat up, retrieved his mug and took a tentative sip, then a larger gulp. 'Actually, that's pretty good,' he muttered. It was as close to a 'thank you' or a compliment as I was going to get from Bay, but it was enough. He glanced around for a bedside clock only to find the digital display blank. 'What time is it?'

'I'm not sure; I don't have a watch; maybe half eight... nine...?'

'And you only just finished work?' His damp hair stuck up in every direction and I had an urge to try and tame it, comb it with my fingers, though of course I refrained.

'No, I went clubbing with the girls after my shift.'

He cocked his pierced eyebrow at me in surprise. 'Good night?'

'Yeah, it was OK I guess. My feet will need time to recover, though.' I flexed them as I said it, wincing slightly. 'And I stubbed my toes on that wretched ashtray of yours, which doesn't help. Why do you leave your stuff all over the floor?' I was surprised at my own boldness;

chiding him as if he were a naughty child, but I was still flustered from seeing his naked body, the sight of which was now burned into my brain. And the way he looked at me was unnerving. And anyway, he deserved it.

'Let me see,' he said, setting down his mug and reaching out his open palm.

'No, it's fine.' The thought of Bay handling my feet in the same tender way that he touched my hands only made me more jittery.

'Let me see, I might be able to help—'

'I don't want your help,' I snapped.

Rolling his eyes he went back to drinking his coffee.

Chapter Fourteen

What a scumbag! It wasn't enough that I'd broken into Cally's home and snooped through her things, I'd then got trashed and let *her* deal with the fallout. The mere sight of me should have had her running away screaming, but she'd stayed. And I'd let her.

After a difficult start we settled into stilted conversation – I plied her with innocuous questions about her job and she told me about the club, the other girls she worked with and the music the DJ played. I didn't let on that I was familiar with The Electric Fox; that I'd been a regular visitor in the past; in the days when all I did was bar-hop, get high and fuck lots of women. She already had enough reasons to dislike me.

Cally looked exhausted. As she began to relax I shifted over to the other side of the bed so that she could stretch out and rest her head. My shirt did a good job of covering her, but it was too little too late – I'd already had a tantalising glimpse of the body hidden beneath and I couldn't get it out of my mind, despite how shitty I felt.

Before long it was Cally's turn to question me:

'Which band is this?'

'Nine Inch Nails.'

'Why do you play it so loud?'

'I can barely hear it now you've turned it down so low. It's good loud – even better live.'

'If you say so. Was that your girlfriend who just left?'

'I don't have a girlfriend. Why?'

'No reason,' she blushed.

I cruelly left her defensive response hanging awkwardly in the air while she tried to think of something else to say.

'Tell me about your tattoos.'

'What do you want to know?'

Her ultramarine eyes travelled across my skin as she considered where to start, and the hairs stood up all over my body.

'Why do you have so many?'

'You don't approve.'

She didn't try to deny it. 'When did you get this one?' She pointed to the moon on my left shoulder, but stopped short of actually touching me, though I wanted her to.

'When I was fifteen.'

'Fifteen? Is that legal?'

'No.'

'Oh.'

'The artist was a friend of my brother's and knew I wouldn't rat.'

'I bet you were a real hell-raiser as a teen.'

'You have no idea.'

She smiled. 'How old's your brother?'

'Now? About forty-one I think.'

'And you?'

'Thirty-six. You?'

'Thirty.'

'Do you have a brother?'

'No.'

The rugby player from the photo in her bedroom flared up in my mind and I worked to keep a ridiculous sense of disappointment from my face.

'So why did you get it – this tattoo?'

I shrugged. 'I just liked it.' I could tell she didn't believe me, but she let it go and I steered the conversation back to her. 'When did you start dancing?'

'My Mum signed me up for ballet classes when I was five.'

'Five! Fuck.'

'Yeah, but I loved it – it made me feel like a princess and a part of something; I made good friends there. When I was thirteen I almost gave it up. Ballet dancing wasn't 'cool', but I missed it too much – the steady discipline and the physical challenge of it. So I kept going to ballet classes and took up other forms, too – contemporary, jazz, hip-hop, even pole dancing.'

We talked for a while, or rather Cally did and I kept prompting her so that she would continue. As far as I could tell, her background was typically middle class, suburban, and uneventful. She was an only child, but her parents were still together and had recently retired to Spain. Cally's conventional upbringing had resulted in an intelligent and seemingly well-adjusted woman with the freedom and potential to do anything she wanted, but she was no less intriguing for all that. Her passion for dancing went some way towards explaining her current bizarre career choice, but nothing she said made sense of her sudden move to London. Of course I couldn't ask her personal questions without expecting her to do the same, so for the most part we stuck to safe topics; music, art and movies. I revealed nothing of my past or my family; why should I? We were never going to be best buddies. It was bad enough that I'd let slip I had an older brother, even that was too much.

Cally made buttered toast, which helped to settle my stomach, but I was still wrecked and at some point, much to my consternation, I must have fallen asleep.

When I woke up in the evening, Cally was gone. She'd washed up, turned off the lights and taken her dress, handbag, and heels next door with her. And my T-shirt. I felt too ashamed to knock on her door and thank her for looking after me – I thought about it constantly, but something always stopped me. Self-preservation, perhaps. And yet I found myself hoping that she might bring my shirt back.

As the days crawled by I lost that hope.

Listening to Muse albums on repeat I threw myself into my work instead. On my windowsill I found a peacock butterfly. I had no idea how it had managed to fly in through a twelfth floor city window, but I carefully trapped it under a glass so that I could study it's velvet markings more closely. It reminded of Cally; the vibrant cadmium scarlet of its wings; a clear warning; both delicate and alluring, and the whorls; cerulean blue and softly hypnotic, like her eyes. Inspired, I embarked on a new set of paintings; recreating parts of the butterfly; weaving the patterns and the sense of flight and fragility into the canvas with a fresh intensity that left little time to sleep or think about anything else.

Chapter Fifteen

As the music built towards a climax I unhooked my bra and let it slither to the floor. I kept dancing; brazenly; as if I was used to baring my nipples to strangers, as if this wasn't my first time. The resulting increase in enthusiasm from the three young men, who'd been plying me with tips and encouragement all evening, was evident. It was in their eyes; the slackening of their jaws and the way they adjusted themselves. I was determined to go the whole hog tonight – to get over myself and finally strip – I'd convinced myself that I was confident enough and that it would be liberating.

Of all the strippers in The Electric Fox I wasn't the youngest or the prettiest and I certainly didn't have the biggest boobs, but I liked to think I was the best dancer, from a technical point of view. Not that it mattered to the punters – they didn't come here for the dancing – but it mattered to me. As one tune morphed smoothly into another I ran my fingers suggestively around the edges of my frilly knickers. They whistled appreciatively in response and I kept dancing; lifting myself high up on the pole, arching my back and pointing my breasts as I lowered myself in a slow, sweeping spiral under their combined gaze.

All three guys looked to be in their early twenties; still boys, really, with a shared celebratory mission and an eager, puppy-like excitement. Though drunk, they were not unattractive, and their avid attention was flattering.

Once they had tucked more notes under the elastic at my hip, I rewarded them by shimmying out of my undies to a roaring cheer of approval. Despite all the mental and physical preparation I'd put into this moment, my cheeks flamed with embarrassment under the spotlights. But I kept moving; braving it out; focusing on the rhythm of the music and grateful for the vodka in my system.

At the next song change I smiled goodbye to the boys, gathered my tips and clothes, wrapped myself inside my robe and fled to the changing room for a break. I was proud of myself for doing it at last; I was done letting fear rule my life, and the money was good; I counted sixty quid and I was only two hours into my shift. But as I washed and re-dressed, I didn't feel as elated or liberated as I'd expected to. Did I just need more practise? Or was this all a big mistake? I'd been sure this was what I wanted, so why was I doubting myself?

My next-door neighbour popped into my head, catching me off guard as I was freshening up my make-up. Where did he come from? Why Bay? Maybe because in his bathroom he'd shown no embarrassment about his own nakedness whatsoever, and he was the only person, outside of the club, whom I'd talked to about my new job.

That was a fortnight ago now, and I'd not seen him since, which bothered me more than I wanted to admit. I'd left him sprawled out on his bed, sleeping; looking so different. I suppose everyone did when they were asleep, but he looked markedly so; without his mocking smile and the dark glint of his eyes. And yet he didn't look peaceful in slumber; he looked melancholic; a sadness lay between his eyebrows and at the corners of his mouth.

Not that I'd observed him for long. To avoid any awkwardness I'd returned to my own bed and resolved never to knock on his door again; he was clearly unstable and the last person I needed in my life.

But it annoyed me that *he* had not made any attempt to see *me*. We'd spent hours talking; the two of us alone together on his bed, and despite our mutual dislike of each other, I couldn't shake the sense of intimacy the memory evoked. Thoughts of him plagued my mind more doggedly with each passing day. Was I really so desperate and lonely that I now wanted to befriend an anti-social, drug-addled, self-confessed arsehole? I'd cut myself off from my old life so successfully that I had no-one else to talk to. Having downed some water and freshened up my make-up, I returned to my podium where the three young men from earlier had been replaced by a group of six sweaty, middle-aged men. Reaching out for the pole I smiled as genuinely as I could manage, spinning myself around it with gritted teeth and fresh determination.

*

It was after 3 a.m. when I arrived on the landing outside my flat, and something, or rather the absence of something, caught my attention. The day before, I'd placed a potted palm tree on the landing windowsill, along with a scented room freshener to combat the stale cigarette smoke which seeped out of Bay's lair. But they were gone; the plant and freshener both; the landing was bare again. Surely no-one had stolen them, why would they? I could only conclude it was Bay's handiwork.

I'd never considered myself to be an argumentative person; I despised conflict and usually went out of my

76

way to avoid it. But a furious sense of injustice had been brewing inside me for weeks, and a missing plant was all the excuse I needed to vent.

'Where are they?' I demanded, as Bay opened his door to my hammering.

'Good to see you too, Cally.' He'd recovered since the last time I'd seen him. He was barefoot, as usual, and loosely dressed in a sleeveless T-shirt and paint-splattered combats; his short black hair in tufty disarray. But he looked fresher; clean-shaven; his inked skin glowing, his eyes bright and a teasing smile on his lips. The shock made me falter slightly, but I clung on to my indignation.

'Where are they?'

'What?'

'You know what; the plant and the room freshener.' With a pointed finger I gestured to the empty space in the window. He deliberately leaned closer to me to look and my nostrils filled with his masculine scent.

'Oh that; I removed them,' he said lightly, shifting his gaze to mine without moving back.

'Why?'

'Well for one, I don't wanna have to look at your tedious, suburban crap every time I leave my apartment...' I gaped at him, '...and two, they're a fire hazard.'

'What? That's ridiculous.'

Bay kept a straight face but I could see amusement alight in his eyes as he shrugged. 'Rules are rules, but you can have the plant back as long as you keep it out of sight.' He smiled, which seemed to suck all the breath out of my lungs, making me angrier still.

'You're unbelievable,' I muttered. In my head I was swearing and calling him names, but, as usual, an inbred sense of propriety prevented me from cursing aloud.

'It's over there by the window,' he said, standing back and gesturing inside his flat with an exaggerated sweep of his arm.

Scowling, my arms crossed, I stomped my way through the gloom of his apartment, temporarily distracted by the changes; the lack of clutter on the floor, the neatly made bed and the tidy kitchen. Even the music, which I now recognised as Nine Inch Nails, was playing at an acceptable volume. But it was the panoramic view of London out of the windows – a thousand lights sparkling and St Paul's glowing in the moonlight – which really captured my attention. Letting my shoulder bag slither to the floor, I dragged my eyes away from the view as I reached my potted plant and inspected the leaves for signs of damage. It appeared to be unharmed. The door closed, and while Trent Reznor sang softly in my ears, Bay sauntered, with that lazy swagger of his, barefoot across the vast, shadowy space towards me.

'What about the room freshener?' I demanded.

He pulled a face. 'Seriously? It stank.'

'It's citrus scented.'

'Smelled like loo cleaner – I tipped it down the bog,' he said with an insolent shrug. He stopped a few feet away from me, his gaze locked on mine and my skin prickled with heat and anticipation.

Chapter Sixteen

Fuck me, she was beautiful. Cally stood by the window in a crimson dress, glaring at me, one whole side of her body picked out in moonlight and shadows. 'Don't move,' I said, reaching for a sketchpad and a stick of charcoal.

'What?'

'Just stay there.'

'Why? What are you doing?… Are you *drawing* me?' She sounded incredulous – almost appalled – but I stayed silent in concentration as I sketched, my eyes flicking between her perfect curves and the page as I rushed to capture her. 'Why are you drawing me?' she said, her voice more subdued.

I shrugged one shoulder without pausing. 'I'm an artist – it's what I do.' For several valuable minutes she didn't move.

'You look so serious,' she said at last.

'So do you.'

She laughed then – out of the blue – her head back and her whole body relaxing in the wake of the soft, swelling sound. I stared at her transfixed, my fingers temporarily frozen over the paper in awe. And then the desire to capture this new side of her became all-consuming and I turned the page and began again; tracing the contours of her smile and the light in her eyes with almost frantic haste. 'Did you really tip all that essential oil down the toilet?'

'Yeah.'

'Did it flush?' she was still chuckling softly.

'Yeah, eventually; it took a few goes,' I admitted, unable to hold back a grin of my own.

'I bet.'

'Whole bathroom stinks now.'

'Good. Serves you right.'

The truth was I'd deliberately taken Cally's things to provoke her – in order to see her again. I wasn't too sure *why* I'd felt compelled to see her again, but it had worked and now, as I scrutinised her with my eyes, my fingers recreating every line in black dust, every shadow with a smudge, I was glad she was here.

She sighed and wiped a rogue tear of amusement from her cheek. 'Do you mind if I make myself a drink?'

'Help yourself,' I muttered, still focused on my sketches.

'You want one?'

I nodded absently.

From the freezer she extracted a bottle of vodka, carefully pouring modest measures into two glasses before opening the fridge. 'Wow, you actually have food in here,' she said, removing a chilled bottle of lemonade.

'I'm not completely incapable of looking after myself.'

'You could have fooled me,' she muttered under her breath. I bit back a cutting retort, discarded my sketchbook on the bed and made my way over to her. She shifted uneasily as I stepped close to her to take a swig of the drink she'd prepared for me. It was sickly sweet. She clutched her glass close to her chest as I added more vodka to mine. Cally smelled delicious – light and floral –

and radiated disapproval. I fought the urge to goad her into another altercation.

'How was work?'

She hesitated before answering, a shadow flickering across her features. 'OK.'

'You don't sound sure, did someone hassle you?'

'No, nothing like that.'

'What then?'

'I don't know... I haven't being doing it very long – I think I just need more practise.'

'Maybe it's not right for you...' It was the wrong thing to say – her face flushed with indignation.

'How would you know?' she snapped. 'I'm a bloody good dancer!'

'I'm sure you are; I just meant—'

'You don't know me; you don't know anything about me.'

'OK, OK, I take it back – you were born to be a fucking stripper – happy?'

She pierced me with an icy look of loathing, but there was hurt behind her eyes, too, and I wished I'd kept my mouth shut. She finished her drink and poured herself another.

'You can't keep practising pole dancing on trees; it'll damage your hands.'

She closed her eyes, sighed, and raised an arm; squeezing the back of her neck beneath her hair. 'I know.' Cally's arms were slender and toned; the muscles feminine but well-defined, and the skin on the underside was as delicate, pale and flawless as virgin snow – crying out for me to touch her, taste her, mark her...

'How's your painting going?' she said, lowering her arm, opening her eyes and snapping me back to reality.

I drained my glass and poured myself another drink, this time with only a splash of lemonade. 'Good, I think.' Cally was already making her way across the room to my current work in progress – a three foot by three foot canvas; an impressionistic, acrylic version of a peacock butterfly trapped in a spider's web. It had a darker edginess to it than I'd originally intended, and it was still missing something; an element that I hadn't yet identified – but it was salvageable. I'd long since set the butterfly from my windowsill free, and watched it flutter off into the dawn.

'Wow, you're really talented,' Cally said softly as I gravitated to her side. 'Do you sell them online, or in galleries?'

'Both I think. Felix – my agent – he deals with all that shit for me.'

'And you make enough to live on?' She turned to me and I could see her thoughts processing; colour staining her cheeks. 'Oh, but, maybe you don't have to, if you own this building and everything…'

'I do OK.' As she returned her gaze to the canvas, I retrieved my sketchbook and settled on my bed, this time choosing a soft pencil over charcoal.

'Can I have a look at the others?' she said, gesturing to the other canvases lined up and leaning back-to-front, against the wall.

'Knock yourself out.'

By the time Cally had retired next door, my blinds were drawn, the sun was high in the sky, and I had sketched whole pages full of her; standing, bending, crouching, peering, preparing pasta carbonara, sitting cross-legged at the end of my bed, eating, sipping coffee, and politely yawning with a delicate hand to her mouth.

Alone once more, I lifted some weights and rowed several miles on the machine in my home gym before switching off the music and wearily collapsing into bed. But sleep would not come easily. My fingers still tingled with the thrill of having fresh material to play with; a new subject; different shapes, lines and forms in which to lose myself. I had to admit, my preliminary drawings were good; they gave me a buzz; I was onto something and my mind was already running ahead with anticipation, exploring the possibilities in other media; pastels, acrylics, oils…

And yet she was just a girl – the girl next door – prudish, ordinary and irritating. Why her…?

Chapter Seventeen

I was physically exhausted by the time I got into bed – my limbs, my head, and my eyelids all ached. I stared at the ceiling for ages, but I couldn't sleep. Fleetingly I wondered if insomnia might be a new symptom, but quickly dismissed the idea – even if it was, I didn't want to know.

No-one had ever drawn me before; my neighbour was the only artist I'd ever met. Were they all like that, or was it just Bay? The way he gazed at me intently, for hours, was disconcerting. He didn't ogle my body the way the men at the club did; as if I was a thing; an object to be bought and toyed with, and I don't think it was just because I'd kept my clothes on. Bay had really *looked* at me; openly; attentively; with steady concentration, as if trying to see inside me, and without apparent shame or judgement. It was unsettling, but it was also intensely flattering to be regarded so thoroughly by another person. Especially after years of being invisible.

But why me? I wasn't unattractive but I wasn't model material either – I was plain-looking with gappy front teeth, bony knees and a washed-out complexion, even in summer. Bay must have many more interesting friends to hang out with; people as bold, quirky, and as artistic as himself. As much as I'd like to deny it, my new job and new clothes didn't fool him – he'd seen straight through me from day one. Bay knew exactly who I was, or rather who I wasn't. So why paint me?

When I finally managed to sleep, it was restless, and it was evening by the time I roused, showered, and dressed myself. Acutely aware of Bay's brooding presence lurking just the other side of the wall, and having wasted the day in bed, I decided to escape – to leave the flat and go exploring – make the most of being in the capital, now that the evenings were getting lighter.

Upon reaching street level I realised I was hungry, but the thought of enduring a sit-down meal without company or a good book to read didn't appeal. In a grocery shop I bought myself an off-the-shelf packaged cheese sandwich, and devoured it on the tube on my way to Hampstead Heath. Once there, I spent some time roaming about; discovering woodland walks, walled gardens, swimming ponds and, of course, spectacular views across London. But it didn't escape my notice that out of everything this great city had to offer, I had gravitated straight to a green space filled with trees, grass, and wide open sky.

It had been six weeks since I'd left Wildham, and though I was reluctant to admit it, I was starting to feel homesick. I missed walking through the town square and seeing faces I recognised from childhood; I missed after-match drinks at the pub with the Wildham Warriors; and I missed taking the pretty path through the woods to the corner shop to buy milk on a Sunday morning, and being greeted by at least ten different muddy dogs and their owners along the way. Hampstead Heath was surprisingly busy and the proliferation of picnicking families, Frisbee-players, and romantically-strolling couples only increased my sense of solitude.

I thought of Liam. He would have brought me here if I'd asked him to; held my hand; bought me ice-cream; probably even picked me flowers – he was sweet like that. But I never got around to asking him. We rarely ever tried new things. He did his job and I did mine; we looked after each other and stuck to our routine. It was safe and familiar, much like our sex life.

Lately, with the stripping and everything, sex was suddenly on my mind. It had never been a priority in my relationship with Liam and, blinkered by contentment, it hadn't occurred to me that I might be missing out on anything – I doubt it had crossed Liam's mind either. But now I couldn't even recall the last time we'd done it in our usual missionary position with the lights off. Clearly it wasn't memorable. I was starting to realise sex was a whole subject area I'd never properly explored.

And if I was honest, these new thoughts also had something to do with my neighbour. It wasn't just the streak of danger in him that piqued my curiosity, it was the raw and uncompromising masculinity he exuded; potent, intriguing, and unlike anything I'd ever experienced. It made me wonder what sex with someone like Bay would be like. Not that I had any intention of finding out – I wasn't stupid – but I couldn't help wondering. Despite the cruel way I'd left Liam, I hoped it had been a catalyst for him, too; I hoped he would take the opportunity to let loose a little; go a little crazy; try something new. But maybe that was my guilt talking.

As the sun began set, and the rosy glow faded from the sky to be replaced by drizzle, the last dog walkers drifted away until I was entirely alone. Unwilling to give up and head home, I made my way back to the West End in search of distraction. But I couldn't seem to settle on anything; the bars and pubs were rowdy and intimidating, and by now it was too late to catch a show, or even a late cinema screening. I sat on a bench in Leicester Square for a while, people-watching, but mostly I kept walking. London, the 24-hour party city, did not feel that way to me. Not on a damp Sunday night.

By midnight the theatres, restaurants, bars and clubs had closed, and even the drunks and prostitutes had cleared the streets in search of shelter. When I finally found a late-night cafe that was still open, I discovered that my purse had been stolen right out of my bag. It had only contained about thirty quid in cash, but tears of shame and frustration stung the back of my eyes. Pick-pocketed! Like some lame, naive tourist!

Saturated with rain and humiliation I cancelled my coffee order and squelched back out into the street, resigned to crawling back to TMC Tower in defeat.

*

What on earth…! In the middle of the day I was rudely awoken by shrill intensive drilling; the sound vibrating through my pillow and grating inside my already-aching head. Surely that wasn't coming from the offices below; not on a week day? Stumbling into the living area, I blinked in the light with increasing irritation. The din was coming from next door.

'That no-good, self-serving, egotistical arsewipe…' I marched out of my flat and in through Bay's open door, by-passing his kitchen and his bed until I was close enough to be heard. 'What the hell are you doing?'

The noise stopped abruptly and my feet faltered as three sets of eyes turned to look at me. The two men in Bay's flat were clearly builders, complete with tool belts and heavy duty boots. One guy even had a pencil perched behind his ear. I folded my arms across my chest and ignored their raking gazes as I took in the construction project between them, my mouth dropping open in astonishment.

'I believe that's my T-shirt you're wearing,' Bay said, smirking. He was leaning against the window frame, smoking; wearing boxers and a sleeveless T-shirt as if he'd recently got out of bed himself.

I glanced down, mortified to be caught wearing his shirt, but relieved that I was at least wearing pyjama shorts beneath it. I probably had crazy bed hair and yesterday's make-up smeared across my face, too. 'It was just the nearest thing to hand,' I muttered, traitorous heat rising to my face.

'I'd quite like it back at some point.'

'That's a pole.' I said, gesturing to the metal shaft and podium the workmen were mid-way through installing in Bay's living space. All three men grinned at my words and I mentally chastised myself for not having woken up properly before coming over.

'Well spotted,' Bay said, flicking his cigarette butt out the open window.

'I don't understand...'

The builders where still standing there, following our exchange with open curiosity. 'Carry on, guys,' Bay said over his shoulder as he sauntered towards me. As the whine of the drill re-erupted in my ears, Bay steered me over to the kitchen area out of earshot. 'You needed somewhere to practise.'

'Yeah, but… you're installing that for me?'

Bay shrugged, but his expression was now serious. He filled the kettle and used a palette knife to transfer instant coffee granules into two broken mugs. 'I could paint you while you dance.'

'What?' I said, appalled at the idea of stripping in front of him.

'*Dance*, not strip,' Bay emphasised, correctly interpreting my expression.

'Oh.' Bay poured in boiling water and stirred the contents of the cups with a paintbrush handle, while I tried to imagine him watching me pole dance in his living room. 'What if I don't want you to?'

'Why wouldn't you?'

God he was arrogant. 'I don't know, it's just…'

'What?'

'Weird.'

He stared at me as he took a prolonged gulp of hot coffee; his eyes boring into mine as if he were trying to read my mind, or change it.

'Your eyes are green,' I said.

'Yeah, so?'

'I've never noticed before – this must be the first time I've seen you in daylight…' He kept staring at me without reply, but even the rich emerald hue of his eyes, like sunlight through leaves, could not distract me from his proposition. Because, secretly, I was thrilled that he'd gone to so much trouble just to paint me. Admittedly it would have been nice to be asked first, or given a choice in the matter, but then Bay was never polite as far as I could tell.

'All done, mate,' one of the workmen said, releasing us from our silent staring match. At some point the racket had stopped and they had gathered up their tools.

While Bay showed the men out I went over to inspect their handiwork; stepping up onto the carpeted podium and testing the pole with two hands; it seemed rigidly secure. Reassured, I positioned my right hand higher up and slowly spun myself around in a wide arc. I landed softly back on my toes to find Bay watching me.

'Well?' he said in a low voice.

'It's perfect, thank you,' I said, unable to keep a smile from my face, my headache now gone.

Chapter Eighteen

The sight of Cally twirling daintily around that pole did something to me. She had morning breath, panda eyes, messy hair and most of her figure was disguised under my ill-fitting shirt, but for a moment I couldn't breathe, or move, or think straight. All the blood had rushed to my cock and I thought I might pass out.

Sternly I reminded myself that I wanted to paint her, not fuck her. I didn't want to be one of those clichéd arsehole artists who fucked around with their muse; especially when I had nothing good to offer in return. God I needed another smoke already. Her smile hurt my eyes so I turned back to the kitchen to retrieve my coffee and put some distance between us. She took a few more experimental turns around the pole while I calmed myself down enough to take a coffee back for her.

'Thanks,' she said stepping down, wrapping her palms around the mug and sipping gratefully.

'Do you want some music on?'

'Yeah that would be great; do you have anything suitable?'

'Probably not, but have a look, see.'

'I should go change and freshen up first.'

'No. Just stay as you are.'

'Oh… OK…'

While she scrolled through the music on my phone I mounted a large sketchpad on an easel and positioned it near the pole along with a trolley full of painting equipment. Settling myself on a stool I located a tin full of oil pastels and picked out some neutral colours. By the time the melancholic strains of Portishead's 'Glory Box' filled the room, I was ready.

'I'm going to pretend you're not here and try out some new routines, if that's OK?' she sprung back up onto the podium and immediately threw herself into her work.

Cally looked nothing like a stripper – she made no effort to be seductive. In fact, there was no eye contact at all. Stopping and starting, she repeated the same moves over and over again and even muttered to herself – lost in concentration. And I filled page after page with quick preparatory sketches, in a vain effort to capture her graceful movements, analyse her methods and understand the peculiar effect she had on me. Despite the fact she was only rehearsing and not performing, I could tell she was good – *really* good – formally trained, technically skilled and naturally gifted. I knew fuck-all about dancing, but there was poetry in the way Cally moved.

My hand was cramping by the time she stopped and came over to see what I'd achieved. She was breathing hard and the sweetly-scented sheen of sweat on her skin made my groin twitch. As a rule I didn't allow anyone a glimpse of my work at the first stage of the process, but Cally was so much a part of it; almost living, breathing and writhing within the paper, that it would be churlish to exclude her. I let her look while I fetched her a pint of cold water from the kitchen and she gulped it down noisily while I sorted through my scattered drawings, discarding some in favour of others. Now that I had a good stock of sketches to use, I wanted her gone so that I could take a long, cold shower and get high.

'So, how is this going to work, then?' she asked.

I cocked an eyebrow at her.

'I mean, when do you want me to come and dance? I won't want to practise on the days I'm working; I'll be too tired, but what about the other days? Do you want me to come over at a set time or something? How did it work with your previous models?'

'Models?'

She blushed. 'You know – the other women that have... sat for you or whatever...'

I wish she'd sit on me. Before I could contain it the errant thought spawned a delicious mental image of her butt nestled in my lap, and she squirmed with embarrassment as if reading my mind. 'You're the first to sit for me,' I admitted, her mouth popping open in surprise. 'Just come over when you like.'

'Oh... but... I wouldn't want to interrupt you when you're working or sleeping or...'

'Fucking?' Her face blanched and I fought the urge to adjust the tenting in my pants. 'How about this: I'll leave the door on the latch when it's safe to come in, and I won't when it's not.'

'OK,' she said, uncertainly, unable to meet my eye.

The intercom buzzed. A brief check of the screen showed it was Tom making a delivery, so I pressed the door release button to let him in, my hard-on subsiding. Cally moved over to my bed and perched on the edge, while I answered the door.

'Alright, Bay? Just two boxes today.' Tom cheerfully set the parcels inside the door at my feet and handed me a device to sign. 'Oh, hello again,' he called over my shoulder. 'It's Cally isn't it?'

'Yes. Hi…'

I glanced back at her. She was blushing again and self-consciously attempting to stretch my T-shirt further down over her finely-curved knees. Tom was beaming like it was his birthday. He was a nice enough kid; still in his twenties, blonde and good-looking, but cocky with it.

'You two know each other?' I said.

'She's your neighbour isn't she? She sometimes signs for your post.' Cally nodded behind me and Tom smiled at her again, making me want to deck him. 'I never forget a pretty face,' he added.

'Get out of here.'

Tom backed away towards the lift, his hands raised in amused surrender. 'Sorry man, I'm just saying, you're a lucky guy.' He was trying not to laugh as I slammed the door.

Chapter Nineteen

At 3 a.m., at the end of my Saturday night shift, Zena called me a cab and Leroy saw me safely into it. Sinking into the back seat, I listened to the dull rhythmic pulse of the windscreen wipers and let the watery lights of London wash over me. It was almost June; I'd been in the city nearly two months – I was already a third of the way through my time here – and I'd not visited half the places on my list, or saved up enough money to venture abroad, or even started writing my book. But at least I was free; independent; a dancer, of sorts; and now an artist's muse.

As a result I saw Bay most days. True to his word, he left his front door on the latch each night and I would wander in to find him painting, or smoking, or perusing a random book on violent crime, philosophy, or wildlife photography. Some nights I would dance for a couple of hours – either around the pole or without – while he sketched or painted me. But often we would simply talk, eat, drink, and listen to music. I was starting to believe we might be friends. I still missed people from back home, Marguerite and Liam in particular, but Bay was surprisingly good company.

That said, he was still sarcastic, evasive and hard to get to know. I'd barely managed to glean anything about Bay's past, and he refused point blank to discuss the mysterious woman in white; the girl who haunted so many of his paintings, cropping up again and again, delicate and disturbing. Of course his most recent studies were of me, or rather abstracted, stylised parts of an anonymous figure in red, dancing. But I hadn't seen anything approaching a finished, full-sized version yet; I wasn't sure if Bay was deliberately stalling, or simply hiding canvases away in one of the bedrooms.

At least he wasn't as dangerously intoxicated as he had been in the past. He still drank and smoked too much, and I regularly smelled marijuana in the air, but he no longer seemed to be taking it to extremes like before. Of more immediate concern to me was the stark realisation that I had never seen Bay beyond the top floor of his building. Did he ever go out at all?

Everything was delivered – groceries, booze, cigarettes, books, art supplies and who-knows what else. Bay was on first-name terms with the postal and delivery guys, and they catered to his antisocial schedule – meaning his parcels usually arrived early in the morning, before he went to bed, or in the evening once he was awake again. On the odd occasion that a courier tried to deliver while he was asleep, he would ignore them completely, forcing them to buzz me instead. It was infuriating when that happened – I didn't like being woken in the middle of the day any more than he did, but I was too well-mannered not to let them in.

On a hunch I'd Googled agoraphobia, and I now had it in my head that Bay needed coaxing out of his apartment like a hermit crab from its shell. Clearly I had too much time on my hands because I fancied myself for the job, but if not me, then who else would do it?

My taxi pulled up outside TMC Tower, the rain tapping gently against the windshield. The moment I paid the fare and shut the door behind me, the driver took off into the night, leaving me alone on the wet pavement. London cabbies were not like the cab drivers in Wildham, who at least waited to see a woman safely through her front door before disappearing. With a sigh I let myself in through the side door before travelling up in the lift.

There was a stranger standing outside my flat as the lift doors opened on the twelfth floor. He was dressed casually in jeans and a shirt, sporting a Beckham-style mohawk circa 2000, and swigging from a beer bottle as he gazed out the landing window. I gaped at him in surprise, before hurriedly stepping out of the lift as the doors began to close again.

'Alright? Come for the party?' he said with a warm smile.

'Party?'

'Yeah, it's in there,' he said, gesturing over his shoulder to where loud rock music was emanating from Bay's flat. 'I was just checking out the view from this side of the building. I'm Matt, by the way,' he held out his hand and I shook it reflexively.

'Cally.'

'Good to meet you, Cally, come on inside and I'll get you a drink.' He was moving before I had a chance to say anything so I followed him inside.

There were a dozen or so different people in Bay's flat – stretched out on his bed, cross-legged in a circle on the floor, draped across a couch that I'd never seen before. Two women were dancing together by the windows. All Bay's sketches and canvases had disappeared from the room and his paints and materials were piled up in a corner out of the way. Bay himself was sat up on the breakfast bar, his legs dangling and head bent as he nimbly rolled a joint between his fingers.

'Everyone, this is Cally,' Matt announced. 'Cally, this is everyone,' he concluded with a sweep of his arm. Several people smiled and said hello and I smiled back nervously. But when I glanced across at Bay, his expression, the look in his eyes, was impassive, as if he didn't know me. Did he not want me here? Before I could react, Matt was helping me out of my damp coat and putting a cold beer in my hand. I took a swig, enjoying the cold bubbles as they slid down my throat.

It was a long time since I'd been to a party. I gripped my drink tightly and automatically slipped into wallflower mode – my default setting – quietly listening to other people's conversations with nods and smiles, but contributing little.

I learned that Theo was a fashion photographer, working for some big names I'd never heard of, though I tried to appear suitably impressed. Fashion had never been my forte. His Australian girlfriend, Dionne, was a pretty aromatherapist who talked passionately about her work, but unfortunately she smelled of garlic and I had to fight not to wrinkle my nose. But the girl she was speaking to, a nurse, I found particularly interesting.

Willow could have been mistaken for a surfer chick with her hair like ropes of wet sand. I'd never seen dreadlocks up close before, but there was nothing dreadful about them as far as I could see. Quite the opposite in fact; they were textural, sculptural, and attractive against her golden-brown skin. She also had a pierced nose and the most beautiful tattoos that I'd ever seen. A sinuous weeping willow tree curled around her left bicep in ribbons of grey and soft green, but it was her other tattoo that really captured my attention – an intricate arrangement of wild-flowers winding their way up her right forearm from wrist to elbow. As she raised a can of beer to her mouth, I glimpsed delicate cornflowers, daisies, harebells, and buttercups displayed so beautifully and with such a lightness of touch that they almost looked real enough to gather with my fingertips.

Faced with these new people, I'd immediately relapsed into my old shy self; afraid to speak for fear of saying the wrong thing. And I hated that. The new me was supposed to be fearless. Luna wouldn't hesitate to speak her mind.

'I love your tattoos,' I blurted out, interrupting the girls' conversation.

'Oh, thanks, Sweetie,' Willow said, turning her warm smile on me. She shuffled closer, placed the beer can at her feet, and stretched her arms out like a contented cat, rotating them slowly to allow me an unhindered view.

'This one reminds me of Charles Rennie Mackintosh's botanical watercolours,' I said, my hand hovering in mid-air.

'Yeah, I know what you mean. It's OK you can touch them if you like.' Taking Willow at her word I gave into my impulse, gently tracing the twining stems and translucent petals with my fingertips, her skin soft and smooth beneath my touch. To physically experience such fine art work on a stranger's body felt extraordinarily intimate and made me shiver. And yet Willow looked entirely unfazed – as if it were a daily occurrence.

'You don't hate *all* tattoos then… Just mine.' Bay's gruff voice made me jump – he'd snuck up close behind me.

'I never said I hated yours.' Heat rushed to my cheeks at the accusation and the grim expression on his face. He loomed over me, a tumbler of something alcoholic in his hand, his eyes darkly dilated. 'Yours are beautiful, what I've seen of them, it's just that they're a bit…'

'A bit what?'

'Scary.'

'Scary?' Bay's eyes narrowed as Willow laughed.

'OK, not scary, that's the wrong word; they're a bit… morbid.'

'Morbid,' Bay echoed, his voice flat.

'Yes – as if designed to keep people away.' Surprise flickered in Bay's eyes, but mostly he looked angry with me, and I wasn't sure why.

'And what makes you an expert all of a sudden? I bet you'd never even consider getting one yourself.'

'I never claimed to be an expert, and what makes you so sure I don't have one?' I snapped back, unable to refrain, but mortified to have been drawn into a petty argument in a room full of strangers. Bay's unwarranted antagonism only seemed to provoke my own. He was silent for a moment, his eyes burning into mine, but I refused to look away.

'Let's see it then,' he said, calmly calling my bluff.

'No.'

'Oh, so it's OK for you to pass judgement on everyone else, but when it comes to—'

'I'm not passing judgement! You invited my opinion – it's not my fault if you don't like it.' Bay's jaw tightened with tension, his free hand fisting at his side. Willow rested a placating hand on his arm, but his eyes didn't stray from mine.

'OK guys, ease up, this is a party,' she said, clearly amused.

Without another word Bay downed the contents of his drink and stalked off back to the kitchen for a refill. I took a deep calming breath, aware that my pulse was racing.

'Sorry,' I said turning back to Willow.

She shrugged and smiled, glancing down at her tattooed forearm and running her own fingers over it. 'You know, Bay designed this.'

'What…? Really?'

'Yep. It was a few years ago now, but I told him what I wanted and this is what he came up with.'

'Why didn't he say?'

'I have no idea – it's not like the great Bailey Madderson to be modest.'

'You've known him a while then?'

'Yeah, we hook up from time to time,' she said, cupping her hand in front of her face as she lit up a menthol-scented cigarette. I nodded nonchalantly, but turned away to hide my face. The idea of Bay and Willow sleeping together had caught me completely off guard. It shouldn't have – they seemed well suited, both boldly creative types – and yet I was oddly upset at the thought. They'd probably had sex in the very bed I was now sitting on. Lurching to my feet and looking to escape, I was grateful to spot Matt's friendly face across the room. He grinned and waved to me and I made my way towards him.

Chapter Twenty

I could tell there was someone else in my bed the moment I came to. For a split second Cally crossed my mind and my eyes sprang open, but it wasn't her. I quickly shut them again against the harsh sunlight that filled the room, piercing my head with pain. During the night it had stopped raining and I'd obviously not managed to draw the blinds this morning before stumbling into bed. The room was now warm and stuffy, despite its vast size. I swallowed down the bad taste in my mouth and, with considerable effort, thought back to the party the night before, but as the recollections rolled in, I soon wished I hadn't.

I'd been hoping that Cally would show up after her shift, but the sudden sight of Matt leading Cally in, touching her and introducing her as if she was his, had filled me with rage. She'd quickly gotten cosy with my other friends, too. What was she doing caressing Willow's ink like that, when she wouldn't even touch mine? And how dare she suggest my tats were to keep people away. She was dead right of course, hit the nail on the fucking head, but to just announce it like that; flay me open; in front of everyone… it just wound me up. Maybe it wasn't Cally, maybe it was bad weed, but it was the last straw when I overheard Matt asking for Cally's number. I wanted to kill him. In retaliation I grabbed hold of Willow and kicked everybody else out. In my addled state I'd decided I needed to fuck it out of my system, whatever 'it' was. Now I just felt sick and ashamed and I couldn't even remember the fucking. Why did Cally rile me up so much?

Willow stirred from sleep and stretched a hand across the bed towards me. Rolling out of reach I sat up, planting my feet on the floor and narrowly missing the used condom lying there. My head was pounding, but as hangovers went, I'd survived worse – it was nothing a good work out wouldn't fix. Swiping my boxers up off the floor I pulled them on, noting from my mobile phone display that it was just 2 p.m.

'Time to go,' I said over my shoulder.

'Uuugh. What time is it? Can I have a coffee first?'

'Help yourself. You know where the kettle is,' I said, leaving her to get dressed.

I spent twenty minutes pummelling the hell out of my punch bag and then took my time in the shower. When I re-emerged from the bathroom I was relieved to find Willow had gone. Having taken extra pharmaceutical measures to further subdue my hangover, I opened a window, pulled down all but one of the blinds, and then dragged the canvas I was currently working on out of storage and into the patch of natural light. Once it was fixed to the wall I stood back, smoking several fags and contemplating it for a while.

It was entirely different to everything else I was working on; more figurative than anything I'd produced for years, and uncompromising in its clarity of subject. It was a portrait of Cally dancing, minus the pole. She looked vibrant, graceful and confident as she leapt from the shadows and into a pool of light, the motion almost alive within the oils. It was verging on brilliance, I was confident Felix would agree, but it needed more work, and I couldn't make myself get on with it. I was prevaricating; afraid to put more paint to the canvas. But knowing that didn't change anything. With a frustrated sigh I returned the canvas to the bedroom and re-covered it in a sheet before locking it inside.

Returning to the main room I put on some music, discarded the condom, changed the bed sheets and, in a fit of optimism, set the front door on the latch. Through lack of anything else to do I rooted about in the kitchen, searching for something to fill the hollow space inside me.

Chapter Twenty-one

When I crawled into bed this morning I'd been adamant I never wanted to see Bay again. I was hurt by the way he made me feel so unwelcome, embarrassed by the way he'd spoken to me in front of his friends, and angry about the way he'd rudely ejected us all from his flat. But what really made me furious was having to listen to Willow's cries of pleasure as he had sex with her. Admittedly it hadn't lasted long, it was all over rather quickly from what I heard, but it had grated on me none-the-less. I'd been sorely tempted to call my best friend – to vent my frustration and perhaps gain some much-needed advice – but how would I even begin to explain Bay to someone as put-together as Marguerite?

Now that the alcohol had dwindled from my system, I could see my reaction for the over-reaction that it was. I should be accustomed to Bay's bad manners by now, and I'd enjoyed meeting his friends. Why should I care who he slept with? He wouldn't give a second thought to my sex life. If I had one.

Picking up the scrap of cigarette packet which had Matt's name and number scrawled across it in blue pastel, I tore it in half and then dropped it in the bin. No matter how nice Matt was, I simply didn't have the time, energy, or inclination to even think about dating.

It was eight in the evening and I was restless. I wanted to go next door and dance; stretch my legs, practise my latest routine and prove to Bay that he couldn't hurt me that easily. But would he want to see me? Was Willow still there? Two hours later I knocked on his door and found it open as usual.

The flat was in total darkness and atmospheric orchestral music was softly playing, brooding and creepy. It took my eyes a while to adjust to the gloom, but when they did, I found Bay by the glowing ember of his cigarette. He sat alone on the floor, in a corner by the window, observing me from beneath his brow.

'I didn't think you were coming,' he said.

'I wasn't sure I would.' I tried not to look at the bed as I picked my way through a minefield of empty cans, bottles and overflowing ashtrays, but I couldn't help noticing, with relief, that the sheets had been changed. 'What's this music?'

'Hans Zimmer's *The Dark Knight* soundtrack.' Bay didn't look his usual intimidating self as I stood looking down at him. He looked tired and defeated, his gaze resting on the floor.

'Do you know, I've never once seen you wear shoes?' I said.

He stubbed his cigarette out on the parquet floor and then, in a practised move, flicked it backwards out through the open window.

'Do you even own shoes?'

He sighed. 'Yeah.'

I sat down cross-legged in front of him and his eyes met mine at last. 'Do you ever get out of here?'

He shrugged. 'Not often.'

'Why not?'

'No need.'

'Really? Well, what do you do for exercise?'

Raising one eyebrow he looked at me and my face heated with realisation. 'I believe I got a cardio work out in last night.'

'I'm not sure that counts – do you even remember it?'

He sighed. 'I have a home gym, Cally – I can run or row for miles without leaving the flat – I don't have to go out to stay in shape.'

'So there's no other reason? Nothing else stopping you from going out?'

'I'm not fucking phobic, if that's what you're asking.'

'You sure?'

'Yes!'

'OK, let's get out of here then.'

'Why?'

'Why not? It's a beautiful night and it's stuffy in here – let's go get some fresh air.'

'Where do you wanna go?' he said suspiciously.

'Not far... what about that lovely big garden you've got downstairs – it seems a shame not to make the most of it.' He shifted uncomfortably, picking at a smear of dried paint on his knee, but his hands looked cleaner than usual. 'I'll dance for you if you like... or not... whatever.'

He nodded, almost to himself, and used the wall at his back to drag himself up onto his feet. 'I'm still not putting fucking shoes on.'

I smiled. 'OK, I'll go barefoot, too.'

It was strange to be going somewhere with Bay; to be walking side by side and leaving through the door together; like normal people. 'Do you want to get a sketchbook or something?'

'No.'

An awkward silence descended as we waited for the lift and Bay radiated tension. I was starting to wonder if he could really do this when the lift arrived with a ding, making us both jump. The doors slid open and Bay entered without hesitation. Turning to face me, he leaned against the back wall, spreading his arms wide and resting his hands on the handrail; deceptively relaxed. His eyes were mocking as I joined him in the small space, the doors closing behind me.

The shiny floor was cool beneath the soles of my feet and my skin prickled. Bay's distinctive, but now familiar, scent soon pervaded the air around me; musky tobacco and soap with a hint of turpentine. As I inhaled it seemed to spread inside me, warming me, making me ache somewhere deep within. In an attempt to hide the effect he was having on me, I closed my eyes against his intense gaze. I wanted to say something light-hearted or reassuring to break the silence, but I didn't trust my voice to sound normal.

And then the lights flickered, the lift lurched to a stop and I opened my eyes with a breath of relief. But it was short-lived. Bay stared at the number display above my head, his eyes wide with alarm. There was no *ping* – no opening of doors – nothing.

'You are fucking kidding me,' Bay said. I spun around and surveyed the doors, helplessly, but there was nothing to see; no explanation; the lift had simply stopped. 'No, no, no,' Bay growled, pushing past me and stabbing at the buttons on the wall with a finger. He hit the emergency button and it lit up red, but that was it – there was no accompanying ringing alarm, no reassuring voice to say that help was on the way, no phone or other means of contacting the outside world. 'Fuck!'

A sense of panic swept through me and I fought it back. 'What happens now?' I said.

'The night duty guard down on reception will see it's stuck and call out the engineer.' Bay had his back to me.

'But it's Sunday night...'

'Yeah but there's always someone on duty – they'll see it.'

'OK,' I said. He was breathing hard and I started to worry that he was losing it. 'Are you OK?'

'No I'm not fucking OK!' He rounded on me. 'You and your stupid fucking ideas – this is *your* fault.'

'I'm sorry – I didn't know this was going to... does it happen a lot?'

'No. Never. It never fucking happens. The other lifts, yes, but not this one – I make sure it's regularly maintained, like clockwork, so that this can't happen. I can't fucking believe it,' he added, turning back to the wall panel and prodding at the buttons again.

'Try to keep calm,' I said. As soon as the words left my mouth I regretted them. He turned on me again, his eyes flashing dangerously, darkly dilated with raw anger, his voice raised.

'Don't fucking tell me to keep calm! Why don't you just fuck off? I was fine until you showed up with your poncy clothes and your superior attitude.' I flattened myself back against the wall to create some space between us, but Bay loomed over me, his breath hot on my face, his fists clenched at his sides. 'And I wouldn't be stuck in this fucking thing if you'd just stayed away from me, minded your own fucking business.'

'I was just trying to help…'

He smashed his fist into the metal wall beside my head, making my teeth rattle, and I flinched in terror silently praying he wouldn't hit me. 'I don't need help! Why do people keep saying that? I can't *be* helped! There's no fucking cure for what I have.' His choice of words surprised me and I recognised the fury in his eyes for what it really was – fear. Bay was messed up and hurting and now he was trapped in a confined space dangling above an abyss. I needed to distract him. Without another thought I did something I'd secretly wanted to do for weeks – I kissed him.

His mouth parted in surprise; his lips soft and warm and his body frozen in shock, but he didn't pull away. Raising my hands to his stubbled jaw I tentatively probed his mouth with the tip of my tongue, tasting him, testing him, and then, with a savage growl, he was kissing me back; roughly grabbing my bum in his hands and forcing me close up against him. I gasped, thrilled by the all-over sensation; the hard heat of his body pressed to mine, the possessive grip of his hands, and the greedy ravaging of his tongue. As troubled as Bay was, and as much as we fought, I could no longer kid myself – he was staggeringly sexy. On some carnal level that was new to me, I wanted him. And despite everything he said, right now, he wanted me, too.

Abruptly Bay pulled away from me and I sucked in a gasp of much needed air. 'What the fuck.'

His words stung and I tried to reach for him again, but he backed away, increasing my growing sense of rejection.

'You want me to fuck you, is that it?' There was a hard edge to his voice – he was still angry.

'No,' I said, gripping the handrail with both hands, my whole body aching, throbbing and screaming "yes!"

'No? You sure…? So I don't make you hot…?' He stepped closer, slipping his left hand under the hem of my dress and dragging his fingers up my bare thigh. 'I don't make you wet?' I closed my eyes to shut out the mocking expression on his face, while my legs parted for him, seemingly of their own accord. He cupped me there, discovering my arousal for himself. 'I think you do want me to fuck you – why don't you just admit it?' he murmured, brushing his lips lightly along my jaw.

He was toying with me, the arrogant bastard. Gripping the handrail tighter I stubbornly shook my head, while my breathing deepened and my legs began to tremble. Deftly hooking my knickers aside he stroked me with his fingertips. The sensation was extraordinary and I bit back a moan.

'Say it, Cally. Say you want my cock inside you.'

'No.' I knew I should tell him to stop, or push him away, or both.

Cupping my left breast, he used the pad of his thumb to rub my nipple through my clothes and it stiffened eagerly at his touch. I vaguely wondered if his hand hurt from punching the wall, but then he eased two fingers inside me and I groaned, appalled by how spectacularly good it felt.

'Say it.'

'No – you've just been with another woman,' I pointed out in disgust.

'So?' He pressed his mouth to my other nipple and nipped me damply through the fabric. I cried out and he began to slide his fingers in and out of me. 'Look at me,' he said.

I shook my head again, my face burning and my breathing erratic.

'Cally...' he growled in warning. Afraid that he might stop, I opened my eyes and glared at him and he chuckled humourlessly. 'You hate me right now, don't you?' he said, increasing the steady thrust of his fingers.

'Yes,' I hissed.

'Good.'

At last he returned his malicious mouth to mine, kissing me again, and my hands relinquished the safety of the handrail and plunged into his hair; my fingers raking across his scalp and clinging to him as my internal muscles wound tighter and tighter. My mind fought to deny what was happening even as my body physically begged for more. Grinding down against his hand, I rocked my hips, shamelessly meeting him thrust for thrust, harder and faster as I raced towards release... and then I came; crying into his mouth; my whole body shaking and my legs buckling as waves of pure pleasure eclipsed all else.

As my orgasm abated and my senses returned, I gradually became aware that Bay was holding me up with one arm around my waist. Transferring my weight into my own wobbly limbs again, I straightened up and he withdrew his fingers. He may have brought them to his lips, but I couldn't be sure, I was too ashamed to look at him. I might never be able to look at Bailey Madderson ever again.

Chapter Twenty-two

I sucked my fingers on impulse. Fuck me, Cally was sweet – I'd never been so aroused. I feared I might lose my mind as she was detonating in my hands – the smell of her, the eager probe of her tongue, the damn sound of her moans and her hands in my hair urging me on… fuck… I'd never been this hard in my life. But she didn't want me – not really. She was better than that; too proud to admit any attraction; too proper to stoop to my level. And I didn't blame her for that – not really.

But what now? I was stuck in this fucking lift with nowhere to go and all I wanted to do was strip her naked, bury myself balls-deep inside her and feel her whole, goddamn beautiful body wrap around me. Fuck. This was gonna be the longest night of my life.

While she was catching her breath she smoothed down her dress and combed her fingers through her hair; steeling herself. And now, at last, she opened her eyes and looked at me. Her cool blue gaze was a shifting mix of shame and defiance, her lips flushed and swollen from my kisses. Neither of us spoke, and the silence hung heavily in the stuffy confines of the lift. Slowly she sank to the floor, her knees drawn up and arms wrapped protectively around them. I followed suit so that I was sitting across from her, my bare toes millimetres from, but not quite touching, hers. I leaned my head back against the wall and released a long slow breath, slowly flexing the bruised knuckles of my right hand and silently willing my uncomfortable hard-on to subside.

'Can we just pretend this never happened?' she said.

'Sure.'

'I mean… getting stuck in a lift is enough to make anyone crazy.'

So that was how she wanted to play it. 'Sure.'

'I don't want you to think that I—'

'I'm already over it.'

'Good, so am I,' she said, bitterly.

We sat in uncomfortable silence for what felt like hours, but was probably only minutes. I could still smell her, taste her, and hear her orgasm echoing in my head. I wished I was tired enough to fall asleep, but I was brutally wide awake.

'Do you have the time on you?' I said.

'No, sorry.'

A voice suddenly erupted into the space making us both jump: 'Hello? Is there anyone there?' I scrambled to my feet and pressed my head to the panel on the wall.

'Yes we're here, where the fuck have you been?'

'I don't know if there's anyone in there, or if you can hear me, but just to let you know, I've sorted the problem and we should have you out of there in a jiffy.'

'Thank fuck,' I muttered, turning back to Cally, who was also on her feet, the relief evident on her face. A moment later the lift jolted into action and continued its descent to the ground floor.

A middle-aged engineer in blue overalls was there to greet us as the doors finally opened and we stepped out into much fresher air. 'Howdy.'

'What the fuck happened?' I was fighting the urge to punch him.

His smile faltered and he glanced down to where he was wiping his hands on an oily rag. 'Just a minor power cut,' he said. 'It was long enough to stop the car but not enough to trigger the re-start mechanism... just a glitch.'

'So what are you doing to ensure it never happens again?'

The engineer sighed. 'Look mate, I know you've just been through a bad experience and I'm sorry about that, really I am, but it's one in the morning and I—'

'Sorry to interrupt,' Cally said, stepping between us with her hands up, just as I was preparing to deck the guy. 'Is the lift safe to use now? Because I'd like to get back upstairs.'

'Yep, perfectly safe,' he said.

'Great, thank you.' Marching back into the car, she pressed a button and folded her arms across her chest as the doors closed. We stared after her, listening to the whirr of the lift as it rose smoothly to the top floor.

'Nice girl,' the engineer commented.

I glared at him, jabbing the button to recall my ride.

'Just saying,' he said, warily stepping back away from me.

Chapter Twenty-three

As I danced I imagined Bay's touch searing my skin; his fingers inducing a sultry heat as they tracked up my thigh. Arching my spine I let my head fall back, exposing my neck to the burn of his kisses, oblivious to those around me. In my mind, Bay's dark eyes followed my every move as the undulating rhythm of Bitter:Sweet's 'Drink You Sober' swirled around the club.

No-one had ever manipulated my body like that before; dragged an intense orgasm out of me so quickly, and with such apparent ease and disdain. It was almost as if Bay was trying to punish me in that lift; using my own body against me, in the most pleasurable of ways – and now it was all I could think about.

Until now, Liam was the only guy I'd ever been with. All my prior relationships had fizzled out before they became physical; my shyness and fear always holding me back. Liam was polite, patient and considerate – inherently gentle and always reluctant to pressure or offend. The exact opposite of Bay. With Liam it was always missionary, but with Bay... anything might be possible. I'd hardly scratched the surface, barely been granted a small taste, and yet the man in that lift had aggravated, challenged and aroused me like nothing else on Earth.

Of course I hadn't actually seen Bay since then – I'd gone back to avoiding him and more than a week had already passed. My bodily attraction to him unnerved me and I had no intention of getting romantically or sexually involved with anyone, let alone someone so clearly volatile. At one point I'd been afraid he would hit me for goodness' sake. Bay had violent tendencies – the fist-shaped dent in the wall of the lift served as a daily reminder. No, I was not naive enough to get involved with a person like that.

But ironically, our heated encounter had helped my stripping massively. I no longer had to pretend to feel sex-starved, desirous and horny – Bay had awoken all that within me. I now danced naked with newly-found abandon and the tips were rolling in. I could earn several hundred pounds a night simply by fantasising about my neighbour as I worked. Extraordinary but true.

*

Bay was leaning against the door to our building when I climbed out of a taxi in the early hours of the morning. He was wearing headphones and a dark hoodie, his hands shoved deep into the pockets of his combats and his shoulders hunched against the rain. It was a shock seeing him outside on the pavement, making me stop mid-step and my pulse race.

'You OK, love?' The driver said through his window 'You want me to wait until you're safely inside?' Maybe not all London cabbies were heartless after all.

'No it's OK, thanks; I know him.'

'OK, love, if you're sure…' He didn't sound convinced, and watched us in his rear-view mirror as he slowly drove away.

Bay slipped his hood and his headphones down around his neck as I approached him.

'What are you doing out here?' I said.

'Waiting for you.' He looked tired; the shadowy sockets of his eyes matching his unshaven jaw, but he was still as disturbingly attractive as ever.

'Why?'

'About what happened in the lift the other night – you were right – it made me a bit crazy.'

'Oh.' I waited, but he didn't say anything else. 'So... was that it?'

'What?'

'Was that an apology?'

'Yeah.'

Though I tried, I couldn't hold back the smile that spread across my face. I'd missed him; in all his frustrating, moody, petulant glory. 'Apology accepted.'

'Good. I need you to come back so I can paint you again.'

'I don't know, Bay, I... there are other things I should be doing with my time here.'

'Like what?'

'Well, when I knew I was going to be in London for a while I made a list of all the things I'd like to see and do, and I haven't got very far with it yet.'

'A list?' Now it was his turn to look amused.

'Yes.'

'What sort of things?'

'Oh, you know; the usual touristy things.'

'So what's the problem? I'm not stopping you.' I looked away down the street, unsure how to explain without sounding like a complete loser, but he leaned around me, obstinately re-establishing eye contact. 'What are you afraid of?'

'Nothing.'

'Just say it, Cally.'

His words made me flush with heated flashbacks and I hoped it was too dark for him to see. I took a deep breath. 'I don't want to do it all on my own – I hoped you might come with me.'

The silver barbell in his eyebrow lifted in surprise. 'I am *not* agoraphobic for fuck's sake! Look – I'm outside!' he said, spreading his arms wide in exasperation.

I laughed. 'I know, I believe you, that's not why I'm asking, I promise. It's just boring visiting all these places on my own and I don't have anyone else I can ask...'

'Right... so... if I do lame touristy shit with you, you'll sit for me in return?'

'Yes.'

Bay sighed. 'You're a fruit loop, you know that, right?'

'Charming, thanks.' I looked down at the pavement to hide my big grin. 'Oh my god, your feet are bare!' I said, looking back up into his face. 'Aren't you cold?'

'Yeah, and wet,' he said suppressing a shiver.

Shaking my head I laughed.

'I'm glad I amuse you,' he said dryly, failing to hide the smile in his eyes.

'Tell me honestly, do you actually own any shoes?'

'Of course I do.'

'Then why aren't you wearing them?'

He shrugged. 'Just stubborn I guess. Come on,' he said, entering the code to unlock the door and steering me towards the lift.

By the time we'd reached Bay's flat my laughter had subsided into the occasional chuckle. I fetched a dry towel for him from the bathroom while he made coffee, but he waved it away.

'I'm fine, stop fussing.'

'You'll get pneumonia.'

He rolled his eyes. 'It's the middle of June, get a grip.' I set the towel down on the end of his messy bed in the hope he would at least dry his feet. 'Go get this special list of yours,' he said over his shoulder.

'I've got it here in my bag, actually.' Sitting down I rummaged about until I found it.

'Read it out, then.'

I cleared my throat, feeling self-conscious. 'Well, I've already been to the Royal Ballet, so you'll be glad to be spared that...' Bay's face remained impassive as he brought our coffees over to the bed and settled opposite me. I clocked the ugly bruising on the knuckles of his right hand but refrained from mentioning it. '...And I've already been on the London Eye – it was a bit cloudy but the views were still amazing, have you been?'

'Skip to the things you haven't done yet.'

Sighing, I returned to my tatty scrap of paper, scanning for the item most likely to appeal. 'Tate Modern...?'

'Go on.'

My cheeks burning I rushed through the rest of the list: 'A boat trip on the Thames; shopping in Harrods; a film at the Imax 3D cinema; Madame Tussauds; Afternoon Tea in Claridges; The British Library; Borough Market; Highgate Cemetery, and the Ceremony of the Keys at the Tower of London, although I'm not sure about that last one – I've heard there's a really long waiting list.'

'What was the one before that?'

'Highgate Cemetery?' I rolled my eyes. 'I should have known you'd go for that one.'

'Will it be open later this afternoon?'

'I expect so.'

'OK, let's start with that.'

I grinned at him over my mug of coffee and he shook his head with a grudging, but no-less breathtaking, smile.

Chapter Twenty-four

I woke at 3 p.m. to the sound of Cally hammering on my door; I'd slept more deeply than I had for days and slumbered straight through my alarm. I refused to accept that my insomnia was in any way related to my loopy neighbour – the idea was fucking ridiculous – but within hours of apologising to her, I'd slept like the dead.

As I staggered over to the door I lit up a fag before letting her in. She scowled at me in irritation as she checked me out – I swear I could actually feel her Prussian blue gaze tingling on my skin as it roved over my bare chest, snagged on the morning wood barely concealed in my boxers and then darted back to my face. A rosy pink glow of awareness bloomed in her cheeks and I tried not to smirk too much.

'I know, I know, I overslept – I'll be two minutes,' I said, heading for the bedroom in search of clothes. Of course I could really do with a wank and a shower, or even a wank *in* the shower, but if we didn't make it to the Cemetery before closing there was a good chance Cally would refuse to sit for me. And I needed to paint – it was all I had.

It was warm outside, the sun irradiating through a hazy sky and rinsing the streets in an unforgiving light. I kept my hood up as we made our way to the nearest tube station. The truth was I hadn't been out in daytime for months. Even at night I'd only ventured as far as the local bars. Anyone worth speaking to could be contacted by phone or email, and I'd seen enough of the outside world to know it didn't need a shitbag like me in it. And yet, here I was. The bright daylight made me squint, despite my shades, my scruffy black trainers rubbed on my feet and my general appearance drew suspicious looks. Feeling disorientated and exposed I buried my urge to hide behind a grim expression and my usual swagger.

Strangely, as we descended into the underground on a steep metal escalator, swept along by a tide of jabbering foreign students, I began to relax. Cally stood on the step below smiling up at me. With her there, the stuffy, artificially-lit tunnels didn't seem so claustrophobic. I still had to fight the instinct to step in front of the train as it approached, but I managed it by keeping my eyes on her.

'Thank you so much for doing this,' Cally gushed, settling into a seat next to me. She was dressed casually in a fitted pair of cropped trousers, a cherry-red halter-neck and a matching pair of converse. She smelled of peaches and summer sunshine. Her rich, dark hair was tied up in a high ponytail leaving her pale, perfectly sculpted shoulders bare for all the world to feast their eyes on. I wanted to sink my teeth into them.

'Don't thank me yet, there's still time for you to regret it,' I said, shoving my sleeves up above my elbows. The woman sat on the other side of me shifted uncomfortably at the sight of my tats, and Cally smiled.

'I'm enjoying myself already,' she mused.

We surfaced at Archway where I paused to drag my sweatshirt off over my head and light up. Cally laughed, reaching a hand up to tame my scruffy hair with her fingers while I stared at the soft swell of her lips from behind my shades. Her touch felt amazing and gave me goosebumps, but going by the frustrated expression on her face, her efforts to impose some order on me were futile.

At the top of Highgate Hill we turned into Waterlow Park – all green lawns, mature trees, duck ponds and sky. I queued at the cafe to buy coffee while Cally wandered around the parterred gardens; perusing the sensory borders, smiling at kids as they chased around the benches, and idly trailing her fingers through the fountain. She looked so at ease here – so happy. It still surprised me how much I enjoyed watching her; how much her mere presence calmed me and made me feel less… lost.

Re-fuelled with caffeine and nicotine, I accompanied Cally to the far side of the park, grateful that the sky had clouded over and softened the harsh glare of the sun.

'It's four pounds each to get in.'

'Does that include that part over there?' I said, indicating the imposing, Gothic gatehouse across Swain's Lane.

'No. You can't get into the West Cemetery during the week unless you're booked on a tour.'

'That'll be where all the interesting bits are, then.'

She pulled a face at me. 'What do you want me to say? Tickets book up weeks in advance and I didn't know we were coming until this morning… let's just go into the East Cemetery.'

'Or… we could sneak into the West,' I said, lowering my voice.

Her eyes widened comically as she glanced nervously across the road. 'You are joking? There's no way… it's like a fortress, Bay – fifteen foot walls and spikes on the gates…'

I shrugged, amused by the horrified tone of her voice. 'We could walk further round, see if there's another way in…'

She stared at me, incredulous, so I turned and started to walk up the road and she hesitantly followed. The one-way street was narrow with cars parked along one side as it wound its way up hill, but the cemetery boundary wall was stepped to follow the incline and therefore lower in places.

'What about here? You could get up there if I gave you a boost…'

'Are you crazy?' Her words hissed through her teeth.

'Oh come on, it's not like we're gonna trash the place, I just wanna have a look around. What are you afraid of?'

'Getting caught, being arrested, or falling and breaking something; possibly my own neck.'

'You'll be fine if you're careful – there's a tree right on the other side to shimmy down, and we're less likely to get caught if we stop hanging around arguing and just get on with it.'

Her bright blues darted across my face, jittery with indecision. By removing my dark glasses I let the force of her gaze lock onto mine. 'OK,' she breathed.

Without further delay I helped her up onto the wall and jumped and hauled myself up behind her. Together we eased ourselves down into the murky depths of the other side.

Chapter Twenty-five

It was dark and cool on the other side of the wall. A forest of trees had taken over the space, rising up and crowding out the light, effectively separating us from the outside world. And below the canopy was a churning sea of undergrowth; brambles, ivy and weeds surging up to our waists in places, in a slow scramble to bury all signs of the dead lying beneath our feet.

My blood thrummed with the exhilaration of breaking the law – unchartered territory for a goody-two-shoes like me. We were both silent while our sight adjusted to the low light and our other senses acclimatised to the sombre but intensely peaceful atmosphere.

'This is incredible,' I said at last, conscious of my voice in the waiting silence. Bay nodded his agreement, still speechless. 'It's far more overgrown than I expected – these trees are amazing. They remind me of the woods behind my grandmother's house where I used to play as a child.'

'Your parents let you play in the woods alone?' he said, finding his voice at last.

I nodded. 'Wildham's a very safe sort of place.'

He frowned but didn't comment.

'What about you? You must like trees, too – the tattoo on your arm; the trees in your paintings…?' I stepped closer to a weathered stone plinth, almost entirely concealed in ivy, with an ornate-looking draped urn poking out of the top, and touched it with my fingertips.

'Be careful where you stand,' Bay warned, 'You could easily fall into a crypt in here.' I shivered and looked back at Bay but he was avoiding both my eye and my question. 'I think I can see some sort of path over there – let's head towards it,' he said.

As I followed, a large bird, possibly a crow, pierced the silence by screaming high up in the branches above, and my foot snagged in a lasso of undergrowth. I almost lost my balance, but Bay was at my side, his hand at my elbow and his firm grip warming my skin as he steadied me. He relinquished his hold as soon as we reached the safety of the path, which was bordered by a concentration of ornate and varied statuary, and only just wide enough to admit a hearse. For a while we wandered uphill, marvelling at the striking Victorian monuments to the dead expressed in a bewildering array of sarcophagi, obelisks, crosses and angels. I stopped at a tomb guarded by a beautifully carved sculpture of a dog. He was lying with his head resting mournfully on his front paws, his body dappled with lichen.

'Thomas Sayers,' Bay said over my shoulder, reading the engraved name aloud. 'I bet that's *the* Tom Sayers.'

'Who was he?'

'A famous bare-knuckle boxer.'

'Are you into boxing?'

Bay shrugged. 'He was notoriously good.'

'I think my favourite poet is buried here somewhere, but there's no way I'm going to find her in all this,' I mused.

'Who's that then?'

'Christina Rossetti.'

'Really?' Bay turned his attention on me, bright with interest.

'Yes, why?' I said cautiously, bracing myself for a derogatory comment.

'Maybe Lizzie Siddal's buried here too then.'

'Who?'

'She sat for Millais – you must have seen his painting of Ophelia in Tate Britain?' Bay's eyes glowed as he looked at me, making my skin tingle.

'Yes?'

'That's her. She nearly died of pneumonia posing in a bath of cold water for that piece, but she mainly sat for Dante Gabriel Rossetti, Christina's brother. They married eventually, but he wasn't very good to her; she gave birth to a stillborn baby and then died of a Laudanum overdose.'

'How awful.'

He nodded. 'Rossetti had her buried in the family plot along with a journal full of his poems.'

'That's kind of romantic, in a sad way.'

'Yeah, except that he had her coffin exhumed a few years later so that he could retrieve the poems and publish them.'

'Oh.'

Bay's knowledge on the subject surprised me – though it shouldn't – he was a painter himself, after all. But what really stunned me was his apparent emotion. He seemed genuinely angry at these Victorian artists and their maltreatment of a woman I'd barely heard of. I made a mental note to Google her.

As we ventured further inside the cemetery we encountered a grand avenue of elaborately carved tombs flanked by an impressive Egyptian-style entrance, and beyond that, a circular arrangement of buildings built into the slope and topped with a grand old evergreen tree. I gazed around in wonder, quietly astonished that such a place existed. But the adrenalin that had got me up and over the cemetery wall was now waning, and anxiety was creeping back in. So far we hadn't seen another living person, but how long would it be before our luck ran out?

As the sun began to set behind the hill, Bay sat down on a weed-infested grave where a low shaft of sunlight penetrated the trees. He leaned back against the large headstone with a contented sigh.

'Isn't it disrespectful to sit on someone's grave like that?'

'These guys have been dead a long time – I doubt they'll mind,' he said. I glanced around awkwardly, warring internally with my innate sense of propriety in the face of Bay's casual logic. 'Sit down; have a rest,' he said, patting the lush green foliage beside him.

With forced confidence I did as he suggested, settling beside him as if we were two people sitting in bed, a gravestone for a headboard. I made sure to leave a gap between us, so that we were not touching. Bay took a tin of tobacco from his pocket and removed what looked suspiciously like a joint from inside. He put it to his lips and ignited the twisted end with his sturdy metal Zippo lighter.

'What are you doing? You can't light that here!'

'Relax – I'm not carrying enough to get me arrested – it's purely medicinal.'

'Oh yes, and what is it that ails you?'

'Agoraphobia,' he said, deadpan. I snorted and looked away. 'Want some?' he said, proffering the spliff in his hand.

'No thanks,' I said reflexively.

'Why not?'

I scowled at him.

'No pressure, I'm just curious,' he said through a lungful of smoke. All the usual reasons crossed my mind: it was illegal, potentially addictive, and I'd never tried it before. But none of those excuses seemed good enough. They belonged to the old Cally – the one I'd left behind in Wildham.

'Give me that,' I said, snatching it from his fingers before lifting it to my lips and cautiously taking a drag. The smoke burned as it hit my lungs, but I held back the urge to cough and released it slowly, lost in Bay's dark eyes as he stared back, a small smile teasing his lips. Exhilarated by my own daring, I had a second toke. He didn't comment and neither did I, but I sensed my whole body relaxing inside my clothes – as if I was sinking into the ground beneath me and the headstone at my back. In slow motion I passed the joint back to Bay and he tutted at the lipstick-stained tip, amusement still dancing on his face.

'Why *do* you have the Grim Reaper on your back?'

My question caught Bay off guard and his smile vanished. He took a thoughtful drag, holding the smoke deep in his lungs for what felt like an age. 'He's an old friend – he and I go way back,' he said exhaling at a leisurely pace.

'Don't you think it's a bit risky? Like you're tempting fate or something?'

Bay shrugged. 'He'll come for me one day, but I'm ready for him.'

'You're not afraid?'

'Life hurts way more than being dead ever could.'

'You can't know that for sure.'

'No, but I believe it. And if there is a Hell, I'll fit right in.'

'Why do you say that?'

'Because I'm a bad guy, remember? Hence the trespassing; grave desecration, and corrupting young innocents with narcotics.'

'I'm not an innocent!' I said, heat rising to my face.

'No? You act like one sometimes,' he said, casually, glancing past me into the distance.

'What's that supposed to mean?'

'Shit,' Bay mumbled, abruptly shoving me sideways to the ground.

'Hey! What do you—?'

'Shh…' he whispered, clamping a warm hand across my mouth, '…there's someone over there.' My stomach dropped and my eyes widened at the thought of being caught and arrested, but I was distracted by the physical weight and warmth of Bay's body as he lay half across me, pinning me to the ground. As he followed the progress of a guardian of the cemetery with his gaze, I studied Bay's face in minute detail – the neat silver barbell that transected the heavy curve of his eyebrow, the emerald irises ringing dilated black pupils, the violet bruise-like shadows beneath his eyes; the coarse stubble over his top lip and across his jaw, the soft pink curve of his mouth… his breathing deepened and I flicked my eyes back to his to find his dark gaze trained on me.

'He's gone,' he said, slowly removing his hand from my mouth. Instinctively I moistened my lips with my tongue, tasting the salt from his skin and his eyes zeroed in on it. At my hip his groin stirred and my breath caught in my throat, heat spreading through me. I really wanted him to kiss me. Or did I? Maybe it was simply the drug in my bloodstream impairing my judgement. 'You're stoned,' he said.

I had an urge to laugh. Here I was, illegally sprawled across a grave in a cemetery with a self-confessed bad guy, smoking dope and thinking about kissing him. As I started to giggle, Bay sighed and rolled off me. With my own hands I re-covered my mouth but I couldn't stop, and as my quiet giggles escalated, my whole body quaked, tears streaming down my face. Bay shook his head and shushed me again, but he was grinning – a rare and uplifting sight to rival any artificial high.

Eventually my fit subsided and Bay offered me the sleeve of his sweatshirt to wipe my eyes.

'Hungry?'

'Absolutely starving,' I said, standing up and dusting myself down.

'Let's go get something to eat.'

*

It was a different kind of crowd on the underground in the evening. Thankfully we'd missed the worst of the rush hour, mainly by loitering in the park and having a go on the swings, and now there were fewer pushchairs and a higher proportion of inebriated office workers clogging up the platforms and carriages.

As we sat side by side on the northern line, several attractive, stylishly-dressed business women eyed Bay openly. Even unshaven, scruffy and scowling, he was undeniably handsome, and the bad-boy effect was particularly potent on females whose inhibitions had already been lowered by alcohol. I experienced a childish sense of smug satisfaction at being his companion for the evening – which was pathetic. In an effort to counteract these feelings I smiled at a suited gentleman sat opposite me, but when he smiled back, Bay glared at him until the man promptly alighted at the next stop.

I'd never been to a Street Feast before, I didn't know such a thing existed, but the place Bay took me to in Shoreditch was fantastic – a quirky assemblage of outdoor diners, bars and fast food outlets arranged over two floors around a central communal eating area. The whole place was decorated with artificial grass, parasols and fairy-lights and a DJ added to the party atmosphere. I ordered a 'Yum Bun'; a soft steamed bun filled with slow-roasted pork belly, sticky Hoi Sin sauce and spring onions, while Bay opted for an enormous burger stacked with freshly barbecued meat and a mess of tasty-looking garnishes.

'You've got sauce all round your mouth,' I said cheerfully, picking up my coke can and taking a sip.

'So have you,' Bay said with his mouth full.

I half-heartedly licked my lips, but couldn't stop smiling; it tasted too good.

In the crowd I caught sight of a familiar face and, taken by surprise, instinctively ducked down lower in my seat, initiating a curious lift of Bay's eyebrow. But it was too late, she'd spotted me, and she was making her way over. Bay looked bemused as I swallowed hastily and wiped the corners of my mouth with a paper napkin.

'Has it all gone?' I asked him. I tried to rein in a flush as he perused my lips with a lingering gaze, and then nodded, swallowing his own mouthful of food.

'Cally! I can't believe it's you! It's been ages!' I smiled as Marguerite descended on me with a big hug and delicate air kisses. 'How are you doing?' she said, pulling back to appraise me at arm's length. 'You look different.'

I wondered if she could tell I'd been smoking a joint only hours beforehand. 'I'm good, thank you, really good, how about you?' I said, nervously scanning the crowd over her shoulder to see who she was with.

'Don't worry, I'm here with work friends; no-one you know.' Relief swept through me, I wasn't ready to face Liam yet. 'How is the flat-sitting going? You said everything was fine in your messages but it's so long since we've actually spoken...'

'Yes, everything's fine – the plants and fish are still thriving; I haven't killed anything...' I tailed off. Marguerite wasn't really listening to me – she was too busy glancing uneasily at my dining companion. 'Marguerite, this is Bay, Bay – Marguerite.'

Bay drew himself up to his full, imposing six feet, dwarfing my petite friend as he flashed a devastating grin and proffered a greasy hand. Marguerite blinked under the visual assault of his smile and accepted his fingers on autopilot. 'Charmed to meet you,' Bay said.

I cringed as Marguerite masked her impulse to recoil in horror with a polite smile. 'Nice to meet you,' she said, snatching away her hand and stepping back.

Bay was still smiling as he sat back down and returned to his burger, his amused eyes passing casually between us.

'Bay's an artist,' I said, as if that explained everything. Marguerite nodded distractedly and I passed her a paper serviette which she accepted gratefully and discreetly used to wipe her hand. 'He's really talented,' I added.

'What about you – have you managed to find work yet?' she said.

'No…' My cheeks heated with the lie. 'I've just been so busy with sightseeing and so on…' In my peripheral vision Bay had stopped chewing and was listening intently, but I avoided his eye.

'Oh, well, that sounds like fun, as long as you're not getting unduly… side-tracked,' she said, glancing at Bay again. What she really meant was 'led astray'. She was doing what most people did – what I had done – judging the book by the cover. She saw Bay's tattoos, piercings and clothes and assumed he was dangerous; the wrong crowd; a bad influence. In this instance most of her assumptions were probably correct – Bay was offensive, volatile, and almost certainly an addict. But there was so much more to him than that. The more time I spent with him, the more I admired his 'don't give a damn' attitude, his dry humour and his raw, tumultuous emotions. Respect and affection were not freely granted by Bay –

they were hard-won – rewards all the more precious for that. In short, he had become a friend,, and I had an urge to defend him.

'No, not at all – it's been great to let my hair down a bit and Bay's been looking out for me…' *"Corrupting young innocents"* his words from earlier crept through my mind, making me want to laugh. Marguerite looked unconvinced and I changed the subject. 'How's everything at home? How's…' I didn't want to say his name.

Her eyes softened. 'He's not great, Cally, I won't lie. He doesn't say much – he never does – but it has hit him hard, I can tell. He's been looking for you, he knows you're somewhere in London, but…' guilt filled my stomach, cold and soupy, '…I haven't said anything, obviously…'

'I'm so sorry,' I said.

'It's not me you should apologise to.'

'I know, but I'm sorry for putting you in this position, really.'

She gave a small shrug of her shoulders. 'We miss you at dance class, you know, it's not the same without you…' For the first time in the two-and-a-half months since I'd left, I felt properly homesick and tears pricked the back of my eyes. I hugged Marguerite again as I blinked them back. 'Can't you just call him?' she said over my shoulder. 'You don't have to tell him where you are, but you could at least let him know you're OK…'

I released her and took a deep breath to steady myself, aware of Bay's curious and penetrating gaze on my face. 'Yes, you're right, I should do that.'

She nodded, searching my eyes for reassurance. 'OK. Well, I'll leave you to your dinner,' she said, 'but call me if you need anything, any time.'

'Thank you, Marguerite – for everything.'

'Nice to meet you, Bay,' she said stiffly.

'You too,' he muttered unconvincingly, his attention fixed on me and all trace of humour gone.

'Please don't ask,' I said, settling back at the table opposite Bay as Marguerite retreated into the crowd.

'Drink?' he said.

'I've still got this,' I shook my half-empty coke can.

'A *real* drink.'

I finally looked Bay in the eye and the dark intensity of his gaze took my breath away; simultaneously surprising and soothing me with its heat, like stepping in front of a fire. 'A double Jack Daniels and coke would be great, actually.'

'Don't move,' he said sternly, getting up and walking away.

Chapter Twenty-six

On Monday evening I was settling on my bed with a selection of pencils and a sketchbook on my knee, when a classical piece of cello music floated unexpectedly out of the speakers and across my dingy flat. Cally positioned herself in the centre of a cleared space on the floor, standing upright, with her shoulders back, but her head down and her hands joined loosely before her. As the music swelled, she began to move with light steps and fluid grace, the full skirt of her summer dress fanning out around her as she danced.

This was no practice session; this was a ballet, properly choreographed and executed to perfection right in front of me. I sat speechless; mesmerised; paralysed. Actually not entirely paralysed – as the music grew steadily faster and louder, building to a crescendo, heat surged into my lap making me uncomfortably hard. Why did this girl do this to me? I don't think I even blinked for the entire duration, not until the music faded and Cally finally came to rest on the floor, her chest heaving – the only outward sign that her graceful performance had taken any effort.

Willing my erection to subside, I wondered if Cally's sudden return to her classical roots had been triggered by bumping into her friend from home the other day. I couldn't recall her friend's name – something long and posh-sounding – but she had mentioned dance classes. Interestingly, Cally had been too ashamed to admit to her job as a stripper, which had me speculating, yet again, as to why she was doing it. They'd referred to Cally's ex-boyfriend too, though not by name. Had she called him yet? I itched to ask her about him, but it was too personal. We didn't do personal. *I* didn't do personal.

At length Cally raised her head and looked at me.

'What was that?' I said into the silence, my voice hoarse.

She rose to her feet, hands on hips. 'Bach. Something I came up with for an audition a few years back.'

'You choreographed it yourself?'

'Yes.'

'What was the audition for?'

'A place in a dance troupe.'

'You must have got it, if you performed like that?'

She smiled. 'Yes I did, but I had to turn it down.'

'Why?'

She shrugged lightly. 'I had a job to do, bills to pay, a boyfriend... I couldn't just drop everything and go off on tour.'

'Fuck that, you could have found a way—'

'Yes, well, I didn't,' she snapped.

Setting my blank sketchpad aside, I fetched a tumbler full of water from the kitchen sink and passed it to her. 'So, what's changed?'

'What do you mean?' she said, accepting the glass. Our fingers brushed and I tried to dismiss the jolt of energy that shot up my arm and ignore the sweet, tantalising scent of her sweat.

'The stripping, your list... you've obviously dropped whatever you were doing before – why now?'

141

'Oh. The opportunity to spend six months house-sitting in London, I guess,' she said with a hasty shrug, water spilling from her glass. I could tell she was hiding something, but she changed the subject before I could push it. 'So, did you get any sketches done, or would you like me to do some stationary poses?' Her eyes darted to the blank page on my bed.

'Let's go out,' I said.

*

It was late by the time we reached the club and a queue snaked right around the block, but I by-passed it, confident we could jump it.

'What is this place?' Cally said, eyeing the people in the line – a motley mix of metallers, rockers, goths and punks – with growing unease.

'You'll see,' I said striding up to the door.

'Bay,' the doorman acknowledged me with a nod, his meaty hands automatically reaching to unhook the rope and admit us. 'Haven't seen you in a while.'

'Ian,' I greeted in return. His eyes did a visual sweep of Cally and then returned to mine, his brows lifted in surprise. I stared back at him as if daring him to say something, but he merely stood back and let us pass, Cally close on my heels.

The light was gloomy inside as usual, the floor sticky beneath our shoes where is sloped from the bar area right down to the stage, but most of the space was filled by hordes of people; most of whom were drinking beer from plastic cups and shouting at each other in an effort to be heard above the music. The atmosphere was anticipatory but relaxed – the roadies on stage were busy setting up for the headline act; the occasional thud of the bass drum thumping the air as they tested out the sound system. It was good to be back – better than I'd expected – I'd missed it; the raw aggression, grime and stench of a live metal gig.

But I was here for Cally this time – to shock her, to test her, to push her limits. I wanted to subject her to a corner of my dark soul now that she'd flaunted the pure beauty and innocence of hers. I needed to counteract the effect her ballet dancing had had on me; I wasn't sure why I needed it, but I did.

Having ordered a couple of pints of lager at the bar, I handed one to her.

'Thanks. I'm not sure I'm really dressed for this,' she said with a downward glance at her red cotton summer dress, the small handbag slung across her body and the little black shoes on her feet. 'It wasn't on my list,' she added with a rueful smile. God I was a heartless bastard.

'You never know, you might like it… and if not, we can leave, OK?'

'OK,' she said, beaming back at me before taking a large sip of warm beer. She was right of course, she stuck out like a sore thumb and, much to my consternation, there were at least a dozen men in our immediate vicinity appreciatively checking her out. 'So who's playing?'

'I'm not sure exactly – it's unsigned bands on Monday nights, but the headline acts are usually pretty good.'

'Great!' Her eyes flashed with genuine excitement as she turned to face the stage. Abruptly the lights and music were switched off and we were plunged into darkness. I stepped closer to her, anxious not to lose her in the throng, and felt her jump as an electric guitar chord rang out. Blinding lights came up on the stage to reveal a five-piece rock band. The music exploded into the air around us and as the crowd roared and surged forwards, Cally surprised me by moving in with them. Lurching to follow after her, I elbowed others out of my way while Cally, jostled by people jumping all around her, grinned back at me over her shoulder.

The band were pretty good – you could tell they'd been playing together a long time – they sounded confident and cohesive – rock metal with a punk edge – reminding me of Green Day in the early nineties before they really hit the big time. I positioned myself a couple of rows back from Cally and found myself observing her rather than the musicians on stage.

I wasn't too worried – she was chatting to two middle-aged, leather-clad biker types who were giving off harmless vibes, and she was far enough away from the mosh pit at the front not to be inadvertently sucked in. Besides, I was reluctant to stand too close to her. The sight of Cally here, rocking out with a rough bunch of blokes like me, turned me on. Dammit, every damn thing Cally did aroused me, as if she had a hotline straight to my dick – I couldn't win.

The lead vocalist announced the band's penultimate song, and the crowd jumped enthusiastically along to it, nodding their heads and shouting the words. Suddenly Cally was hoisted into the air by the guys around her and anxiety reared up painfully in my chest. Pushing forwards I tried to get to her, but I was too slow – calmly she spread her arms out wide and lay back onto the heads and shoulders of those around her, as if she had been crowd-surfing all her life. I watched, immobilized with awe, as she was borne away towards the stage on a sea of bodies, in the raised hands of strangers, like a beautiful, modern-day Eurydice being carried off to the underworld.

I was no Orpheus, but as Cally disappeared from view, I launched myself towards the side of the stage, pushing and shoving my way through the masses, heedless of anyone I pissed off in the process, adrenalin pounding in my ears in competition with the music. I arrived just in time to spot Cally being handed out from behind the stage barrier by a bemused-looking security steward. Her eyes were wide with exhilaration and delight, but she appeared to be in one piece, thank Christ.

'What the fuck!' I shouted at her, furious.

Leaping forwards she threw her arms around me, laughing. 'Oh my god, Bay, did you see me?'

'Yes I fucking saw you.' The sudden physical contact was unsettling but I hugged her close to me, shaking with profound relief. Pulling back she beamed at me with such joy and satisfaction that it was impossible not to return her smile.

I shook my head. 'Are you hurt?'

'Nope,' she said smugly.

'Have you still got all your valuables?'

'Yep.' She held up her bag for me to see.

'And no-one groped you?'

'What? No!' she said, her smile vanishing and her mouth dropping open in horror.

'Thank fuck for that, let's go,' I said, taking her sweaty hand in mine and dragging her back through the crowd.

'We don't have to go yet,' she shouted after me. 'I don't mind staying longer if—'

'No, I've had about all I can take for one night,' I shouted back. 'Can't take you anywhere.'

She chuckled and I shook my head again as I walked, lacing my fingers tightly and securely through hers.

Chapter Twenty-seven

In his own bossy way, Bay had made a mockery of my boring 'London To Do' list. He'd subverted it completely by taking me to see and do things that I never would have experienced on my own. Who knew I had it in me to crowd-surf at a live rock gig? OK it was my idea to take it that far, but it was Bay that gave me that confidence – he was so unlike anyone I'd ever known. He was often rude and said harsh things, but his actions were a complete contrast. The way he looked at me, really looked at me, as if searching my soul; the way he cared for me when I was hurt or tired; the way he went out of his way to show me new places... he challenged me on a daily basis and I loved meeting him head on and shocking him in return. We had become friends and, as I'd implied to Marguerite when they'd met, I trusted him to look out for me.

I'd never admit it aloud, but Bay was the coolest friend I'd ever had. Take my idea to watch a 3D screening of *Titanic* for example. From the expression on Bay's face you'd think I'd proposed a trip to the dentist. I'd flushed with embarrassment as I gave it more consideration. Of course he didn't want to go and see *Titanic* – it was one of the most romantic films around – he probably thought I was trying to lure him into a date. But instead of shooting it down he simply said, "I have a better idea".

Three days later here we were lounging on the grass beneath the stars on a mild summer's evening, watching *The Dark Knight* on a large screen. It was ironic that Bay had brought me to The Luna Cinema since I'd never told him my stripper name. The pop-up screen was situated in a royal park, right alongside the Thames, with the Houses of Parliament looming up behind it. Softly lit in all its Gothic splendour, the architecture provided the perfect backdrop to one of Bay's favourite films. It was surprisingly comfortable leaning side-by-side against a wedge-shaped backrest, blankets draped across our legs and plastic cups of warming red wine in our hands.

We sat right at the back of the open space near the tree line with the other smokers, and the atmosphere was both stimulating and pleasantly subdued. Despite being outside, I'd never seen Bay looking so relaxed. He'd brought a sketchpad and a chewed pen with him and had half-heartedly sketched various members of the audience while the movie washed over us. But now his pen had wandered off the page and he was doodling on my left arm; developing an intricate pattern of curved lines, the ballpoint tickling my skin and sending a subtle throbbing awareness throughout the rest of my body.

'Do you think I should get a tattoo?' I murmured.

Bay's pen stilled and he raised his eyes to mine. They glinted in the flickering light of the movie. 'No.'

'Why not?' I whispered, 'I thought you'd approve.'

'Just 'cause I have them, doesn't mean everyone should.' His voice was gravely at my ear and made me shiver. The soundtrack was loud enough to mask our conversation and created a strange sense of intimacy, isolating us from the rest of the audience as we lurked in the semi-darkness. 'Anyway, I thought you didn't like my tats.'

'I never said that, you just assumed. Most of yours are rather dark, but I can still appreciate their beauty.' On impulse I reached across his chest and pushed the sleeve of his T-shirt up to reveal his left shoulder. He stilled at my touch and I tried to ignore the body heat that radiated up my arm and the lure of his masculine scent. 'I love this moon – it's simple, but so powerful...' His penetrating gaze implied he was caught up in some kind of internal conflict, and I withdrew again. Wondering what I'd said wrong I opened my mouth to apologise, but he cut me off.

'It's in memory of my mother – she died when I was fifteen,' he muttered.

My throat tightened with emotion at this unexpectedly poignant and personal revelation. 'I'm so sorry.'

Bay shrugged and looked away towards the screen, his head resting mere inches away from mine. 'She was beautiful and popular and admired, but she was also remote.'

'Remote?'

'She was a writer – poetry mainly – but she suffered with insomnia and always preferred to be alone. She was magnetic, alluring and distant, like the moon.'

'I'm so sorry,' I said again, touching his hand where the pen was gripped tightly between his fingers. But he didn't react. 'Would I have read anything by her?'

He swallowed hard, his Adam's apple falling and rising again, his profile outlined in the silver light of the screen. 'I doubt it – her work was never very commercial.'

We observed in silence as Batman weaved his way through the streets of Gotham on his Batpod in a desperate race to rescue Rachel Dawes. But The Joker had deliberately given Batman the wrong address, and Commissioner Gordon couldn't reach Dawes in time to save her. Harvey Dent's heart-wrenching howl of agony made my eyes cloud with tears.

'How did she die?'

Bay sighed, hooking his lighter and a cigarette out of the packet beside him and lit up. I knew I should take my insensitive question back, but my curiosity prevented me from saying the words. 'Car crash,' he said flatly. 'She was driving. My Dad was asleep in the passenger seat but he was barely scratched. She swerved to avoid an animal or something and they hit a tree. But it was my fault they were on the road in the middle of the night – I was responsible.'

'What do you mean?'

'I'd run away from boarding school. I was stranded in Scotland with no money and threatening to hitch-hike home. They drove out in the middle of the night to get me,' he said.

'That doesn't make you to blame.'

'How would you know?' he was glaring at me.

'Because you were fifteen—'

'Just drop it, Cally—'

'A child, for goodness sake—'

'Shut the fuck up. I don't need you to make excuses for me; you don't know anything about it.' Bay had got up and stormed off, disappearing into the shadows before I had a chance to reply.

I sat and watched the end of the film on my own, Bay's pain ringing in my ears. It was no wonder he was hurt and angry, if he'd been blaming himself for the death of his mother for the past twenty-one years. Maybe I shouldn't have pushed so hard.

As the credits rolled I wondered if he'd left for good or whether I should sit and wait for him to return. Once the audience had dispersed and only the staff were left behind, I collected up my bag and Bay's drawings and exited through the gate. He was waiting for me – leaning casually against a tree, his hands shoved deep down in his pockets. Neither of us spoke as he gently relieved me of his sketchpad and fell into step beside me. The laughter and raised voices of other people in the street only emphasised the awkward silence between us as we walked towards Westminster station. Eventually I spoke up, unable to take it anymore.

'Would you design something for me? A tattoo I mean?'

Bay's shoulders dropped and he rubbed the stubble at his jaw. 'You should choose something yourself – you're the one who'll have to live with it,' he said at last.

'I know, but you're so talented,' I said, extending my arm and twisting it to catch the light so that I could admire the fluid design he'd drawn there. 'Please, for me? I won't get it done if I don't like what you come up with…'

He smirked and shook his head. 'I'll think about it.'

'Thank you.' I grinned, hooking my arm through his. 'Hey, shall we cross the river and walk along the Southbank?'

'Nah, let's walk up to Trafalgar Square, I know a great old pub near there and I need a drink.'

Chapter Twenty-eight

I'd always felt at home in Gibbs' tattoo studio. I used to hang out there in the summer holidays when I was a teenager – soaking up the atmosphere, admiring the artwork all over the walls and on the bodies of the various patrons – biding my time until the day I had enough cash saved up to get my own. And even then, despite the grim circumstances that induced Gibbs to waive the usual rules and gift me my first tattoo, I didn't feel nervous, only excited. The familiar smell of the antiseptic, the firm feel of the leather chair beneath my fingers, the persistent, focused hum of the needle… it all added to the buzz.

Tattooing was personal expression in one of its simplest forms, but for me it was something to do with control; knowing myself well enough to make an indelible choice – having the confidence to scribe a part of my inner soul onto the outer shell of my body, a daily reminder of what lurked within. And it was highly addictive. No, I'd never felt uncomfortable about entering a tattoo parlour – until today.

I took a deep drag on my fag. 'You don't have to do this, Cally.'

'You smoke too much.'

'Don't change the subject.'

'OK, but you know smoking's a filthy habit and bad for you, right? Far more unhealthy than getting tattooed.'

I stared at her, incredulous. 'I've started cutting down, actually.'

'Really?'

'I chain-smoked before I knew you.'

'Oh.' She looked lost for a moment, but then a determined expression settled back in her features as she squinted in the evening sunshine. 'I want to do this.'

'You should really choose your tat yourself; something that really means something to you.'

'But I wouldn't know where to begin, and anyway this...' she said, holding up my drawing of a peacock butterfly, '...this *does* mean something to me; it's perfect, I love it.'

I scowled at her as I dragged more nicotine into my lungs, irritated by her careless attitude.

'What? I assume there's no ugly hidden meaning I should know about?'

'No, of course not, it just reminded me of you, but I've only known you a few weeks—'

'Three months and counting,' she interrupted, cheerfully.

'Like I said – weeks – this might not be the right design for you, are you sure you don't want to sleep on it?'

'I've never been more certain of anything in my life,' she said, her big blue eyes burning into my soul.

What had I done? I should never have shown her that damn drawing; should never have agreed to bring her here. And now, as we stood arguing in the car park, the day's heat radiating off the dusty tarmac as the sun set, all I could think was that her beautiful flawless skin was going to be marred forever, and it was all my fault. I rubbed at my jaw in frustration. 'What's the hurry?'

She sighed and reached out, taking my clenched fist in her warm hand. 'Please, Bay, I'm going in there to do this, right now, and I'd really appreciate it if you'd come with me.'

There was no way I was letting her go through with this alone. 'Fuck's sake,' I muttered, dropping my fag butt and grinding it with my heel before storming towards the shop.

'Yay,' she said with a nervous laugh, running to keep up with me.

Chapter Twenty-nine

Despite its modest size, my tattoo took several hours to complete due to the intricate nature of the design, the vibrancy of the colours, and Gibbs' patient, highly skilled approach. But it was worth all the discomfort. I'd fallen in love with Bay's drawing the moment I'd set eyes on it. I recognised the pretty insect from his paintings, but this was much simpler in form, without the spider webs or dark embellishments. My butterfly was a touch smaller than life-sized, the wing tips slightly raised and a subtle shadow cast beneath so that it would look as though it had just alighted on my left shoulder. To me, butterflies symbolised transformation, and what could be more fitting now that I'd finally emerged from my chrysalis and spread my red wings? It seemed right to mark this moment in my life, and I was privately thrilled to be having a tiny piece of Bailey Madderson's considerable talent branded on my skin.

The interior of the tattoo parlour wasn't nearly as dark and intimidating as I'd imagined. I'd pictured a cramped, dingy, almost squalid-looking space filled with torture-chamber-style equipment, cigarette smoke and the rusty scent of blood. But this studio was bright and airy and spotlessly clean, with what looked like highly-sanitised medical equipment, comfortable leather adjustable chairs, colourful, framed artwork all over the walls and the reassuring smell of antiseptic in the air. Gibbs was a revelation, too – I'd envisaged a large, hairy man, but she was petite and female and had fewer tattoos than I expected. With her shaved head and ears adorned with a multitude of colourful glittering piercings, Gibbs radiated calm and smelled faintly of sandalwood. She donned a wipeable apron and a scarily large pair of dark-rimmed spectacles whilst she worked, but her spectacular talent was evident on the walls around me and, of course, on Bay's bare skin.

Bay's resistance to my getting a tattoo was surprising. As I settled into the chair and Gibbs marked the outline, Bay's usual cavalier attitude was replaced by a strange tension. *He* was more nervous than *me*; his shoulders and face rigid with apprehension as he scrutinised every move Gibbs made. Thankfully the process was not as painful as I had feared, and once Bay began to relax, I did too. He said he'd created a monster; that there was no stopping me now; and that I would probably end up a tattooed lady in a travelling freak show. Before long Gibbs was scolding Bay for making me laugh and ordering me to keep still.

Trudy was a large, curvaceous woman with an enviously ample cleavage and a quiet demeanour. She assisted Gibbs by operating the sterilising machines, preparing the inks, and providing a steady supply of wipes and needles. But it was also clear, by the way the two women interacted with each other, that they were very much a couple in love.

A burly guy called Sol also worked in the shop. He might have been an apprentice of some kind, but he mainly stood behind the counter eating, as far as I could tell. It was apparent that Gibbs, Trudy and Sol had known Bay a long time. He was as rude to them as he was to everyone else, but there was an easy camaraderie in the way they traded insults, as if they were family.

Over the course of the evening several other people in the locality (each with their own distinctive tattoos) popped into the shop to catch up with Bay, having heard on the grapevine that he was there. And I enjoyed seeing him interact with his friends – witnessing the subtle but charismatic way in which he roused others, and the not-so-subtle antagonistic arrogance by which he kept them at arm's length. Bay's wolfish good looks, brooding masculinity, and effortless popularity made a potent combination that was undeniably sexy, and I found myself pondering, yet again, why he was so intent on hiding away from the world.

As the end of my session neared, Bay went outside for a smoke with the others, leaving Gibbs and I alone with the buzz of the needle and Placebo playing on an old-fashioned stereo.

'So this is what it takes to lure Bay out of his cave, huh?' Gibbs said.

I smiled. 'Apparently so.' I wanted to ask her why he was such a recluse, but I was too chicken. 'Has he brought you many new customers in the past?'

'A few referrals, but you're the first he's actually brought along personally. Bay's always been a lone wolf.'

'Oh.' I was pleased to hear I was different; glad that Bay had not accompanied Willow the way he had with me. But it was sad to think of Bay so alone. 'Did you do all of his tattoos for him?'

'It's been a while since I've seen him undressed, but as far as I know, yes.'

I flushed with heat at a mental image of Bay's naked body. 'They're beautiful,' I said.

'Thanks. I'm just about finished here; you want to take a look?' She held a mirror up at my shoulder and my eyes widened. My skin was inflamed, but the butterfly already looked amazing, delicately perched there like an exotic flower.

'Wow! It's perfect, thank you so much.'

'You're welcome.' She set the mirror aside, dipped her fingers into a tub of lotion and began smoothing it into my raw flesh. 'I'll give you an after-care leaflet full of instructions. Make sure you follow them to the letter,' she said, cleaning her hands and then carefully applying a bandage. 'Try not to get it wet until it has healed and keep it protected from the sun.'

'OK.'

'If you notice any signs of infection you come straight back here or you go to a doctor, understand?'

'Yes.'

'But once it's healed, if it needs any touching up, I can do that, no problem.'

'OK, thank you.'

'You're welcome,' Gibbs repeated, her back turned to me while she tidied things away.

'Why doesn't Bay like to go out?' I blurted.

Gibbs turned around, her bespectacled eyes level with mine. 'I don't know for sure. I have a fair idea...' her words came out slow and careful, '...but it's not my place to say.'

'No, of course not, sorry.'

'Look, you seem like a sweet girl, and Bay is clearly fond of you, but just so you know, he has a lot of friends and we care about him a great deal. If you hurt him…' she said, her voice hardening.

I stared back at her in alarm, as her threat hung in the air. 'Oh! No. You don't understand – I think you've got the wrong idea – I'm not… we're not…'

'She's just my neighbour, Gibbs, stop prying,' Bay said, returning through the door.

Gibbs glanced up at him, shrugged, and moved over to the counter while I pulled myself together. 'I didn't think she was your usual type,' she said, as if I wasn't there.

'How much do I owe you?' Bay said, ignoring her remark.

'Hey, I'll pay,' I stuttered, scrambling to my feet.

'No you won't. I got you into this – it's on me.' Bay tossed a bank card onto the counter.

'No, really, let me; I can afford it.'

'Save your tips, Cally, you work hard for them.'

Heat rose to my face as if Bay had struck me. His comment wasn't made with obvious contempt, but on top of being threatened by Gibbs and then dismissed as *just a neighbour*, it stung. 'I'll wait outside,' I said.

Having settled the bill and said his goodbyes, Bay emerged from the shop with a small bag in his hand, his gaze immediately seeking me out.

'What's up? Are you in pain?'

'No, it's sore, but it's fine,' I said, starting to walk.

'What then?' he said, falling in beside me and peering intently at my face.

'Nothing.'

'Did Gibbs say something?'

'Like what?'

'I don't know, something to piss you off.'

I shook my head and he sighed. My fingers tingled with an irrational urge to fight him or grab him or something. Gibbs was right – I wasn't his type – but that didn't mean we couldn't have some fun, did it? If I was honest I was haunted by Bay's kiss and plagued by the way he'd made me come in the lift all those weeks ago. Memories of it assaulted me every night I stripped at the club, and each day while I slept in my bed he touched me again and again in my dreams. My body ached with the need to do or say something about it, but I couldn't; I wouldn't; it would be far too humiliating. And it was driving me slowly insane.

'You're not regretting your tat already, are you?' he said.

'No. I love it; it's beautiful, thank you.' I glanced briefly into Bay's troubled gaze and then looked away again, for fear he would read my licentious thoughts.

'Here's your after-care lotion and stuff,' he said, handing me the bag.

'Great, thanks.'

'So what do you want to do now? We can go get something to eat – I know a diner that should still be open – or we can head back to the flat, order a take-away…?'

'Actually, I think I want to be on my own for a bit, if that's OK?'

Bay stopped and stared at me. 'Suit yourself,' he muttered, thrusting his hands in his pockets and sloping off without a backwards glance.

I took my time walking home, wandering the dark streets instead of catching the bus. When I arrived at the top of TMC Tower I could hear thrash metal coming from inside Bay's flat, but I resisted the impulse to check whether or not he'd left the door on the latch for me. What did it matter either way? What did it really mean? That he wanted to paint me? Why...?

Safely inside my own flat, I took two paracetamol for the throbbing in my shoulder, grabbed a tub of ice-cream and a spoon from the kitchen, and crawled onto the sofa with a duvet. As the opening scenes of *Pretty Woman* played out on Sidney's wide-screen TV, I resolved to push all thoughts of Bay from my mind. Again.

Chapter Thirty

What the hell was she playing at? I'd kept my side of the bargain – taken Cally out to a whole load of public places, just like she wanted; I'd been out more in the last three weeks than I had in the past three years. Admittedly it had not been as nauseating as I'd anticipated; in fact I'd even found myself enjoying it. Revisiting a few of my old favourite haunts and introducing Cally to London's nocturnal delights was kinda fun. But fair's fair – she was supposed to dance for me in return so that I could paint. So where the fuck was she?

Guilt needled at my brain as I recalled how fantastic she had looked, sitting in Gibbs' chair the night before. Majestic in a flowing red dress with a smile of serenity on her lips, as if it was nothing, as if she trusted my judgement completely. She didn't complain once about the stinging discomfort that I knew for a fact she was feeling. While I was catching up with various guys I hadn't seen in ages, I felt her gaze on my skin constantly, like heat from a flame. And I felt acutely sensitive to every nuance of her experience; each new puncture, each needle change and every wince she tried to suppress. I wanted to take her away, or take her pain away, or bear it for her. And yet each time, as I was about to say something, she would smile at me with warm assurance, disarming my fear.

But then she had changed; something had shifted; there was emotion trapped in her eyes which she wouldn't let me read. Regret had come crashing back, hitting me full force, like a kick in the guts. What was I doing to this poor girl? Why couldn't I leave her alone?

She hadn't come over afterwards; she had returned to her flat alone and I had stayed away, swamped with guilt. But twenty-four hours on, there was still no sign of her. And a deal was a deal.

'I thought you were coming over to practise,' I said as Cally opened her door. She was still in her pyjamas, or more accurately, my Alice In Chains T-shirt, but her eyes looked red and swollen.

'Yes, sorry, I—'

'You've been crying.'

'It's nothing,' she said, pausing to blow her nose in a tissue. 'My Mum called from Spain to wish me a happy birthday and she got a bit teary, which always sets me off...'

'It's your birthday...?' A tidal wave of fresh guilt sluiced my soul. 'Why aren't you out celebrating with Marguerite?'

She shrugged, wincing slightly. 'She suggested it but I don't really feel like it.'

'How's your shoulder?' I instinctively reached out and touched the hem of her sleeve, but then stopped, unsure. 'Can I see?' She nodded but looked away as I gently pushed back her sleeve and inspected the raw skin beneath her bandage. 'It looks like it has stopped bleeding and there's no sign of infection. Where's your lotion? I'll put some on.' Cally perched quietly on a stool by the breakfast bar while I gently applied a thin layer of cream. 'Why don't we go somewhere for a drink?'

'I'm a bit tired… and it's raining out,' she said, gazing out of the streaked windows into the speckled darkness beyond.

'I'll drive.'

'Drive? You have a car?'

'Yeah, it's parked in the basement. I pay someone to keep an eye on it and keep the battery charged.'

'Why do you have a car? You never go anywhere.'

'My brother gave it to me. He probably hoped I'd wrap it round a tree or something.' Cally paled slightly and I regretted the comment.

'You don't get on then, you and your brother?'

I shrugged. 'I never see him – he lives in LA. So are we doing this or what? You can't stay in moping on your birthday – it's sad.'

'OK,' she said, granting me half a smile. 'Give me a few minutes to get changed and I'll meet you downstairs.'

*

'Holy crap!' she said, emerging from the lift and stepping into the underground car park.

Her expression amused me, but I couldn't get my facial muscles to work. As Cally stood there openly admiring my DB9, I openly admired her. She was wrapped in a spectacular, figure-hugging dress that clung provocatively everywhere, and stiletto heels that showcased her long, elegant dancer's legs. Standing in the cool air of the ventilation, it was clear she was wearing no bra, and I stifled a low, involuntary groan as I hardened instantly.

'Is this really yours?' she said turning to me and then doing a comedic double take. 'You dressed up!' she said, her searing gaze travelling over my shirt, tie and trousers, right down to the black leather shoes on my feet. The look on her face made my balls ache and my whole body vibrate with need.

'So did you,' I said, my voice strained. This was a bad idea. I'd wanted to cheer her up, but now I was starting to feel like a horny teenager on a first date. 'Come on, get in,' I said, opening the driver's door and surreptitiously adjusting myself, before sliding behind the wheel.

'This is an Aston Martin, isn't it?' The girl knew her stuff. She wriggled in her seat and pulled on her safety belt. 'I feel like I'm in a Bond film.'

I rolled my eyes. 'That would make me a villain, then,' I muttered as I pressed the ignition and the engine snarled into life.

Chapter Thirty-one

I tried not to chew my lip as I perused the smart cocktail menu in my hand – it was a short list of just ten drinks, but I imagined that each and every one would be balanced to perfection and absolutely sublime – they certainly ought to be at the price. And I had never wanted a drink so badly in my life.

Today I had finally bitten the bullet and called Liam – I'd been concerned he might be worrying unnecessarily about me, and equally confident that nothing he could say would persuade me to go back to him. I still cared about him – we'd been friends a long time – but I was no longer in love with him, if I ever had been. Hearing his voice again after three months was tough. Having wished me a happy birthday, he asked me what I'd been up to, and I rambled on about some of the more mundane sights I'd seen. He was calm and composed, and he didn't once suggest I come back. "Are you happy, Cally?" he'd asked near the end of our call. I'd automatically said yes, and only allowed my tears of self-pity to fall after hanging up.

And now, here I was a few hours later, in another life entirely with Bay – who seemed to be on his best behaviour. The brief ride in his swanky car had been surprisingly comfortable. I'd assumed he might be a bit of a hot head behind the wheel, but he was impressively confident and relaxed; gently easing through the traffic, shifting smoothly between the gears and caressing the legal speed limit with steady patience. And the first-floor cocktail bar he'd brought me to was utterly charming.

We sat close together on a red velvet sofa in the corner, surrounded by antique wood panelling, understated glamour, and a smattering of London's elite who chatted politely amongst themselves. Raindrops dripped behind me from the open leaded windows into pretty planted boxes, and a waft of cool air tickled my skin. I was grateful for the breeze, as my body was positively suffused with unnecessary heat.

It was Bay that was having this effect on me; he looked incredible all dressed up. He'd even scrubbed his hands clean of any traces of paint. With his shirt sleeves rolled up to his elbows, and a dark expression on his face, he looked handsome, roguish and good enough to eat. It was taking all of my will power to keep from biting him.

'What would you like to drink?' he asked, and I tried to focus on his question and not the feel of his thigh pressed against mine.

'I don't know. It doesn't seem fair that we've come to a cocktail bar when you're driving.'

'I can have one and still drive you home safely – anyway it's your birthday, not mine. Tell me what you want.' His last five words made my brain stall. What did I want? Being alone with Bay in a place like this made my stomach flip. But that was wrong. I didn't want to date and I certainly couldn't afford to fall in love – that would be disastrous. So what did I want? 'I'll have a Dry Martini,' I said, picking the first drink my eyes alighted on.

'Good choice. Two Dry Martinis coming up – stirred, never shaken.'

There was a large ornate mirror mounted on the wall behind the bar, but Bay stood to one side of it, as if to avoid his own reflection. I feasted my eyes on the tight muscles of his glorious backside, and then admired the way his broad shoulders tapered down to his narrow waist and hips. I could just make out the dark shadow of death through the thin fabric of his shirt and suppressed a shiver. It was obvious what I wanted – I wanted Bay to finish what we'd started in that lift. I wanted to go back in time and beg him to fuck me, like he'd told me to. He'd lit a fuse inside me that day and it had been smouldering away ever since. It was shocking to admit, even to myself, because I'd never been that kind of girl, but I needed to have sex with the man and get it out of my system once and for all. The big question was, had I already missed my chance? Would Bay still take me if I asked him to?

Setting two full, elegantly frosted and garnished glasses on the table, Bay sat back down beside me, the close heat of his body and the tantalising smell of his skin making me ache.

'Happy birthday,' he softly tapped his glass against mine.

'Thank you.' His gaze held mine as we both took a sip, his eyes so dark that I could no longer detect the green in them. 'Delicious,' I admitted, once I'd managed to swallow. I smiled, but he didn't smile back. 'This place is amazing, how did you find it?'

Carefully he set down his drink – the glass already half empty. 'The restaurant downstairs is the oldest in London – more than two hundred years old.'

'Gosh, that *is* old.'

'Edward VII used to bring one of his mistresses here,' he added with a smirk.

'Really?'

Bay nodded. 'Lillie Langtry,' he said slowly, drawing out the Ls with his tongue.

I found myself silently testing out the name myself, tasting it, my eyes loitering on Bay's lips.

'She was a real beauty in her day; dark hair, pale skin, large eyes. She sat for several great British artists: Millais, Poynter, Burne-Jones. The Prince of Wales used to bring her up to this room so that they could dine in private.'

'Wow.' I dragged my eyes away and gazed around in wonder, trying to picture the scene and tingling with the exciting sense of being so close to history. But I could feel the weight of Bay's look and turned back to him, intrigued by his smile. 'What?'

'Apparently the Prince once complained to Lillie "I've spent enough on you to build a battleship", to which she replied: "And you've spent enough in me to float one".'

I laughed, delighted by the wicked and highly-infectious grin on Bay's face. 'I can't believe you just said that.'

'Yeah, you can.'

I shook my head, basking in the rare glow of his smile. 'How do you know all this stuff?'

His smile faded. 'I'm not a complete pleb – I do read.'

'I never said you were. You just don't strike me as bookish.'

'You wouldn't be the first person to see the tats and assume I'm a moron.'

'Hey, I have my own now, remember? Anyway, I'm surprised you care what other people think about you.'

'I don't. I care what you think,' he said, bluntly.

'Oh.'

'Fuck, it's warm in here,' he muttered, downing the rest of his cocktail. 'Another?'

'No, thank you… let's head back.'

Bay looked relieved. 'Are you sure? We haven't been here long.'

'I'm sure – this is lovely, but I think I owe you some dance practise.'

'Yeah, you do actually,' he said, rising to his feet and offering me his hand.

Chapter Thirty-two

'I don't have any gin, how about a Vodka Martini?' I said, already sloshing vodka into a pair of mismatched wine glasses. 'It won't be up to Rules' standards but…'

'I'd love one, thank you,' Cally said, setting her handbag down on the kitchen counter. Now that I'd got her back here to dance for me, I was restless, almost nervous with anticipation.

'I don't have any olives either.'

Amusement flickered around her mouth as she regarded me, her eyes indigo in the low light.

'Cheers!' I clanged my glass a little too hard against hers and took a swig.

She pulled her phone out of her bag. 'Do you mind if I put my music on?' I shook my head, kicking off my shoes and tracking the beguiling swing of her hips as she crossed the room to hijack my speakers. 'I realise Nichole Alden probably isn't your thing, but this song is perfect for pole dancing,' she called back.

'I don't care what you dance to,' I said, dragging off my tie and unbuttoning my shirt.

She did a double take. 'What are you doing?'

'I don't want to get paint on my shirt.'

'Oh.'

Once I'd secured a primed canvas to an easel, I grabbed the nearest trolley full of acrylics and selected a long-handled, round-tipped Da Vinci brush. Still wearing my black suit trousers I settled on a stool. Why did I feel so damn impatient?

As I looked up, Cally's dress dropped to the floor, pooling around her feet and leaving her standing in nothing but heels and a small pair of lacy black knickers. My brush slipped from my fingers, landing with a clatter. 'What are you doing?'

'My dress is too tight to dance in,' her voice was level, no hint of any awkwardness. Having queued up the music she took a long graceful step up to the podium.

Was she messing with me? Could she really not dance in that dress or was she deliberately trying to punish me for something? As I retrieved my brush from the floor, a female voice sang out across the space accompanied by a piano and Cally began to move; slowly, sinuously, her eyes trained on mine. And I stared back, helpless and captivated as she danced in a way I'd never witnessed before – with hunger and overt sexuality. The music was unashamedly seductive, the rhythm hypnotic and the lyrics provocative as Cally silently called to me with her body, touching herself as she moved, and reclaiming me over and over again with her eyes.

I recognised many of her steps; the spins, transitions, gymnastic-style stretches and bends, but they were woven together so seamlessly, her movements so fluid and erotic that it was like beholding something else entirely; something dangerously intimate. It was intoxicating; more stimulating and arousing than any drug; too much to bear. And I hated her for it.

I'd never allowed myself to dwell on Cally's job at The Electric Fox; always refused to picture her like this;

refused to consider all the undeserving bastards that must get to see her naked each week. It wasn't really her – not the sweet, demure Cally I knew – and I'd never wanted those images in my head for fear of what they'd do to me. But now here she was dancing for me the way she must dance for them – shoving her job in my face – taunting me with it – seducing me. How dare she do this to me?

As the song drew to an end, my anger took over and I abruptly stood up, knocking my easel aside. It crashed to the ground as I stalked towards her, trembling with rage. Stepping down she backed away from me, but calmly; her shoulders back and her gaze glowing with heat.

'What are you doing?' I loomed over her, my fists clenched at my sides, forcing her back until she was pinned against the windows. 'I'm not one of your fucking punters.'

'No, you're not—'

'You want paying, is that it? You want money?'

'No, of course not,' she said, her eyes flashing.

'Then what? What do you want from me?'

She raised her chin defiantly. 'Bay, I want you to fuck me.'

Those words, on her lips, detonated inside me. 'Fuck, Cally...'

'Just once; no strings attached... I want you to show me what it can be like – how good it can be...'

Speechless I stared into the deep pools of her eyes.

'You want it, too,' she said, pressing herself up against my erection and making me groan. 'Please,' she whispered.

Begging was overkill – already I wanted her with my entire being – I had from day one. Grabbing hold of her I kissed her hard, stealing her breath with my tongue and crushing her soft breasts to my chest. She saturated my senses; swamping the air in my lungs and the blood in my veins, as if I was drowning from her kiss alone. A voice in my head warned me I was making a huge mistake and I pulled back, unsure. 'Just once,' I stated, searching her face for assurance.

Her eyelids were heavy with desire, her cheeks flushed. 'Yes,' she breathed.

And that was good enough for me. Dropping to my knees I dragged her knickers down to her ankles, unhooking them from a stiletto as she lifted her foot. Pushing her knee out to the side I lifted it high with one hand and buried my mouth between her thighs, impatient to taste her again. She braced her heel on the window frame, clinging to the windowsill at her back and panting as I explored her with my tongue. She was so beautiful; so perfect; so ripe and ready for me and making me lose all control.

The way she shoved her fingers into my hair and yanked at the roots told me she was already close – I had the power to make her fall apart with ease.

As I stood, I undid my trousers and my cock sprang free with an eagerness of its own. Cally whimpered at the sight of it, and I smirked with satisfaction, restraining the beast in one hand. 'I'll just go get a condom.'

'No, don't,' she gasped. 'There's no need, honestly, I won't get pregnant and I trust you; just do it, please.'

I'd never done it without a rubber before – usually when I invited a girl over I was too wasted to move, let alone fuck. But when I did fuck, I always used a condom – always. But Cally wasn't any of those other girls, there was an innocence about her and I trusted her as if I'd known her forever. Either way I was in no fit state to deny her anything. 'Turn around.'

She did as I asked, her breath catching at the glittering view of night-time London spread out before her. Beyond the inky abyss of the garden below lay a jumble of apertures, domes and rooftops; the many lights haloed by raindrops on the glass.

'Hold onto the windowsill and spread your legs,' I said, fighting the urge to bite her pert bottom as she complied and tipped it up to meet me. Steadying her hip with one hand, and positioning myself with the other, I thrust up inside her with an animalistic grunt. She moaned, long and low, and I stilled as her internal muscles rippled around me. Fuck she felt fantastic. While I fought to calm myself and retain control, I reached up to cup and pinch her nipples and she made a keening sound, clenching everything inside her. 'Sweet Jesus,' I muttered under my breath. She was watching me in the reflection of the window pane like a beautiful ghost, her eyes dark, her lips parted and me a sinister black shape, silhouetted behind her.

'Ready?' I growled.

'God, yes.'

I fucked her hard, unhurriedly at first, slowly withdrawing and then driving firmly back up inside her with intense deliberation – as if I was finally receiving, or solving, or finding something that I had needed all my life. And she pushed back to meet me with equal fervour, taking me deeper, moaning with pleasure and asking for more – as if she really wanted me. I knew I should be savouring this moment, drawing it out and making it last longer, but she felt too fucking incredible and my need was too overwhelming.

As our pace increased she pressed her forehead to the cool glass where it misted with her breath. Soon I sensed her body tightening in my arms with her impending release, and I had to focus solely on outlasting her. When Cally came she cried out, her back and neck arching in blissful abandon, her skin flushing with warmth and washed in moonlight. I held her close as a tidal wave of powerful convulsions consumed her from head to toe, dragging my own climax from me with near-violent force.

'Fuck,' I muttered, shaking and breathing hard.

Cally smiled lazily at my reflection, her eyes almost closed. Struggling to catch my breath, I gently eased out of her and she turned to me, her forehead dropping to my shoulder with a sated sigh. Scooping her up in my arms I carried her across the room to my bed and threw her down on the covers. She stretched and purred, kicking off her heels with loose-limbed contentment before leaning onto one elbow and gazing up at me, her dark hair stormy and her mouth a smear of crushed berries against her pale cream skin. Delicately resting her cheek in her hand she smiled knowingly, the epitome of Venus herself.

'Stay there,' I said.

Chapter Thirty-three

So that's what I'd been missing out on this whole time – that's how it felt to be properly, expertly, fucked. My body had never, *ever*, felt so utterly fantastic. Stretched out on his bed like a cat, I couldn't keep the smile from my lips.

Bay took his time setting up – righting his easel, re-securing a canvas, arranging the low lighting and organising his supplies. Retrieving our vodka Martinis from the kitchen, he set them by the bed before switching off my playlist and putting The Fragile album on repeat. This time he stripped off his trousers and settled on to the stool butt-naked except for his wristwatch; a paintbrush in hand, and his expression all business.

I watched him as he worked, his gaze shifting constantly between me and the canvas, even while he was mixing up new colours or incorporating a gel medium to alter the texture. My eyes feasted on the parts of him that the easel didn't block from view – his sexy feet; his long, athletic, hairy legs; his impressive private parts relaxed and weighty against his thigh; the bulge of his inked biceps; his black unruly hair, sticking-up in great tufts where I had pulled it – my fingers tingled at the memory – and his eyes; that dark, intense steady gaze, that turned me inside-out with longing.

'Tell me what you see,' I said.

He kept painting as if he hadn't heard me, and I started to wonder if I had ruined things between us. Shamelessly, ruthlessly, I had taken what I wanted. Would he forgive me? Or would I live to regret it? Abandoning his brush in a jar of water he took up another, kneading the bristles in his palm and then into fresh paint. At length he returned his impassive gaze to me, as welcome as the sun.

'I see the gentle slope of your shoulder...' he said, applying brush to canvas, '...the elegant line of your neck and the way the light burnishes the tips of your knuckles beneath you cheek.'

His measured words physically stirred me, as if he were actually reaching out and caressing my skin. I swallowed. 'What else?'

'I see the shadows captured by your collarbone; the way your breasts rise and shift with each breath, and the deep, wine-red splashes of your nipples, which pucker and harden under my scrutiny.'

I shivered at his words, an aching heat unfurling inside me and pooling low down in my groin.

'Cold?'

'No.'

'Move your right hand up and cup your left breast.'

I did as he said, as if in a trance, and my fingers didn't feel like my own. My skin thrilled at my touch as if it was his.

'Now rub your nipple with your thumb,'

My breath caught in my throat as sensation zinged through me. I had become Bay's willing marionette; in his thrall and at his mercy. Calmly he returned his attention to his painting while I continued to pleasure myself. But I wanted more. 'What else do you see?'

'The gentle swell of your stomach... the feminine curve of your hip... and the soft, dark nest of curls between your thighs, still damp with my come.'

I was breathing harder now, my face felt flushed and I unconsciously squeezed my thighs together to ease the throbbing there.

'Slowly move your hand down your body – *slowly*,' he repeated. His eyes followed as my fingers began their torturous descent. Despite his stern expression, his steady voice, and his determination to paint, Bay was hard again; his impressive shaft restrained in his left fist. Every part of me yearned for Bay to give in, to lose control and take me again. But we said only once – that was the deal – and I didn't want to be the one to break it.

'Raise your thigh and touch yourself there,' his voice was lower and rougher than before.

Sinking my fingers between my legs, I quietly moaned as a shudder of pleasure rolled through me, but I fought to keep my eyes fixed on Bay. His paintbrush now hovered ineffectually in the air, his gaze ensnared by my body, his left hand slowly working his length.

'Taste it,' he said and I withdrew my fingers. They glistened with moisture as they caught the light and I sucked them slowly and deliberately.

I no longer recognised myself at all. But it did the trick.

With a groan of defeat Bay abandoned his work and strode towards me. Nudging me over onto my back, he leaned down, pressed the flat of his tongue to my lower belly and licked all the way up to my neck in one long, slow sweep. I instinctively spread my legs for him as he crawled onto the bed and kissed me on the mouth, tasting our combined desire on my tongue. It was a much gentler kiss than before – soft, warm and probing – a proper long, drawn-out, bone-melting snog. I was so relaxed that it felt entirely natural when he eased inside me – the most sublime feeling in the world.

This time there was no urgency. Bay took his time; moving with a slow, sweet, steady rhythm; stroking me everywhere with his fingertips, lips and tongue. Whenever I grew dangerously close to coming, he would still within me, simply caressing my skin with the dark heat in his eyes, before resuming his internal coaxing. In this way, Bay gradually moulded and sculpted my pleasure, increasing the tension inside me with patient skill; a true artist at work. When at last he drove me over the edge, it was like flying, soaring and then floating somewhere a million miles away. But he was close behind me and climaxed groaning my name, his face contorted as if in pain.

*

The buzz of the intercom startled me awake, and for a moment I was disorientated by my surroundings. Then I took in Bay's naked form spread out beside me and I remembered with a smile. We'd had sex three times in all – a record for me – I had no idea I was capable of so many orgasms in a row. Maybe in Bay's mind it all counted as one session, but now, sadly, it was over. The buzzer made me jump again and I nudged Bay with my elbow to wake him.

'Just ignore it,' he mumbled.

'It might be important.'

180

'I doubt it.'

Lifting his heavy arm I angled his wrist into a patch of light seeping from the kitchen so that I could read his watch. 'It's 3 a.m. are you expecting someone?'

Whoever was outside was now leaning on the buzzer continuously and Bay dragged himself upright with a frustrated growl. 'Can't a guy have a post-sex nap in peace?'

'I smiled to myself as he stomped across the room naked, his dick swinging and his hair sticking up. God he was sexy. I was going to miss this so much.

Bay groaned when he reached the small camera screen. 'What the fuck does *he* want?'

'Who is it?'

'My brother.'

'Really? The one from LA?'

'That's the one.'

'It doesn't sound like he's giving up – do you want me to leave?' Sitting up I slid my feet off the bed.

'No, stay, we might be less inclined to kill each other in front of a witness.' He finally pressed a button and the buzzing stopped. 'What?' he barked.

'It's me,' said a disembodied voice.

'I can see that, what do you want?'

'Buzz me in it's wet out here.'

'No.'

'Bay... I know the code and I have a spare key, I'll just let myself in if you don't.'

Sighing resignedly, Bay jabbed the door release button while I pulled on his white shirt and hastily searched for my knickers. As he stalked towards the kitchen I threw his trousers at him and he paused long enough to pull them on before lighting up and grabbing a bottle. 'More Martini?' he said, raising his pierced eyebrow at me, the cigarette dangling precariously from his lip.

'I think I'll just have a soft drink if you've got it,' I said, slipping a dust-sheet over the unfinished nude portrait of me. Bay shrugged and there was a knock at the door.

'Sorry man, didn't realise you had company,' Bay's brother said, smiling as he noticed me arranging the corners of the dust-sheet.

'Would it have made any difference?' Bay muttered.

'Ashwin Madderson,' he said, walking right up to me and holding out his hand. 'But you can call me Ash.'

'Cally,' I said.

The similarity between the two brothers was striking – same build, same dark hair, same direct gaze. But Ash was the well-groomed, clean-cut, respectable version; with a tan, a polished smile, a short, neat haircut and an expensive-looking suit. He wore a plain gold wedding band on his left hand and his other was dry and firm as he shook mine. Up close I could see laughter lines around his eyes and a dyed absence of grey hair. Ash made me feel shy and uncomfortably conscious of my half-dressed state, even though he was too polite to allow his eyes to stray from my face.

'Why are you here, Ash?' Bay said, standing bare-chested and glowering, his feet firmly planted and smoke drifting from his nose. Ash released my hand and smoothly turned to face him.

'I was in town on business; thought I'd drop by. Are you going to offer me a drink?'

Bay crossed his arms. 'What kind of business are you doing at 3 a.m.?'

Ash sighed heavily.

'What can I get you?' I interjected, stepping into the kitchen.

'A whiskey would be nice, thanks, Cally – I don't mind which sort.' Ash turned back to his brother. 'You know, the usual kind of business; the kind where they invite you to sit through hours of tedious presentations and then take you out for a slap up meal and ply you with alcohol until you're drunk enough to visit a strip club. I ended up blowing a wad of bills on a bunch of college girls in The Electric Fox.'

I started at the mention of my workplace, spilling Jack Daniels on the counter, and glancing up to find Bay's eyes on me.

'The Electric Fox, huh?' he said, a mocking smile spreading across his face as my cheeks flamed with heat. He wouldn't... would he?

Chapter Thirty-four

'Yeah, The Electric Fox, you know it?' Ash was oblivious to the silent exchange between Cally and me. 'It was OK, but nothing to shout about.'

'Maybe Tuesdays aren't the best nights?' I said, enjoying the pretty pink blush on Cally's face, her large eyes imploring me to keep my mouth shut.

'Yeah, maybe,' Ash said, shrugging out of his jacket. 'Man, it's hot in here. Ah, thanks, Cally,' he said, spotting his drink, taking it from her hand and taking a sip. 'So, what's a pretty girl like you doing getting wasted with a guy like Bay?'

I gritted my teeth. 'Thanks for dropping by Ash, you can go now.'

'Hey, come on,' he grinned, spreading his arms wide, 'I just got here.' He walked over to the bed and sat down, tossing his jacket down beside him. 'I haven't seen you for at least a year, tell me what's new.'

'Nothing's new.'

'Why doesn't that surprise me?' Ash glanced around. 'How can you live like this? Are you ever going to sober up and sort yourself out; do something with your life?'

'That's a bit harsh,' Cally blurted out, her cheeks colouring again.

'You think so?' Ash said, his eyes narrowing. 'Let me guess, you've known Bay all of a few hours and you think all of this...' he indicated the room with a sweep of his arm, '...squalor, you think all this is cool, am I right?'

'No, but I think he deserves more credit,' she said, crossing her arms and raising her chin.

'Cally, don't bother—' I began, but Ash cut me off.

'Credit? What on earth for?'

'Well for one thing, Bay hasn't been wasted for weeks,' she said, leaving the kitchen and moving towards my brother. 'And he's been a good friend to me; showing me around town, introducing me to new people and places... and his work! I mean, have you seen his latest paintings?'

I gawped at Cally, momentarily bewildered by the rush of words pouring out of her mouth.

'Actually, no, I haven't,' Ash admitted.

'No?'

'Cally, just stay out of it,' I said, hurriedly stubbing my fag out on a paint lid, but they both ignored me.

'Are you serious? You haven't seen his work?' Cally's eyes were round.

'No, now that you mention it, maybe I should,' Ash said, rising to his feet. He reached a hand out to the shrouded easel and Cally yelped, springing forwards and batting his hand away.

'Not that one! It's not finished,' she muttered, her face flaming.

As the CEO of a multi-billion-dollar company, Ash Madderson was not used to being openly contradicted or scolded by anyone, let alone a half-naked stranger with crazy bed hair. So far he was coping well under the circumstances.

'Very well, which painting would you recommend?' he said stiffly. Cally spun around, squinting into the shadows, before realising that all my finished pieces were shut in another room. I took the opportunity to intervene.

'Just leave it, please,' I said moving close to her, lowering my voice and squeezing her hand. Her fingers were soft and warm in mine and the tantalising scent of sex on her skin made my head swim.

'But… he's your brother and he doesn't even—'

'Please?' I repeated, holding her determined gaze and watching it soften.

'Afraid I'll be disappointed, Bay?' Ash piped up.

Cally's eyes hardened and I spoke quickly before she could open her mouth. 'Ash wouldn't recognise fine art if it fucked him in the arse.'

'Watch your mouth, you little shit,' Ash said, setting aside his empty glass and rising to his feet. 'Dad would belt you for that if he were still alive.'

'I'm not a fucking kid anymore,' I said, stepping around Cally so that she was no longer between us.

'No? Grow up then! Look at this place – as far as I can see all you do is lie around getting high and sleeping with skanks.' My free hand bunched into a fist, my teeth clenching together as the blood roared in my ears. But I was aware of Cally lacing her fingers firmly through mine and I didn't want her getting hurt. 'You're wasting your life away,' Ash went on, '…it would break Mum's heart if—'

'Just fuck off back to America, Ash, I'm not your fucking responsibility.'

He stared at me for a moment, as if debating whether to push it. 'No, you're not. Not anymore,' he collected up his jacket and walked towards the door. 'You're supposed

186

to be family, but if that doesn't mean anything to you, I'm better off without you.' He opened the door and turned. 'Cally,' he said, stiffly nodding in her direction. Then he left, the door clicked shut behind him and he was gone.

Picking up Ash's empty glass I hurled it across the room with a roar of exasperation. As it exploded against the door Cally jumped and cowered behind me. Shit. Why didn't I just let her leave when she offered to? Ash and I might've been better off beating the crap out of each other after all. And Cally didn't need to get dragged into my mess. She even tried to stick up for me – *me* for fuck's sake, how fucked up is that? The pitiful truth was I'd asked her to stay because being inside her turned out to be the best feeling in the world – the high to end all highs – and I hadn't wanted our one night together to end. But with Ash's help I'd killed it completely. I needed another drink.

'Bay, stop!' Cally cried out. 'Your feet – there's glass everywhere.' With a shrug I kept walking, indifferent to the pain.

Hoisting myself up onto the kitchen counter I poured myself more booze while Cally slipped her heels back on, disappeared next door, and returned armed with a dustpan and brush.

'Just leave it,' I said.

'I can't, you'll cut your feet to ribbons,' she grumbled, crouching down, sweeping up the broken shards and neatly depositing them in the bin. By the time she'd finished I'd downed enough vodka to feel comfortably numb. Kneeling down where my feet dangled above the floor, Cally gently inspected them, gingerly removing a couple of slivers of glass from my skin with her fingernails and carefully setting them aside. 'We should clean these cuts,' she muttered in concentration. Even through a haze of numbness the tender caress of her touch was a bitter and painful reminder of everything I was going to miss about her from now on.

'Stop fussing for fuck's sake,' I said, jerking my foot out of her grasp. As she stood I pushed a glass of vodka along the counter towards her, but she shook her head, gazing at me with a sombre expression. 'What? Don't like what you see? You got what you wanted, didn't you? I gave you what you asked for – maybe you should just go now.'

She hesitated. 'Is that what you want?'

'Yes.' Even as I said it I regretted it – hated myself for being such a gutless bastard – but I couldn't look her in the eye.

'OK,' she said. Collecting her bag, her dress and Sidney's dustpan and brush, she left. The sharp click of the door as it shut behind her echoed like a gun shot in the silence.

Chapter Thirty-five

As usual my mind was elsewhere as I danced around a pole in the club. It no longer thrilled me the way it had in the beginning – it didn't seem to matter who my audience was, unless it was Bay I felt nothing. Nowadays I probably carried the same bored expression as the other girls. Donning a mask of cheerful seduction was difficult to sustain for prolonged periods, and therefore best held in reserve for the big spenders. Hell, some nights it took all my effort simply to smile. But at least this punter was turning out to be generous with his cash. He was young and attractive, a suited and booted business man, who reminded me a little of Ashwin Madderson.

The contrast between the two brothers had been a shock at first, especially since Gibbs was originally Ash's friend – I'd been expecting someone rougher around the edges. Was Ash always as polished as he now appeared? Or might there be a rogue tattoo hidden beneath his suit; residual traces of a rebellious past?

I'd dreamt about the two brothers after their altercation the night before. Meeting Ash had come so closely on the heels of sleeping with Bay that the two things had tangled in my head. The dream was a strange, confusing and erotic affair, in which I slept with both men at the same time. In reality I wasn't the slightest bit attracted to Ash – he'd come across as a pompous arse – but I couldn't deny that aspects of the fantasy itself were exciting. Three months ago I never would have entertained the notion of a threesome, and now, with what little time I had left, it seemed unlikely I'd ever get the chance to try one – it wasn't exactly the sort of thing I could stick on my bucket list. Had I ever really known myself at all?

Bizarre, inappropriate fantasies aside, it seemed ridiculous to me that the Madderson brothers were so antagonistic towards each other, especially if they were all the family each other had. I longed to know more about their history and to understand how Ash could be so blind to his sibling's considerable artistic talent. Did their father really used to beat them? With an actual belt? The idea made me ache with sorrow.

Smiling half-heartedly over my shoulder at the customer in the chair, I wrapped up my routine. He appeared to be sober and had followed my moves with an oddly courteous attention rather than the usual vacant stare I'd grown accustomed to. As I was about to walk away he stood up and straightened his tie.

'Luna?' He leaned closer, raising his voice above the music. 'Can I speak to you for a moment?'

'What about?'

'I just wondered if you choreographed your routines yourself?' He was well spoken, with a transatlantic accent and kind eyes.

'Oh, yes, why?'

'They're fantastic – you've clearly had professional training, but the way you've put everything together is inspired.'

'Oh, thank you.' His compliment surprised me.

'Listen, I'm not coming on to you, I promise, but I'd like to give you my card – I own several clubs, a bit like this one, but all over the world, and I want my dancers to be the best they can be; elegant; classy; a cut above the rest. Have you ever done any teaching?'

'Teaching?'

'Yes – have you taught dancing or choreography before?' I shook my head, dazed. 'Would you like to give it a try? I'm not knocking your job here, but I'd love for you to come and teach my dancers how to move the way you do. I'd pay well – I can offer you a good salary, health benefits, travel expenses…'

'You're serious?'

'Yes.'

I stared at him in shock, gutted by his generous offer. 'I'd love to, but, I'm so sorry, I can't.'

His disappointment was clear in his face, but no match for my own. 'Well, will you take my card and think about it anyway – just ring me if you change your mind…?'

I struggled to keep my deep regret from spilling into tears as I accepted his card, said goodbye and hurried back to the changing room. Could life really be this cruel?

*

Bay's front door was firmly locked when I got home in the early hours of Thursday morning. I could hear music through the wall and fervently hoped he was painting or working out rather than drinking himself into a stupor or getting stoned. But when I ventured onto the landing to check his door later that evening it was still closed. And that hurt.

Clearly Bay was still angry with me and he had a right to be. Using all the skills I'd learnt at the club I'd shamelessly manipulated him into sleeping with me to satisfy my own selfish curiosity – risking our precarious friendship in the process. And now, when he was upset and needed a friend, he was shutting me out. It was what I deserved but I couldn't help fretting about him. Bay had several good friends he could turn to – Willow, Gibbs, even his agent – but in my gut I knew he wouldn't. He was stubborn and hurting and had gone back to hiding himself away again.

Almost without meaning to, I found myself calling Marguerite. Her phone rang several times and when she answered she was shouting to be heard. 'Cally? Is that you? Finally! How are you?'

Just hearing her voice, so warm and familiar, almost had me bursting into tears. 'I'm good! Sorry I haven't been in touch, how are you? *Where* are you?'

Marguerite giggled. 'I'm at a wine tasting in a bar in Ealing and—' she broke off to speak to someone else, her words drowned out by music, chatter and clinking glassware, and then she was back again. 'Cally, you should come down! There's still a few rounds to go and I haven't seen you in *so long*!'

Now that I had her attention I realised that calling her was pointless – I couldn't share any of the things I wanted to – not the amazing choreographer job offer I'd received, not the stripping, and definitely not Bailey Madderson. 'Thank you, but I was just calling for a quick catch up.'

'Are you sure? You're welcome to join us…'

'Another time maybe.'

'Really? I'm holding you to that! We need to talk in person – soon – I worry about you – that man you were with last time I saw you—'

'I'm fine – really,' I said, cutting her off. 'See you later, take care…' Once I'd hung up I felt desolate and resolved not to call Marguerite again if I could help it.

At around 9 p.m. as I was fixing myself a sandwich, I heard someone leave the flat next door and the whirr of the lift as it bore them away. Rushing to the window, I leaned outside and was rewarded with a glimpse of Bay as he emerged on the pavement, twelve floors below. I would know him anywhere. Dressed all in black with a gym bag over one shoulder, he paused to light up a cigarette, then shoved a hand in his pocket before sauntering away out of sight. It was a relief to see he was alive and not limping, but I wished he'd taken me with him.

A couple of hours later my buzzer rang and it took me a second or two to place the face I saw on the screen. It was Gibbs' partner, Trudy.

'Hi, Bay's not in, if that's who you're looking for.'

'No, I'm here to see you, actually.'

My mind hummed with impatient curiosity as I stood at my door waiting for the lift to carry Trudy up.

'I'm sorry to just turn up like this,' she said as I ushered her inside.

'Not at all, it's nice to see you – what can I do for you?' She was breathing hard, her bosom heaving as if she'd been rushing, and fear prickled at the back of my neck. Having offered her a drink I fetched her the requested glass of water while she sat down heavily on the sofa.

Taking a long swallow she looked at me as I sank into the seat beside her. 'It's Bay. I don't know what the deal is between you two — whether you're really just neighbours or… or whether you have any influence over him.'

'Influence?'

She took a steadying breath and exhaled slowly. 'Bay's at the club right now, volunteering to stand in for someone who's dropped out last minute. I know because I sell tickets on the door.'

'Sorry… the club…? What club? What do you mean he's standing in—'

'Fight; he's going to fight. It's a club for white-collar professionals to train up like boxers and beat the hell out of each other.' My mouth fell open and I gaped at her. 'The thing is, I know Bay; he's been fighting since he was a kid and I know he can handle himself, but Gibbs doesn't like him doing it, and she'll kill me if she finds out I didn't try to stop him. But he won't listen to me, he never has. And then I remembered the way he was with you the other day, and I wondered if he might listen to you?' She took another sip of water while I tried to process what she was telling me. 'How's your shoulder by the way?'

'It's fine, thanks,' I murmured. 'What…? Is this club legal?'

'Yeah, the club's all above board and they have rules and regulations and so on, but it can still be pretty brutal, and the mood Bay's in tonight, I'm afraid he could do some real damage.

'You'd better take me there,' I said, rising to my feet in a daze. 'I don't know if it will do any good but…' I glanced down at my skimpy top and floaty red skirt. 'Should I change into something else?'

Trudy looked me up and down. 'We don't have a lot of time...'

Shoving my feet into the pair of heels by the door, I quickly slipped my handbag on over my head and locked the flat behind us. As we stood side by side in the lift, I tried not to picture Bay lying beaten to a pulp while a crowd of people looked on for sheer entertainment. The thought of mindless violence had always turned my stomach, but imagining Bay in pain was worse.

'I don't suppose you know why he's so riled up?' Trudy said, distracting me from my building anxiety.

'Maybe. He fell out with his brother a couple of nights ago...'

'Ash? He's here?' She tutted. 'That would explain it – like chalk and cheese those two.'

'I don't know, they both seem pretty stubborn.'

'Yeah, true, and they're both experts at pushing each other's buttons. They used to be close, but Ash changed when their dad died; moved overseas to run the family business. Now whenever Ash comes back, he and Bay are at each other's throats.'

'Bay said that Ash and Gibbs used to be friends...?'

'High school sweethearts.'

'Wow, really?'

Trudy nodded grimly. 'Like I said – Ash has changed a lot, but Gibbs still considers Bay the little brother she never had.'

*

The club was a dark, crowded basement with a smart, corporately-branded boxing ring lit up in the centre like a stage. A match was in progress; two men in sports clothes, headgear and gloves were going at each other with focused intent. Until now the only real violence I'd known was second-hand from TV news reports or fictionalised in books and films. I stared in shock as two real live fighters, amped up on adrenalin, attacked one another in a brutal competition to see who could damage each other the most. The standing, predominantly male audience was loving it; the atmosphere was thick with primitive excitement, it was almost animal, and the din generated by the bellowing crowd was immense. I could almost taste the testosterone in the air.

While I was frozen in fearful fascination, as out of place as a little girl in a den full of wolves, Trudy was consulting a match schedule.

'We're too late,' she said, her voice raised over the noise.

A chill swept through me. 'What?'

'Looks like we already missed Bay's fight.'

'Oh god, is he OK?'

She huffed out a breath. 'Probably – I'm more concerned about the other guy,' she shouted. 'Looks like Bay took him out cold in the first round.'

'Oh.'

'Yeah. I'm going to the office to find out more details – check his opponent is still breathing,' she added, turning towards the ticket booth.

'OK. Wait,' I put a hand out to stop her. 'What about Bay?'

'He won't be fighting again tonight – club rules. Changing rooms are back there.' She pointed to a dimly-lit doorway just visible in the shadows towards the back of the basement, and when I nodded my understanding she moved away. The spot-lit brightness of the boxing ring made it virtually impossible to make out anything beyond or around it. Clinging on to my handbag I plunged into the gloom, avoiding the animated faces around me as I burrowed my way through the crowd. The door wasn't labelled, and I'd been expecting it to lead to a corridor and a further choice of doors beyond – so it was a shock to find myself bursting straight into a men's changing room lined with lockers and benches and several large men. Conversations broke off and all eyes turned in my direction as the door swung shut behind me, muffling the din of the arena.

'Hey there, gorgeous, you lost?' the nearest guy said, taking a step towards me. Thankfully he had clothes on, I didn't dare check the others as I tried to formulate a reply.

'She's with me.' Bay's voice, deep with conviction, sliced through the room, brooking no argument. My eyes found his and while the other men returned to their conversations, I clung to the sight of him as if he were a rock in a stormy sea. The sexiest and most frustrating man alive was standing alone, at the back of the room, wearing nothing but a pair of shorts, a sheen of sweat, and an uncompromising expression. His arm and chest muscles looked harder and meaner than ever, the distinctive ink of his tattoos reading like a health warning. Any normal person might have hesitated to approach such an individual, but my relief at finding him conscious and not bleeding made me brave. Ignoring the other men I walked up to him, scanning him for signs of injury, while trapped in the laser-like beam of his stare.

'What the hell are you doing here?' he said in a low voice.

'Trudy said you were here.'

'So?'

'So, I came to talk to you.'

'Why?'

'I… I was hoping to talk you out of fighting.'

He snorted. 'Bit late for that. What's it got to do with you anyway?'

His face bore faint red indentations, presumably left behind by the head gear in his hand, and the boxing gloves, discarded on the bench behind him, seemed to have done a good job of protecting his knuckles, but an area of pink inflammation was slowly blooming across his ribs. Confronted with Bay's blunt question I decided to be honest. 'I don't know I just… you're pretty much my only friend right now and I didn't want you getting hurt.'

The shouting in the arena rose to an almighty roar preventing Bay from delivering what was almost certainly a mocking retort. He eyeballed me until the noise level had subdued again but seemed to think better of saying whatever he was going to say, opting for a warning instead.

'You need better friends – ones less likely to get you hurt.'

Suppressing a shiver I folded my arms across my chest. 'What's that supposed to mean? I'm not afraid of you.'

'Well you should be.' Snatching up his T-shirt he pulled it on over his head, punching his arms through the sleeves and dragging the fabric down over his bruised torso.

'You're not going to shower?'

'No,' he said shoving his feet into a pair of trainers. 'You'll just have to put up with the smell. Let's get out of here.' Grabbing his bag in one hand he put the other to my back and guided me towards the door.

We made our way back to TMC Tower in silence – Bay smoked while I quietly pondered his warning. From the first moment I met Bay he'd struck me as trouble – that was the vibe he exuded. But over the intervening weeks as I'd got to know him – earned his trust, unearthed his grudging generosity, basked in his artistic appreciation and revelled in his coarse sense of humour – my initial impression had been overwritten, if not erased. But there was still so much I didn't know about him.

'Is the other guy OK?' I enquired as we entered the lift. Being in there with Bay still made my skin tingle.

He raised an eyebrow at me.

'You know – the guy you fought – is he OK?'

'He's fine. I didn't even hit him that hard – he feigned a black out to end the match.'

'Why?'

Bay shrugged. 'Got scared I guess.'

'Does that happen often?'

'Sometimes. A lot of the guys who sign up there don't have much real experience.'

'And you do.' It wasn't a question, and Bay didn't reply. 'You scare them,' I added, finally understanding Trudy's concern – apparently Bay was so dangerous in the ring that his mere reputation was enough to intimidate other men.

The realisation should have appalled me. I'd never approved of grown men threatening and beating each other in the name of sport – it sounded moronic – but having been to a legal club and experienced the atmosphere for myself, I was starting to reconsider.

Though I still didn't know the root cause, I knew for certain Bay suffered emotional pain and struggled with anger. Most of it he seemed to take out on himself with drugs and booze, but when he did need to lash out, like tonight, rather than recklessly instigating a brawl in the nearest bar, he'd chosen to unleash his aggression in the controlled environment of a club – one with rules, restrictions, and protective headgear. And there was virtue in that – a strength in Bay's character that I couldn't help but admire.

The fight, though brief, seemed to have taken the edge off his anger, and as I accompanied him into his flat I hoped he had forgiven me enough that we could still be friends. The intimacy we'd shared two nights ago, that close sense of easiness between us, was gone. Naked in Bay's bed I'd discovered a playful side to him; a lightness, an openness that almost rivalled the sex itself, and I already missed it. But Ash's impromptu visit had ended what was only ever going to be a one night stand – a sexual relationship with Bay was out of the question – it would only complicate things in the long run. Now, if I could just get our friendship back on track, everything could go back to how it was before…

'When was the last time you ate?' I said, discarding my handbag on his unmade bed and making a beeline for his kitchen. When Bay didn't answer I turned back to look at him. He was leaning against the far wall watching me with a distracted look on his face, as if he was trying to figure something out. 'Bay?' I prompted.

He shrugged.

'I'll make us something, then.' Opening the fridge I cast an eye over the meagre contents. 'Go and have a shower,' I added over my shoulder. Without a word Bay sauntered off to the bathroom, his hand buried in the wild tufts of his hair.

Chapter Thirty-six

Standing with my back to everybody, I took another gulp of the over-priced, too-sweet, barely-alcoholic beverage in my hand, and stared out at the glowing horizon. I'd ordered Aperol Spritz because it sounded like the sort of drink Cally might enjoy, but she was late, I was restless, and having finished my own Spritz I was now downing hers. Where was she?

Recently Cally had been hanging out with me on an almost daily basis. She kept dropping round unannounced and making meals in my kitchen, or she'd bring her laptop and tap away on it, or lie there reading books on my bed as if she owned the place. For a recluse like me it was unnatural to have so much company – I should hate it – I should put a stop to it; throw her out; keep my door locked – for her own safety, if for no other reason.

But I'd warned her I was bad news – she'd come to the fight club for fuck's sake – if anywhere was a clue to my true nature it was that shit hole. Cally hadn't seen me fight, but she'd witnessed enough to understand my bad rep. Yet, when we got back to the flat, she acted like nothing had changed. And apparently I'm too fucking weak and selfish to push any harder.

It didn't help that the chemistry between us was staggering. Usually the moment I'd had a woman, I was done with her – sex was a release; a means to an end, nothing more. But it was different with Cally – our 'just once' had involved doing it three mind-blowing times in one night – I couldn't seem to get enough of her – and ever since then, for the past eight days, I'd been trying hard to forget. I may not be able to get rid of Cally, but I was determined to keep my dick in my pants – some things were a risk too far.

In the early hours of this morning, before she'd retired to the flat next-door to sleep, she'd said she'd be going shopping and asked me to choose a place to meet her afterwards. I wanted to impress her, so I'd suggested the roof top of this multi-storey car park in Peckham, with its quirky pop-up bar, spectacular views and trendy hipster crowd. Festival-style toilets aside, it had a good vibe and the distinctive scarlet tarpaulin alone made it very Cally. But I was regretting it now; she was late, there were too many people and I had a growing urge to throw myself off the edge. Was she lost? Had something happened to her? Why didn't she ever have her phone switched on? And why was I letting it bother me so much? This was another good reason not to get close to people – they couldn't be relied upon.

Awareness prickled the back of my neck as someone came up behind me and I hoped it was her.

'Guess who?' she said, a smile in her voice as she clumsily covered my eyes with her fingers while bashing me round the shoulders with her shopping bags. I took a moment to savour her, now so familiar, sweet floral scent and let the tension start to ease from my muscles with relief.

'You're late,' I muttered.

Cally sighed as she removed her hands and I turned to face her. 'I know, I'm sorry, I had to get a bus and it took longer than I expected.' Her cheeks were flushed and stray tendrils of her hair were sticking to her neck and temple. I longed to taste her there; run my tongue over her skin, feel her pulse race and see her head tip back in pleasure…

Slipping her bags off her arms she bent down to neatly line them up between her feet before straightening up again.

'I'll have to get more drinks,' I said pointedly, clutching the two empty glasses. Now that she was here I didn't care that she was late, I just couldn't forgive her for the way she made me feel.

'I can get them…?'

With a shake of my head I dismissed her offer and stalked off.

'Can I just have a soft drink? I'm really thirsty…' she called after me.

There was a queue at the bar and as I stood there, suffused in the rosy light created by the awning, I had time to regret being an arsehole. Ruefully I glanced over to where I'd left Cally standing alone, patiently gazing out at the sunset. My fingers itched with the urge to paint and I quickly tried to memorise the details of the scene; the simple eloquence of her posture, the quality of the light glowing in her hair and the fragile serenity she exuded, so that I might capture it all on canvas later. Then I told myself to get a grip.

By 10.30 it was dark, the crowds had begun to thin and I'd managed to nab us an empty picnic bench. We were sitting in a corner of the rooftop car park, away from everyone else, and Cally was excitedly showing me her purchases. She'd picked up a few bargains for herself in the sales, but she'd also bought something for me. The T-shirt was black, my colour, with a retro print of a charcoal grey, green-eyed wolf on the front. It was exactly my size and I liked it immediately, but it had been years since anyone had given me anything, and for a moment I was struck dumb.

'I just saw it and thought of you – but you don't have to wear it – in fact I can return it if you don't want it,' she said, trying to shove it back into a bag.

'No,' I said, snatching it back. 'I want it. But this doesn't mean you get to keep my Alice In Chains shirt.'

She grinned. 'Damn.'

I lit up a fag and the scrutiny of her gaze was warmer on my skin than the flame.

'I thought you were giving up.'

'I've cut down – I doubt I'll ever give up completely.' She looked disappointed and I changed the subject. 'How's work going? You haven't mentioned it in a while.'

'It's fine,' she said. 'There's not much to mention – most nights are the same. The other girls are friendly enough and I usually do OK for tips…'

Now that I'd seen her dance – properly pole dance in only a pair of knickers – I had to try even harder not to picture her at the club, doing the same thing for strangers. On the nights she worked her shifts, I painted and drank or got high; anything to keep busy and stop myself from worrying about her. 'So the punters aren't giving you any trouble?'

205

'No – the club has strict rules and Liam is quick to throw out anyone who tries to break them.'

'Liam?'

'Oh God,' she said, briefly covering her face with her hand. 'Did I say Liam? I meant Leroy – he's a bouncer on the door, I think I've mentioned him to you before.'

'So who's Liam?'

She sighed, rubbed her forehead and closed her eyes, as if that might shut out my curiosity.

But it didn't. 'Cally?'

'He's my ex-boyfriend. Leroy reminds me of him, that's all.'

Shifting sideways I straddled the bench to better see her face, but she kept her eyes closed and half hidden behind her hand. Suspicion and suppressed rage simmered through my veins as I intently studied her profile. I fought to keep my voice steady. 'Is he the reason you left home? Did he hurt you?'

'No!' She glared at me.

'Are you sure?'

'Yes! If anything I hurt him, OK?'

I wanted to believe her. 'Are you still in love with him?' The question slipped out before I could catch it, surprising us both. 'Fuck. Actually forget that, I don't want to know.' Wrenching my eyes away from her I stubbed my fag out with ill-concealed irritation.

She didn't reply, and in the ensuing awkward silence I internally berated myself with a string of expletives. I *did* want to know, and we both knew it – I wanted her reassurance that she was over him. But why? Why? I liked to paint Cally, and yes the sex with her had been fantastic, and OK, I'll admit, I enjoyed her company too, but that was it. Why should I give a shit who she loved?

Leaning down, Cally rooted around in one of her carriers and removed a small paper bag full of cherries. Throwing one leg over the bench, she straddled it, mirroring me, her skirt riding up above her knees. She set the cherries on the seat between us in mute offering – they looked almost black in the low light. With a shake of my head I declined, but watched, rooted to the spot, as she plucked one, sank her front teeth into the ripe globe of flesh, delicately removed the stone with her fingertips before launching it off the rooftop and into the dark. Popping the rest of the cherry into her mouth she smiled hesitantly at me as she chewed, a blood-like trickle of juice escaping the corner of her mouth. She caught the fluid with the tip of her tongue and swallowed, while I stared, helplessly transfixed.

'Bay, you know whatever this is between us, is just… ' *killing me*, my brain supplied, '…temporary.' My hand strayed to her knee of its own accord, my fingers spreading out across her warm skin. She shivered slightly at the contact but didn't move away. 'I'm so grateful to you for the company and all the new things you've introduced me to… I just don't—'

'Like what?' I interrupted, keeping my voice low, though there was no-one close enough to overhear us.

'Well, you know, like the street feast, the rock concert, the outdoor cinema, the fight club…' Her voice wavered as my fingertips caressed the inside of her thigh. What was I doing? This was dangerous. My head was telling me to stop, to abstain, but it was addictive witnessing the effect I had on her.

'And...?'

She swallowed heavily but held my stare. 'Tattooing... smoking dope...'

'Anything else?'

'Sex,' she whispered, blushing like a virgin bride.

'You've had sex before.'

'Yes, but not like with you...'

'You mean fucking,' I said, tracing small circles on her skin. 'You liked the way I fucked you.'

'Yes,' she breathed, her eyes closing, heavy with arousal. God I wanted her.

'What else haven't you tried? I bet you haven't come in public before?' I said, slowly inching my fingertips under the hem of her skirt.

She gasped, her eyes snapping open and darting self-conscious looks over my shoulder as she pushed my hand away. 'No! I... I don't think I'm ready for that...'

I shouldn't tease her, but she was the embodiment of temptation. 'Then what, Cally? What else do you want to try? What's the filthiest, dirtiest fantasy that's ever crossed your mind?' I kept a hold of her hand and her fingers absently twined around mine.

'I can't.'

'Why not? What are you afraid of? If you can't tell *me*, then who? There's no strings between us and I won't—'

'A threesome.'

I stilled at this entirely unexpected revelation. Fuck. 'With another woman?'

'No, another man.' Her eyes flashed defiantly as she said it, as if laying down a challenge. Whether she realised it or not she was goading me; daring me; testing my resolve and the limits of my physical need for her. She had no idea who she was dealing with – no clue how dangerous I could be.

'I'm sure that could be arranged,' I said with a smirk.

She laughed and shook her head, dismissing it all as a big joke. 'Oh and I've never been on top,' she added, as an after-thought.

'Really? Hell, we can remedy that right now,' I said, dumping the bag of cherries on the table, grabbing her hips and dragging her along the bench towards my lap.

She yelped in surprise, 'Stop it! Don't you dare!' She laughed, batting at my arms, flustered with embarrassment and I released her. I was only half serious, but my cock throbbed and balls ached with frustration. 'I believe it's your round,' she said, rearranging herself demurely with her legs together on one side of the seat and plucking another cherry from the bag.

'Don't go anywhere.' Standing up I adjusted the front of my trousers and headed back to the bar, the sweet aroma of cherries now trapped in my nostrils and taunting my every step.

By the time I returned with our drinks I'd calmed down, but Cally was no longer alone at our table; there was someone in my seat.

'Willow?'

'Hey,' she said, smiling lazily up at me as I sat down. 'Second time I've seen you in less than two months, must be a record, huh?'

'It wasn't intentional,' I muttered. 'Why are you here?'

She shrugged, smoke escaping from her mouth as she tapped ash from the menthol cigarette in her hand. 'Same as you, I expect – having a drink with friends. It was me that told you about this place, remember?'

'Was it?'

'Yeah, a while ago now. It's good to see you out and about for a change – it suits you – you've almost got colour in your cheeks.'

'Don't let us keep you,' I said, hoping she would take the hint and bugger off.

'You're not. Cally here was just showing me her new butterfly tat – it's lovely – another Madderson masterpiece! Welcome to the club,' she said, leaning in to Cally and nudging her shoulder.

Cally smiled back but it didn't quite reach her eyes.

'How are you, Bay?' Willow said, reaching across and giving my forearm a squeeze. 'You seem a little tense?'

Usually I didn't mind Willow's openly flirtatious ways; her casual approach to sex had always suited me. But right now, with Cally in my orbit, it was all wrong. Before I could respond, Cally stood up, excused herself, climbed out of the bench and walked off to the toilets. Was she upset? Willow's touch was irritating and I yanked my arm out of her grasp.

'What? What's wrong?'

Ignoring her I lit up a fag of my own, inhaling deeply.

'Shall I come back to yours tonight? You look like you need to unwind.'

'No.'

'Why? You're not planning to get Cally into bed are you?'

I glared at her. 'No.'

'I hope not 'cause she's a sweet girl, Bay, and she's got a crush on you – you know that, right...? Don't go there.'

'Who are you, her mother? You don't even know her.'

'No, but I know you – you'll fuck her and drop her and it'll break her heart. You'll hate yourself afterwards.'

'I already hate myself, what's the difference? Just mind your own fucking business.'

As I knocked back my drink, Willow stood up to leave. 'Fine, but don't say I didn't warn you.'

Cally looked peaky when she returned, as if she might have been sick.

'You OK?' I said.

She nodded. 'Where's Willow?'

Standing up I shrugged. 'Shall we go?'

Questions hovered in her expression, but I avoided her eye by gathering up her shopping bags and we left without another word to each other. Willow didn't have to say it – I was well aware that Cally deserved better than the likes of me. I would not fuck her again.

Chapter Thirty-seven

Out of the corner of my eye I noticed Bay go to the intercom, check the screen and press the door release button without bothering to speak to whoever he was admitting into the building. He left the door on the latch and padded barefoot back to the kitchen, rummaging in his pocket as he went.

'Delivery?' I enquired from his bed where I was sat cross-legged, still typing away on my laptop.

Bay hopped up onto the kitchen counter, flicked on his lighter, cupped his hand and lit up. In my peripheral vision I could see his hairy, naked calves idly swinging in time to Linkin Park. 'Nope, it's someone for you.'

I looked up and he smirked at me. 'Who?' He didn't reply but I heard the lift opening out on the landing. Seconds later the door swung open and in strode my best friend in fully professional business mode; buttoned-up blouse, pencil skirt and heels; her hair in a neat up-do and a smart leather briefcase in her hand. I gaped at her in surprise, feeling under-dressed in a small pair of shorts and a vest top. 'Marguerite!'

'I thought I might find you here,' she said, marching right up to the bed and ignoring Bay entirely. 'Why haven't you returned my phone calls?'

'I ... I'm sorry... I kept meaning to...'

'What are you doing?'

'Writing! At last.' I grinned triumphantly. 'You know how I've always wanted to write a book but didn't know what it should be about? Well I've started jotting down my experiences of London, and it's fun, and I'm hoping I might be able to make something out of it...' I tailed off, my smile fading. Marguerite was slowly shaking her head, her lips pressed into a line. 'What?'

'Why are you here?' she said, wrinkling her nose and waving her hand in front of her face, even though Bay's cigarette smoke had yet to reach her. Nowadays Bay made a conscious effort not to smoke in my personal space.

'Oh, Bay's painting me...' I said, pointing at the easel before realising that it now stood empty. He must have finished for tonight. A glance at my laptop showed me it was 9.30 a.m. No wonder I was tired, my nausea had abated and I'd completely lost track of time.

'Have you only just got up?' Marguerite's voice was snipped and sharp.

'No, I haven't been to bed yet,' I muttered, glancing over at Bay. He looked shattered, too – why hadn't he kicked me out?

Marguerite was shaking her head again. 'I don't know what's going on, Cally, but this isn't you.'

'I'm fine, honestly. And I called Liam and he knows not to worry about me—'

'Good Lord, is that a tattoo?' She grasped my shoulder, angling my skin towards the light. 'I think you need help, Cally.'

'Help...?' I laughed. 'What is this, some kind of intervention?' My smile faded at my best friend's stern expression. 'Why do you think I need help?'

'Just look at you!' she said with a flail of her hand. 'You've thrown away a nice home, a kind, decent man who loves you and a perfectly good job, and for what? This?' It was déjà vu the way she glanced disparagingly around Bay's apartment – Ash all over again. 'Staying up all night and doing Lord-knows-what with Lord-knows-who? What are you going to do when the six month contract is up? Have you even thought about that?'

'No,' I admitted, looking down and quietly closing my laptop. 'I haven't thought about that at all.' A heavy sense of inevitability sank like a stone in my stomach. I'd always known this new life of mine wasn't going to last, but I'd deliberately avoided thinking about it.

'Right, well, I think we need to sit down and work out how we are going to get you back on track.'

'Can't you just believe me when I say that I'm happy as I am?' I offered gently.

'No. I know you better than you know yourself, I always have and we've been friends too long for me to just—'

Bay snorted loudly. 'Are you fucking kidding me?'

Marguerite spun round on one heel. '*You* stay out of this,' she said, jabbing a finger in Bay's direction. 'You've done enough damage already.'

'What damage?' he said, sliding off the counter. 'She's just said she's happy as she is – who are you to decide what she does?' He prowled across the floor towards us.

'I'm her best friend, that's who! I love her and I look out for her, isn't that right, Cally?' she added, turning back to me. I nodded and smiled weakly at her. She was right – she had always been there for me – Marguerite had always been my strength.

'But she doesn't need you *right now*.' Bay pointed out, towering over her, smoke smoothly escaping the side of his mouth. But Bay's height alone would not be enough to intimidate Marguerite.

'She needs me *now*, more than ever – so that she doesn't get taken advantage of.' My cheeks heated with shame; I didn't want Bay knowing the real me, and here she was spelling it out for him, as if I wasn't even here. I wanted the ground to swallow me up. 'She needs…'

'Are we talking about the same person?' Bay interrupted, looking at me and then back to my friend with a confused expression. 'Cally's the bravest woman I've ever met.'

I glanced up at him, shocked by his words and his eyes locked onto mine, glowing with something I couldn't decipher.

'I don't care what you think,' Marguerite said dismissively, taking my hand. 'Come on, Cally; let's go next door where we can talk in private.' Unconsciously I rose to my feet to follow her, Bay's unexpected compliment still ringing in my head.

'Hang on,' Bay said, tossing his cigarette butt into an open tin of paint and stepping up close to me. He cupped my face in both hands and stared into my eyes, filling my vision, his warm familiar scent stirring my blood. 'What's going on? You don't have to do what she tells you.'

'No, I know; it's not like that – she's my best friend…'

'So why have you gone so quiet? Why aren't you standing up for what you want?'

'I…' Good question. I'd always let Marguerite take the lead; it was automatic.

For a split second I thought Bay might slap me, but instead he kissed me on the mouth, urgently; as if to wake me, resuscitate me, or remind me of something. A fortnight had passed since we'd slept together and the strength of my latent desire rushed to the surface, making my head swim and my knees weak.

'Urgh, what are you doing!' Marguerite cried, trying to pull me away.

'Whatever else happens, you still have two and a half months here...' Bay said, his dark eyes holding mine.

'Yes,' I said, breathless. He was right – my time hadn't run out yet. Reluctantly stepping back out of Bay's hands I dragged my eyes over to Marguerite's disgusted expression. 'How about we go next door and I make us a cup of tea,' I said brightly. She looked relieved as I gathered up my laptop and we made our way over to the door. Bay silently followed, his steady gaze unrelenting.

Once Marguerite was safely through my front door I turned back to him. 'I'll see you later, get some sleep.' The worry on his face receded at my words, and on impulse, unable to resist, I reached up and stroked my fingers through the stubble at his jaw. An arrogant smirk slowly spread across his lips, warming me inside.

'Later,' he said, winking playfully at me before stepping back inside his flat and closing the door.

Over the course of half an hour I worked to convince my best friend that I was not in need of saving. I distracted her with all the pretty new dresses and shoes I'd bought, and regaled her with tales of all the amazing places I'd seen. Obviously I left out the more colourful details: my job as a stripper, illegal trespassing, smoking

216

weed, crowd surfing, fight clubs etc. But I was able to reassure her with complete honesty that I was not piercing my body parts, injecting myself with heroine or prostituting myself, which helped put her mind at ease.

Marguerite had been my rock growing up – she had given me the direction and protection I craved and I'd pledged my unswerving friendship and loyalty in return. But somewhere along the way, the balance between us had shifted too far in one direction. It was my fault as much as hers. I had let her carry me, simply because it was easier than standing on my own two feet, and she had grown more controlling in response. But things were different now – my eyes had been opened and I couldn't afford to capitulate any longer.

Thankfully Marguerite had a meeting to get to. We made firm plans to meet up for a girly night out later in the week, and she left far happier than she had arrived. Collapsing into bed, exhausted, I felt grateful for my devoted old friend, and grateful for my new and unpredictable one. If only I could wipe his breathtaking kiss from my mind, I might get some sleep.

Chapter Thirty-eight

Why the hell was I doing this? What was wrong with me? I'd never had the urge to follow anybody before, but then I'd never met anybody like Cally before. She'd become a bad habit and I wasn't sure what, short of moving into a hotel for the next two-and-a-half months, I should do about it. Since meeting her I'd tried ignoring her, swearing at her and repeatedly exposing her to all my bad vices, but it didn't seem to have any effect. The woman had infiltrated my work, my bed, my network of friends. She'd even met my brother for fuck's sake. Worst of all she was in my head – making me want to confide and confess things – things that were none of her damn business. It scared the shit out of me.

So why was I skulking at the back of this pub in a baseball cap, watching my neighbour from across the room?

It was probably a nice pub once upon a time, with history, character and soul, but it had been taken over by a chain; had its guts ripped out and been modernised so thoroughly that, sitting here, you could easily be in any city in the western world. The service was lousy, the food was worse, and the so-called music was giving me a headache. Even the beer was decidedly average – I usually avoided the hard stuff and stuck to lager when drinking in public to better keep my wits about me. At least Cally hadn't spotted me. But then she seemed oblivious to most of the pub's punters; including the two middle-aged men at the bar eyeing her up while they worked up the nerve to approach her; and the young guy at the next table who kept checking her out over his date's shoulder. I couldn't blame them – she was particularly alluring this evening in a cadmium-red, Grecian-style maxi-dress that hugged her torso and billowed around her legs when she walked.

But Cally had all her focus trained on the straight-laced, uptight brunette sitting opposite her – Marguerite. I wondered what they were talking about; whether they were discussing Liam, the ex she'd left behind, or whether Cally's thoughts were elsewhere. Her fingers repeatedly strayed to her shoulder where, beneath the fabric, I knew her tattoo was nicely scabbed over and itching like mad. So far she had refrained from actually scratching it. Was she thinking of me?

I told myself I was here to look out for Cally because I didn't trust Marguerite – she was snooty and controlling and hated me on sight. I suspected she would try and do something to lure my next-door neighbour away from me for good. But so far there were no signs of kidnapping – they were simply having a quiet drink, while I trailed them like a sick dog.

I was losing the plot.

As I took another sip of my pint and started to destroy yet another beer mat between my fingers, a blonde with a lip ring and an undercut slid into the seat beside me.

'Hey, I'm Jen.'

'Hey, Jen, fuck off.'

'There's no need to be an arsehole.'

'But I am an arsehole.'

'Fair enough. Buy me a drink and you can tell me all about it.'

As I was shaking my head, two young guys approached Cally's table. Marguerite greeted one of them enthusiastically with air kisses before shaking the other by the hand. I didn't envy the guy; I'd been on the receiving end of that limp-fish handshake myself. Marguerite proceeded to introduce the newcomers to Cally and then, to my increasing irritation, invited the men to sit down. I say 'men' but really they were boys – fresh-faced, no muscle bulk to speak of, and wearing chinos for fuck's sake. I could flatten them both with my thumb. I certainly wanted to. So this was Marguerite's cunning plan…

'Hell-oo,' Jen said, waving a hand in front of my face.

'What?' I growled, without taking my eyes off Cally.

'Are you gonna buy me a drink or what, grumpy guts?'

'If I do, will you piss off?'

Yep,' she said cheerfully. I passed her a tenner and told her to get me another pint while I continued to observe my Greek goddess making polite conversation from afar.

An hour and two pints later I was confident that Cally wasn't into her blind date. She seemed perfectly at ease in the guy's company as she steadily made her way through two half pints of lager, but the eye contact was fleeting, her smiles half-hearted, and so far he had only made her laugh once. I was debating whether to slip out the rear exit and leave them all to it, when Cally suddenly stood up. Excusing herself from her seat she squeezed her way between the crowded tables and approached the jukebox idling in the corner.

I loitered, curious to see what she would choose, noting that she was a little flushed, as if the beer had gone straight to her head. As she returned to her friends the main music clicked off and I listened with anticipation. As the familiar first line of 'Bohemian Rhapsody' leaked out of the speakers, a ripple of awareness swept through the pub, triggering memories and associations within the collective minds of the pub's patrons and lifting the atmosphere.

Cally's 'date' was a picture of surprise and Marguerite wrinkled her nose, but several other people, including the men at the bar, whooped and cheered with appreciation. I couldn't help grinning as Cally enthusiastically sang along to the words, encouraging others to do the same. By the middle of the song she had her friends up on their feet and was half-hidden in a throng of strangers that jumped along to the music, head-banging and swinging their hair.

'Supermassive Black Hole' came on next and I tried to recall whether Cally had always been a Muse fan or whether my taste was starting to rub off on her. Marguerite took herself off upstairs to the Ladies' while Cally and the others carried on dancing; the various different groups mingling and getting to know one another as if now at a party. But on her way back, Marguerite slipped on the stairs and twisted her ankle. After much gentle prodding and debate, it was decided that Cally would take Marguerite to A&E for an x-ray, effectively ending their night out.

I observed from the shadows of the pub as a taxi drew up outside and the patient was helped into it, but then Cally ran back inside alone, as if she'd forgotten something. Except that she bypassed their table completely, quickly weaving her way through the makeshift dance floor, her head down as she advanced towards the back of the room. Before I had a chance to move she was grabbing me by the scruff of my shirt, leaning up on her tiptoes and kissing me beneath the peak of my stupid cap. Had she known I was here all along?

Impulsively taking hold of her butt I pulled her to me, groaning into her mouth with shame and pent-up frustration. But after only a couple of minutes she backed out of my grasp and hightailed it as quickly as she had arrived, gliding away through the masses and into the waiting taxi without a word. I stood for a moment, stunned, and then Cally's final song choice started up on the jukebox.

Though a classic, The Police's 'Every Breath You Take' wasn't enough to keep the crowd on their feet – people gravitated back to their seats, their enthusiasm for dancing disappearing along with the woman in red. But I chuckled to myself, shaking my head and grinning like an idiot, the stalker's anthem serenading my ears as I ordered myself another pint at the bar.

Chapter Thirty-nine

I snuck into Bay's flat unheard over the music. He was standing with his back to me; legs spread, bare feet firmly planted and arms crossed at his chest, seemingly lost in thought as he surveyed a selection of paintings propped up all along one brick wall. Stepping up behind him, I recklessly tucked my hands into the pockets of his cargo shorts, pressing my chest to his lean, hard back and subtly inhaling his warm scent though his shirt. Outwardly he showed no reaction to my presence, but I felt him stirring; swelling and hardening inside his shorts and shivered with satisfaction.

'What you up to?'

'Felix is sending someone over tomorrow to collect some paintings for an exhibition.'

'Felix?'

'My agent.'

'Oh! That's exciting.'

'Is it?' His voice sounded far away.

Withdrawing my hands I moved to stand beside him, running my eyes over the fine array of work before me. 'How many does he want?'

'Fifteen.'

'Ah.'

Several of the forty-or-so canvases featured the peacock butterfly theme or early versions of me dancing – though I was abstracted enough that I wasn't easily recognisable. Presumably Bay had omitted all the larger and more recent depictions of me because they were unfinished or otherwise unsuitable. I still danced for him occasionally – with my three shifts a week at the club I didn't need the practise, but I enjoyed dancing when Bay was watching. He seemed equally content to paint me whether I danced or not; even when I cooked food, read books, brushed my teeth or dozed on his bed. That was Bay. I think he'd paint me while we fucked if he could, except that he hadn't fucked me since that one night.

We were both refraining, which was good; sex would only confuse things in the long run, but I couldn't seem to stop wanting it – wanting *him*. And it wasn't just me – we were both growing increasingly tactile with each other – skating close to the line but never crossing it. Sexual tension crackled like static electricity between us and yet, I was fairly certain there had been no other women in Bay's bed since me. And if he wasn't going to have me, then why not someone else? Why was Bay abstaining from sex completely? Was it something to do with his artistic process?

There was no way to ask without sounding horny and obvious, and it's not as if I wanted him to sleep with anyone else. So it just hovered between us – the sexual tension – as ripe and unspoken as the ache between my thighs.

At least I wasn't the only one struggling with the parameters of our friendship. The other night Bay had literally followed me, while I spent an evening out with friends. It should have bothered me – if it was anyone else it would have been stalkerish and creepy – but I was so used to him watching me. And more than that – I liked it –

it felt good having him there, keeping an eye on me from afar, it was oddly reassuring.

My so called 'girly' night out with Marguerite, whereby my best friend tried to set me up with a guy from her office, had ended in a long and boring wait in A&E. I couldn't help thinking it was some kind of karmic justice. Luckily for Marguerite the x-rays of her ankle proved that she had nothing worse than a sprain, and though she wouldn't be able to attend dance classes for a while, she was already on the mend. I think secretly she'd enjoyed all the sympathy and attention her injury brought with it. Either way, she had stopped pestering me with unnecessary concern since then, leaving me free to spend my time as I chose. And I generally chose to spend it with Bay.

The majority of the paintings he had dragged out of storage were part of what I thought of as Bay's 'Trees' series, though they were more involved and compelling than that simple label implied. That ghostly girl in white still haunted that particular grove of trees with an insistence that was disturbing. I often felt as though I was viewing the scattered fragments of a story I didn't understand.

'They're all wonderful,' I said. 'Are you going to focus on just one theme or show a range of all three?'

'I was thinking all three,' he said carefully. 'Three of you, three trapped butterflies, and nine of the rest.'

'Sounds great.' He looked at me and I was surprised by the uncertainty in his eyes. Bay did not do uncertain. Conflicted, sceptical and suspicious, yes, but never uncertain. It pulled at something inside me; made me ache

225

with an emotion I didn't want to define, and I quickly looked away. 'Maybe you should start with a process of elimination – take out those you like least and see how far you get?'

Over the course of several hot, sweaty hours, I helped Bay lift, move, and rearrange his paintings one by one as he completed the torturous task of distilling his genius down to a cohesive collection of fifteen pieces of perfection. The temperature had risen to 28°c during the day, making sleep virtually impossible, and although we had all the windows open and the hot July sun was finally sinking below the horizon, the air was stiflingly humid and still. I made pitchers of home-made lemonade filled with copious amounts of ice to keep us going, privately delighting in Bay's casual acceptance of a soft drink over something stronger. Maybe he wasn't as much of an alcoholic as I feared; perhaps there was hope for him yet.

The bedrooms in Bay's flat were much larger than Sidney's, and there were three of them. Of course Bay didn't use them as bedrooms, preferring instead to sleep in the wide open living space, so I was intrigued to see inside them. The smallest and most homely of the three held a wardrobe, an airing cupboard full of linen, an antique-looking chest of drawers, and his home gym – a rowing machine, punch bag, pull-up bar and a selection of weights. The modest exercise equipment helped account for the muscular, toned, underwear-model physique of someone who rarely left his home.

Thoughts of Bay's body made my already-warm skin prickle with heat, and I focused instead on the jumble of shoes heaped under the window and the odd T-shirt strewn haphazardly here and there. The space had the feel of a dressing room, but there were no ornaments or adornments, no pictures on the walls, and oddly no mirrors at all.

Much of Bay's artistic equipment – tools, mediums and materials – were stored in the second bedroom along with an enormous roll of canvas, a pile of timber and a workbench with a vice for constructing frames. The real surprise was that one whole half of the room was filled with books of all shapes, sizes and genres; crammed haphazardly into bookshelves and overflowing from heavy crates, stacked precariously one on top of the other. I had never seen so many books in one place outside of a library.

'Good grief, have you read all these?'

'Yeah.'

'What even...' I reached into the nearest pile and extracted a book at random, '...'The Brinkworth Guide to Ancient Myths and Legends'?'

He shrugged. 'Yeah, that's pretty good, actually. Anything you wanna borrow, help yourself...' I laughed and thanked him, wondering where on earth I would start.

The would-be master bedroom was kitted out with industrial-sized, wall-mounted racks filled with hundreds of paintings, and a large map-chest full of drawings and sketches. One glance at this room made Bay's quiet but serious dedication to his work obvious, and my fingers itched to rifle through his back catalogue; to discover examples of his earlier work and unravel more about him. But I didn't dare. Bay never left me in there alone and was careful to keep the room locked.

While Bay was in the bathroom I took the opportunity to change the music in the main room. Scrolling through his list of artists I came across a band I'd never heard of; Bleeding Trees. The name seemed appropriate so I put it on and was pleasantly surprised as a gentle guitar riff drifted from the speakers. Pressing my chilled drink to my temple I wandered back to the final fifteen pictures Bay had settled on. The more time I spent looking at his tree paintings, the more a sense of nagging familiarity grew in my mind. At first I thought it was just my general sentimental attachment to trees – they reminded me of Wildham, of home, of the woods behind my grandmother's house and my grandmother herself, whom I still missed every day. But as the female vocals kicked in with the first verse of the song that was playing, it hit me – I *knew* these particular trees; I'd seen them before; down in the garden below.

Bay emerged from the bathroom bare-chested, hair wet, and all but ran at his iPhone, abruptly switching off the music mid-song. His urgency startled me.

'What's wrong?'

'I don't want to hear that,' he snapped.

'OK… sorry… wh—'

Bay silenced me with a look so grim he momentarily appeared capable of murder. I was dying to know what had prompted such a reaction from him, but knew better than to ask. As Bay put another album on, reached for his cigarettes and lit up, I hovered awkwardly, like a guest who'd finally outstayed their welcome. I could swear the reaper on his back was smiling at me. Who was I kidding? I still didn't know this man at all.

Chapter Forty

Setting down my brush I took a few paces backwards to survey the piece as a whole. It wasn't finished yet – the background still needed adjustment – but I'd captured her perfectly; she inspired my best work.

Cally sighed in her sleep and I glanced over at her. How long ago had the music stopped? I hadn't even noticed. She was wearing her Grecian Goddess dress at my request and she'd been posing for me all night, while I aggressively re-created her image on a massive three-by-three-metre stretched canvas on the wall. I'd used cans of emulsion, a range of decorating brushes, and a ladder to reach the top; working my sexual frustration into the canvas with every stroke.

I knew I shouldn't cross that line with her again. I could paint her, look out for her, even be a friend to her if that's what she needed, but nothing more. We couldn't be lovers – I couldn't do that to her; she deserved better. But Jesus I didn't know it was possible to want to fuck another person as badly as I wanted to fuck her. My memories of being inside her were more powerful, more potent than heroin – and I should know. No matter how much I studied her, painted her and jerked-off to thoughts of her, it wasn't enough. I could masturbate a hundred times a day and still want her – it was driving me crazy. Right now she was a vision – a real-life sleeping beauty – and I was tempted to crawl into bed with her rather than wake her up.

The buzzer went and I cursed under my breath, jogging barefoot to the intercom to silence it before she woke. After a few minutes Tom appeared at the door with fresh art supplies and I pressed a finger to my lips in warning.

He smiled when he caught sight of her. 'A sleeping princess,' he whispered.

'Exactly,' I said, surprised by his choice of words. As I signed for the delivery an idea began to form in my mind. I'd known Tom a while now and his dad, John, even longer – he owned an art supply warehouse and could be relied upon to get me whatever I needed. Tom was a budding musician in his spare time; bass guitarist in a rock band. He played for Bleeding Trees before tragedy ripped them apart. The guy was an affable, reliable sort, and I got the distinct impression he swung both ways.

Clearly young Tom was attracted to Cally, who wouldn't be? The question was did Tom appeal to her in return? On a Peckham rooftop she'd confessed to a sexual fantasy. Had she really meant it? Maybe it was time to call her bluff. Perhaps that way I could physically have her without any risk of us getting closer emotionally…?

'When does your shift finish, Tom?'

'Six o'clock, why?'

'Come back and join us for a drink – sleeping beauty should be awake by then, and you never know, she might be pleased to see you.'

Tom's eyebrows disappeared up under a swathe of blonde hair as he registered my meaning. 'Are you serious?' he hissed.

I shrugged. 'I'm not promising anything, but I think she likes you…'

'Jeez… Bay, are you sure? I mean, you don't seem the type to share. I thought…'

Crossing my arms I leaned into the door-frame and cocked a silent eyebrow, impatiently waiting for an answer.

'Fuck yeah! I'll definitely come back then.' His whole face shone with excitement and he returned to the lift with a definite swagger. 'See you later,' he said, turning back to me, grinning from ear to ear as the doors slid shut.

What had I done?

Chapter Forty-one

I woke to find I'd slept the day away in Bay's bed. I was still fully clothed and so was he, but he was spooning me, one arm draped around my waist and his face nestled in my hair. It was something I'd missed since leaving Liam; the warm comfort of waking up in someone else's arms. But right now, wrapped in Bay's delicious musky scent and intense body heat, I was tingling with sexual desire in a way I never had with Liam. We didn't do this, Bay and I, sleep in the same bed together; not since the night we fucked and briefly napped before being woken by a visit from his brother. And this felt different; intimate; cosy. This could not be good.

The buzzer went and I pretended to still be asleep. On the third determined buzz, Bay finally stirred. I sensed the moment he registered that he was holding me; a split second of surprise. But he hesitated before letting go; paused long enough to inhale deeply at my neck and brush his fingers through my hair before getting up to answer the door. It was an unexpectedly tender gesture from him, one that I was not meant to be aware of. It filled me with longing and fear in equal measure.

As Bay showed someone into the flat, I stretched and yawned. It took me a while to recognise him as one of the regular delivery guys because, instead of his usual uniform, he was dressed in washed-out jeans and a tight-fitting T-shirt.

'Hey, Cally, sleep well?' He smiled cheekily at me from the kitchen area while Bay filled the kettle from the tap. Blinking and confused I sat up, heat rising to my face.

'Cally, you remember Tom?' Bay's voice was gravelly with sleep and his hair was sticking up wildly; like some furry animal recently roused from hibernation.

'Hey,' I said, raising my hand in greeting. What was Tom doing here?

'Coffee? Or something stronger?' Bay said.

'Coffee would be great, thank you,' I said, stumbling towards the bathroom.

'I'm happy to start with coffee,' Tom agreed.

Splashing my face in the bathroom sink helped revive me, but there was no mirror to check my appearance. What I really needed was a shower, but all my toiletries were next door. Returning to the kitchen I retrieved my coffee from between the two men, feeling distinctly self-conscious.

'I love your dress, Cally, you look beautiful.'

'Oh, thanks,' I said, taking a sip of much-needed caffeine and trying not to blush.

'How's the band doing?' Bay asked Tom.

'Great thanks. Actually we've got a gig lined up for Friday after next, you guys should come along.'

'Tom's a bassist,' Bay explained for my benefit, before re-addressing him. 'Where are you playing?'

I found myself inadvertently tuning out as Tom talked about Bad Bears' Picnic and the various songs they played. He was slighter in height and build than Bay and looked too pretty to be in a rock band; trendy hairstyle, long girly eyelashes, pale blue eyes and a mischievous smile – a distinct contrast to Bay; all dark, grizzled and moody. Tom's clean white T-shirt hinted at a nice set of muscles and I found myself idly wondering if he had any tattoos – there were none visible.

'Like what you see?'

At Tom's sudden question I realised I'd been staring at his chest and returned my eyes to his face, my face flaming with embarrassment. 'God, sorry,' I mumbled. Catching the smirk on Bay's face, I covered my eyes with my hand.

'Don't apologise, it's a serious question,' Tom said, gently taking my hand from my face and encouraging me to make eye contact. 'It takes a lot of work to look this good,' he added with a smile.

I set down my coffee and laughed. 'You look great,' I said, braving it out and avoiding Bay's eye.

'Why thank you, that's a real compliment coming from someone as pretty as you.'

'Are you flirting with me?'

'Yes, is it working?'

He was still holding my hand and I wondered what Bay was making of all Tom's attention. Was he jealous? 'You're very forward,' I said.

'I like you, Cally,' Tom said, raising my hand to his lips. 'I was hoping you might like me too? Bay thought you might…?'

'What?' I looked at Bay and his gaze locked onto mine, his eyes glowing with a mix of curiosity and something else.

'On the rooftop the other day…' Bay began. Shock and mortification swept through me and my mouth dropped open at the realisation that he had invited Tom over for a threesome without even consulting me. And then I was absolutely livid. Bay must have read the growing fury in face because he raised his hands defensively. 'It's just an idea, we don't have to… it doesn't make a difference to me either way…'

I turned back to Tom, still speechless.

He smiled reassuringly. 'I won't be offended if you don't fancy it – I'll be disappointed for sure – you are seriously hot and I've been trying to get my hands on this dude for ages,' he added, jerking his chin in Bay's direction with a grin.

'Watch it,' Bay growled.

I couldn't help laughing. 'I… it's just a shock that's all…'

'Yeah, sorry,' Tom said. 'He really should have talked to you about it first, I didn't realise he hadn't.' My hand was still in his and he gently squeezed my fingers.

There was no denying how cute Tom was, and the mere notion of seeing these two guys naked at the same time was enough to turn me on. If I was completely honest the idea definitely appealed, and I would never get another opportunity like this one, but… was I really brave enough to go through with it…?

'I'm going next door to have a shower and freshen up,' I said, reclaiming my hand. 'Will you still be here when I get back?'

'Do you want me to be?' Tom said.

I looked up at Bay's impassive face. 'Yes.' The word provoked a glint in his eyes and my belly fluttered with excitement.

Chapter Forty-two

Fucking hell, she was really going through with this. She strode back into my apartment, head held high; wrapped in red satin and smelling of honey and roses. I stood paralysed by the window, my hair still dripping from my shower and a tumbler of whisky and coke in my hand. I should have kept the bottle.

'Wow, Cally, you look stunning,' Tom said as she walked over and sat down on the bed. 'Can I get you a drink? A glass of wine?'

'A glass of red would be lovely, thank you,' she said, her voice quivering with nerves.

Tom looked far more relaxed than I felt, but then he'd done this sort of thing before. I'd warned him that tonight was all about Cally; about making her happy and satisfying *her* fantasies, not his, or mine for that matter. He'd assured me that he understood, vowed to treat her like a princess and promised to wear a condom throughout, but parts of our conversation kept looping through my head:

'Are you really going to let Cally take the lead on this?'

'I think she can handle it.'

'No, I'm sure she can, but can you? You're very alpha male, Bay, are you really going to be able to completely hand over control?'

'I guess we'll find out won't we. But hurt her and I'll break your legs.'

'Yeah, I figured,' he'd said with a grin.

By the time Cally had finished her large red wine, she and Tom were lying together on my bed, listening to Muse, chatting away and giggling like old friends while I observed them from the shadows. Time to get this party started. Walking up to the bed, I took the empty glass from her hand and set it aside.

'Tell him what you want, Cally.'

She gazed up at me; wide, indigo eyes dilated and a teasing smile pulling at her crimson lips. It took all my self-control not to lean down and steal her smile with a kiss. What was she thinking? What was she searching for in my eyes? Did she really want to do this? Did I...? The seconds ticked by and still she didn't speak. Finally Tom reached out and took her hand, interrupting the loaded eye contact between us.

'Strip,' she said to him.

Jumping up to stand beside me Tom did as instructed; quickly and obediently removing his clothes while she watched him and I watched her. Once he was naked, Cally gracefully rose to her feet and stood before him. Placing her fingertips on Tom's chest, she lightly ran them down to his hip and he smiled, his erection twitching. I noted his dick was smaller than mine and had to suppress a smug smirk as I passed him a condom, but he rolled it on without complaint. Her hands shaking, Cally unwrapped her robe and let it drift to the floor to reveal a lacy red bra and a matching pair of knickers. Tom looked like a kid at Christmas. Stepping back, I positioned myself behind Cally – partly to impede my view of Tom's overeager young body, but mainly in order to admire the perfect beauty of Cally's ripe bottom.

'And you, Bay – strip,' she murmured, turning to face me.

I'd resent a command like that from anyone else and my mind instinctively baulked at it. But my body could not deny her. Having reluctantly dragged my shirt off over my head, I calmly dropped my shorts and kicked them aside, internally at war with myself.

Keeping her gaze on mine, she reached back and guided Tom's hands up to cup her breasts from behind. I didn't want to see his hands on her, but I could tell it was turning her on; I could see it in her eyes.

'I want you two to kiss,' she said, her face shining with mischief. She was enjoying this.

Narrowing my eyes I slowly but deliberately shook my head.

'Please, just one kiss, for me…?'

I could feel Tom's expectant gaze but I kept my eyes trained on Cally. She was testing me again. Punishing me. Glaring at her I reached past her shoulder, grabbed the back of Tom's head and drew his mouth to mine. I kissed him hard; crushing my lips to his without mercy. It was strange; completely different to kissing a girl; rougher, baser, and not something I'd want to repeat, but the triumphant spark of delight that flared up in Cally's eyes, the obvious flush of arousal that now suffused her features, made it worth it.

'Wow,' she breathed as I pushed Tom away.

Tom licked his lips, unperturbed. In my peripheral vision I watched him kiss Cally's shoulder, gently hooking a finger under her bra strap at the same time.

'Let me relieve you of this,' he suggested before unclasping it. Her eyes never wavered from mine as Tom slipped the garment off her arms and then peeled her knickers down her legs. Once she was completely naked, she took my length in one palm. Her hold was surprisingly possessive and self-assured, and almost brought me to my knees.

Returning his hands to Cally's breasts, Tom pinched her nipples and she gasped, her grip on me tightening and my cock jerking in response. Fuck, this was madness. Clenching my fists, tightening my jaw and grinding my teeth together, I fought the desperate urge to simply deck Tom and claim Cally for myself.

Chapter Forty-three

God help me, I'd never felt sexier than I did right now, standing between two gorgeous naked men. And seeing them *kiss*... I'd never witnessed such a potent display of masculine sexuality; it rocked me to my core. I could tell Bay wasn't into it the way Tom was, but he'd gone ahead and done it anyway, for me, which only made me want him more, if that was even possible. Lately I wanted Bay all the time – he oozed sex appeal, naked or not. But with him at my mercy like this, and young Tom pressed up behind me, my whole body was trembling with need. If I didn't sit down soon I was going to collapse.

Releasing my hold on Bay, I stepped out from between the two men and sat down on the edge of the bed. Two sets of hungry eyes stared down at me – one man smiling while the other glowered – and I shivered with anticipation. But I had no idea how this should go, or what to say next, and Bay understood my hesitation.

'Kiss her,' Bay said.

Tom looked to my face for approval and when I smiled he wasted no time dropping to his knees on the floor between my legs, cupping my face in his hands, and kissing me tenderly on the mouth. He tasted of toothpaste and aftershave; his lips soft as they coaxed mine. Draping my arms over the smooth, unblemished skin of his shoulders, I traced his back muscles with my fingers. But my gaze was drawn, inexorably, back to Bay's as if magnetised, his black eyes burning into mine.

Dropping his hands to my waist, Tom started to shift away from my mouth, planting a soft line of kisses down my neck. As he worked his way lower I leaned back on my elbows and he kissed my breast. It felt good and I moaned. Bay stood watching; towering over us, naked, his feet firmly planted, his cock in his hand and his eyes blazing. What was he thinking? What was he feeling? How far would he let this go? All the way?

'God, Cally, your skin tastes fantastic,' Tom mumbled between kisses as he moved steadily down to my navel.

'Like heaven,' Bay rasped in agreement.

The pain in his voice as he said those two words sent a shiver right through me and I realised with sudden clarity that the person currently between Bay and I had no place being there.

As if reading my mind, Bay took a step towards me. 'Move aside, Tom.' The command was dangerously low and Tom stilled at once, his eyes darting to mine. Disappointment washed over his features before he gave me an accepting smile, rose to his feet and moved over to lie on the bed beside me. If either of us had ever doubted that Bay was in charge, those doubts had now been now quashed.

Ensnared in Bay's heated gaze, I shifted further back up the mattress as he silently prowled forwards; climbing onto the bed; caging me with his arms; pinning me with his body and possessively capturing my mouth in his with a feral growl. Hesitating only long enough for me to anchor my legs around him, Bay thrust inside; claiming me at last and firmly grinding into me for good measure. I couldn't help crying out with the sheer joy of it.

'Fucking hell, you guys are awesome,' Tom breathed, fisting his own cock in his hand. 'The view from here is mind-blowing...' Sweet Tom, with his angelic looks, free-flowing compliments and easy smiles; he was like steady sunshine, where Bay was all moonlight and shadows. And yet, it was Bay, with all his secrets and demons, that I craved and yearned for. As he took me, each deep drag and plunge, smooth and profound, and the tension and pace rose rapidly, I knew we wouldn't be able to hold back for long.

If I was being honest, this all started out with me wanting to prove something to Bay – to show him that it was simply sex, nothing more, nothing personal between us. I suspect he had similar intentions. But now as he took me; fucked me; owned me right in another man's face – it *was* personal. Whether he would admit it or not, just knowing that Bailey Madderson wanted me all to himself was a far bigger turn-on than any three-way could ever be. Closing my eyes I let Bay consume me, like only he could.

We came hard, the three of us; Tom prematurely, in the latex in his hand, and then Bay and I together, racked with a blissful sense of release. Afterwards, Bay collapsed onto the bed on the other side of me, landing heavily, like a felled tree, breathing hard.

'Jesus that was the most erotic thing I've ever seen,' Tom said. 'You guys are made for each other,'

'Go home, Tom.'

'Don't be so rude!' I tutted, slapping Bay on the arm. 'You're welcome to stay for a drink, Tom...'

'No he's not.' Bay glared across at Tom making him laugh.

'It's OK, Cally, I should be going anyway,' he said, sitting up, disposing of his condom in a wodge of tissue and dragging on his jeans.

Once I'd slipped on my robe and seen Tom to the door, I returned to the bed where Bay was propped against the headboard smoking. Stubbing out his cigarette he loosened the sash at my waist and pulled my robe right off again.

'Don't you want me to leave, too?'

'No,' he said, tugging me down onto the bed beside him.

'Why? Are you going to paint me?'

'No, not tonight.'

'Oh? Why not?'

Bay sighed, took a firm hold of my hips and hauled me on top of him so I was straddling his lap. 'I just want to spend the rest of the night inside you, without an audience or a fucking running commentary,' he growled.

I laughed, thrilled at the prospect. 'It wasn't that bad! I think you liked it…'

'Stop talking,' he said, dragging my head down until my chest was pressed to his, and brushing my mouth with his own.

'I think you were just as turned on as I was.'

'Stop. Talking.'

'I think you enjoyed fucking me right in Tom's face…' his eyes darkened, '…just as much as I did.'

He kissed me and it was everything I shouldn't want, but had been missing; coarse stubble, whisky and tobacco

– dark, latent passion overlaid with stubborn control.
Nothing had ever tasted so good.

Chapter Forty-four

I stared at the three lines of coke on the shelf above the cistern, the bass thundering through the walls of the men's room, a rolled bank note poised in my hand. Did I really want to do this? I'd been clean almost three months. I'd had brief periods of sobriety before, but it was different this time. Since meeting Cally I'd actually been enjoying life in other, healthier ways; and it felt good. Tonight I was just riled up because of the letter I'd received; the condescending, jargon-filled solicitor's letter designed to intimidate, which was essentially a "fuck you" from Ash. Wanker.

Cally was working tonight so I'd gone to the fight club and taken on the first guy stupid enough to let me. He was a hedge-fund advisor; loaded, arrogant and over-confident after twelve weeks of intensive training, but ultimately soft. I roughed him up a bit, put on a show for his mates and let him get a few blows in before I laid him out cold ten minutes in. Afterwards I bought him a pint at the bar, though I'm not sure he deserved it; he'd barely hurt me at all. One brief bout in the ring had done fuck-all to appease my anger and frustration, and they wouldn't let me take on another fight – rules are rules.

Now I was at this gig to support Tom and his new band, but seeing them play only made me feel worse, reminded me of things I'd prefer to forget, and the mosh pit was doing nothing for me either. Would coke help?

Fuck no. I swept the powder off the shelf and into the toilet bowl before flushing it away and washing my hands, assiduously avoiding the mirrors as usual. Would Cally let me fuck her after her shift? She'd be tired and I'd have to remember to hide the bruising on my ribs or she'd start asking questions, but lately it was all I wanted to do. Being inside Cally was intense; a gift of insane pleasure far too special for the likes of me, but I was done struggling against it. The night we attempted a threesome changed everything. Seeing Cally so aroused and uninhibited; the way she carried herself with such elegance was a massive turn-on. But I was done sharing her. At the end of the day, despite my best intentions, I was a selfish bastard; a lost cause; doomed – and Cally helped me to forget.

Chapter Forty-five

'Bailey Madderson and Guest,' Bay muttered at the girl on the door.

She was smartly dressed in black with a serious expression and an air of authority about her. But that changed upon hearing Bay's name and her face split into a smile of incredulous delight, her clipboard temporarily forgotten. 'Mr Madderson! We didn't think you'd come – it's an honour to have you here. I'm Pritti, I work for Felix and I'm a huge admirer of your work. Please come in, and if there's anything I can help you with please just let me know.'

'Cheers,' he muttered, holding the door for me as we entered.

'Help yourself to champagne!' she called back over her shoulder.

Bay grabbed a flute from the nearest table and quickly knocked back the liquid, downing it in one. Setting the empty aside he then picked up two full ones, and handed one to me.

'Thank you,' I said, trying not to laugh. I'd never seen Bay this uncomfortable before. He'd been on edge for days now, but it wasn't tonight's opening that was bothering him, I had a feeling it was something else... only I had no idea what.

He was wearing the same shirt and tie he'd worn for my birthday and, despite grumbling, had allowed me to run a wet comb through his hair. It was still tufty at the front, but tamer at the top, back and sides. He looked devilishly handsome and I was proud to be on his arm. But underneath the surface he was a mess. Tonight could go either way.

Four other artists in addition to Bay were being represented in this exhibition within the walls of a prestigious commercial gallery in the heart of London. The space was larger and crowded with more glamorous-looking people than I'd been expecting, but then I'd never attended a private preview before – maybe this was the norm.

Holding the centre of the floor I recognised Jasmine Reed, the actress who'd dated one of my old friends, and who had in-directly gotten me my job at the club. While she flirted shamelessly with the crowd of men around her, I briefly considered thanking her, but she'd recently been convicted of drink driving – receiving a hefty fine, a twelve month ban and escaping prison by the skin of her teeth. She wasn't someone I wanted to introduce Bay to, so I pretended I hadn't seen her and sipped my champagne – it tickled as it went down.

Bay led me around the edge of the first room at a surprisingly leisurely pace, perusing the artwork with quiet intensity. Beforehand I'd imagined him heading straight to his own work with little regard for the rest, but then I recalled the mountains of books tucked away in his flat and reminded myself that Bay had a genuine interest in many things, and art was just one of them. From a practical point of view he probably ought to be aware of the standard of his contemporaries anyway, though I suspected that was of little concern to Bay, or perhaps he simply trusted his agent implicitly. These pieces for example – impressionistic depictions of wild-flower meadows under blue skies – couldn't be more different from Bay's work in terms of tone and style, but they were artfully done, with generous depth, a clever use of perspective and pretty details. The scenes brought to mind some of the farm land around Wildham, and the flowers in the foreground reminded me of Willow's tattoo, though these blooms were nowhere near as beautiful. All the work was for sale, but there were no prices marked and I suspected each piece was valued at thousands of pounds.

'What do you think?' Bay asked, nudging his shoulder gently against mine.

'They're lovely – uplifting.'

Bay nodded thoughtfully.

'What do *you* think?'

'They're technically good, but there's no truth in them; life's not really like that.'

Abruptly he moved on to the next room, leaving me standing alone and staring at the sun-filled meadows through a film of tears. Life *could* be like that, couldn't it? Not all the time, but occasionally at least? It saddened me that someone as smart, generous, and talented as Bay felt so completely removed from happiness. I wanted to help him, but what could I do? He wouldn't let me in, not really, and in seven weeks' time I would be leaving forever.

Catching up with Bay in the next room, we toured the rest of the exhibition in silence, without interruption, our backs to everyone else. We came to Bay's paintings last, but they dominated the space – dramatically vibrant and compelling. Obviously I was biased and very familiar with them by now, but they looked particularly magnificent mounted on pure white walls and expertly lit from above. The 'Trees' series was attracting a lot of attention and I overheard comments: "a masterful use of light", "exceptional talent", "a unique style, unlike anything I've seen before". It wasn't just me, then. These paintings would almost certainly sell here and I'd never see them again. At this realisation I scrutinised them one last time, more closely than before.

The girl in white was harder to find in these nine pieces, Bay had omitted the ones where she featured more prominently, whether consciously or not I couldn't be sure. As breathtakingly brilliant and well-received as the paintings were, they still emitted an undercurrent of something else; a mystery, dark and disturbing. Who was she? What did she mean to Bay? And why was she hiding in his garden?

'Bay! You made it.' An attractive red-haired guy with razor-sharp sideburns and silver-rimmed spectacles slapped Bay on the back.

'Hey Felix. This is Cally, Cally – Felix. He did all this,' Bay added with a sweep of his hand.

'It's a pleasure to meet you.' Felix pinned me with a curious look as he warmly shook my hand.

'You too – this is wonderful, you must be very pleased.'

'Yeah, so far the feedback's been really positive, but then it usually is on opening night; I'll be interested to read what the critics come up with…'

'I'm sure they'll be glowing with praise,' I said.

'Fingers crossed,' Felix said, with a nervous smile.

'I'm gonna take a leak,' Bay said abruptly, snatching the barely-touched flute from my hand and stalking off. I smiled awkwardly at Felix and he rolled his eyes.

'Between you and me, Bay is a good friend and the most talented artist on my books, but he's also a classic case of tortured genius and a royal pain in the butt.' I laughed and Felix grinned conspiratorially at me. 'I have to say though, he's looking much better than when I last saw him at Easter, I almost didn't recognise him.'

'Yes, he's... doing well, I think...'

'And he *never* comes to these things, ever. How on earth did you get him here?'

'To be honest I think he's only here because he didn't want me coming on my own. I doubt we'll be staying much longer...'

'That's fine, don't worry. If it's OK with you I'll try and introduce him to a couple of influential buyers and some people who admire his work before you go. I'll try not to keep him from you too long.'

'Keep him as long as he'll let you – he's not mine.'

'Oh, sorry, I just assumed...?'

'We're neighbours.'

'Ah, OK...' He stared at me for a moment, as if working something out. 'You must be the Easter Bunny!' he finally said, triumphant.

'I beg your pardon?'

Before Felix had a chance to explain, Bay was back at my side, handing me a fresh glass of champagne. 'Ah Bay, let me introduce you to Darius DeWinter,' Felix said. 'He's a huge fan of your work...'

Bay rolled his eyes at me and grudgingly allowed Felix to steer him away. 'I won't be long... they've got nibbles at the bar...?' he offered over his shoulder. As they disappeared into the crowd I returned my attention to Bay's glorious paintings, still pondering Felix's bizarre comment.

*

'Fuck it's too hot in here.' Crossing the flat, Bay kicked off his shoes and stripped off his tie while I filled a pitcher with cloudy lemonade and lots of ice in the kitchen. As he was flinging the windows open wide, a folded piece of paper fell from his trouser pocket but he didn't notice. Handing him a drink, I went over to pick it up. Simple curiosity had me opening and reading it before I'd considered what I was doing. It was a formal, scary-looking letter from a firm of solicitors, concerning some sort of legal dispute over TMC Tower. It looked serious. 'What's this?'

'Nothing,' he said, snatching it from my hand and stuffing it back in his pocket.

'It doesn't look like nothing. It looks like you might lose this place...'

'It's just my brother trying to fuck me over.'

'Ash? Why?'

He shrugged. 'He's angry at me. Maybe he thinks being homeless would be good for me, I don't know. Don't worry you'll be long gone by then.' His last sentence was painful, but I tried to ignore it.

'Would you be homeless?'

'No. I've got more money than I know what to do with. It's not me he'll be hurting.'

'What do you mean?'

'There's all the people employed in the offices below for a start. I lease the space to charities virtually rent free – I only charge them enough to cover the maintenance costs. And then there's all the people those charities benefit – it's bound to have a knock-on effect…'

I gaped at him, speechless. How did I not know this? I hadn't paid the slightest bit of attention to which companies occupied the floors below me, and the depth of Bay's generosity was astounding.

'What?' he said, a fag hanging from his lip as he lit up.

'Does Ash know?'

Bay shrugged.

'Can he really do this? Take it away from you?'

He shrugged again. 'Probably. I could get myself a fancy lawyer and fight it, but…'

'But what?'

'He'll probably win in the end.'

'Oh God, will you lose the garden, too?'

'Yeah, they come as a package.'

'Is this why you've been so moody lately?' His eyes narrowed. 'You should have said something; I wouldn't have forced you to go along tonight if I'd known.'

'You didn't force me; I thought it would be a good distraction.'

'And was it?' Bay scowled at me and I had my answer. 'Look, it's so hot in here, I feel like I can't breathe. Why don't we go down to the garden; make the most of it – it's bound to be cooler down there under the trees…?'

Bay sighed heavily and then nodded almost imperceptibly, idly scratching his jaw.

'OK good. Can you find us a blanket or something to sit on and I'll grab us something to eat from next door…?'

Chapter Forty-six

Cally was right; it was cooler down here under the trees, but for me it might as well be the fiery pits of Hell.

Before leaving the flat I'd topped up the jug of lemonade with vodka (soft drink alone would not get me through this) and grabbed a dust sheet. I didn't have a blanket as such – I wasn't exactly a picnics kind of guy – so a white, slightly-paint-splattered sheet would have to do. Riding down in the lift I'd tried to mentally prepare myself; tried to convince myself I could do this; that I was OK with it. Maybe it would be different with Cally by my side – better – maybe she would keep the horror away? But as soon as I rounded the corner and the garden came into view, I was assaulted with flashbacks. My legs stopped moving of their own accord; the ice-cubes rattling in the pitcher, and the folded dust-sheet dropping to the ground.

'You OK?' Cally murmured, carefully taking the jug and setting it down on the grass beside the wicker basket she'd been carrying.

Reaching into a pocket I retrieved a spliff and lighter from my tin. The shaking in my hands irritated me as I lit up. My weakness sickened me – I was nauseated by my very existence – but I took a long, calming toke, closed my eyes and concentrated on expelling my memories along with the smoke. Once I was feeling composed I re-opened them to find Cally's concerned, Prussian-blue gaze trained on my face.

'How long has it been since you came down here?'

I tried to shrug but my shoulders were stiff with tension. 'A couple of years.'

'*Two years*?' Her eyebrows arched in surprise.

'Three,' I admitted.

She stared at me. She wanted to ask me why; it was the obvious question and it hung heavily in the air, making me want to vomit with dread, or hide, or both. 'How did you come to own a place like this?' she said at last.

Reaching out with one arm I hugged her to me with gratitude. I didn't deserve her kindness, a monster like me; if she knew the truth she'd run a fucking mile. Banding her arms around my waist she nestled her head comfortably into the space between my jaw and my shoulder; the smell of her shampoo soothing me even further. I wished I could hold on to her forever.

'It's been in my family for centuries,' I began, pausing to take another drag. 'Originally there was a grand old town house here and this was the garden. The house was bombed in the Second World War and my maternal grandfather had an office block built in its place. He wanted to build another alongside it, but my Mother begged him not to. She loved this garden – used to climb the trees as a child – and my grandfather didn't want to break her heart. The oldest trees have protection orders on them now.'

'It's beautiful here,' Cally said, her warm breath tickling my collarbone. 'It reminds me of being back in Wildham.'

'Ash had the cherry tree planted in my Mother's memory when she died.'

'Oh no! I'm so sorry!' She gazed up at me, stricken. 'I never would have danced around it if I'd known!'

I shrugged. 'I think she would have liked the idea actually; found it funny. But the building and this garden – they're the only pieces of property left from my Mother's side of the family. Dad sold the rest off in the course of building his empire. When he died ten years ago he left everything to Ash; the company, capital, assets, property… everything. But that was fine by me. Ash asked me if I wanted anything and I requested this place. I always suspected he might take it back one day – I'm surprised it's taken him this long…'

She kissed me, tenderly, the taste of her lips and the sad light in her eyes helping chase my demons back into the shadows. If only it was enough.

Cally spread the sheet out on the grass in a clearing between the trees, and I sat hunched over my knees, silently urging myself to relax. She was here, I could sense her, hidden somewhere in the trees, calling to me.

Suppressing a shudder I watched as Cally began removing things from her twee little hamper; a couple of glasses, cutlery, napkins, and little pots of marinated olives, mini falafels, cherry tomatoes, stuffed vine leaves… as if life were a fucking picnic. Kneeling on the sheet beside me she poured a couple of drinks, passed one to me and then took a sip of her own. It made her cough.

'You've spiked this!'

'Improved it.'

She sighed and I wondered why she was surprised. Did she really think she could change me? Redeem me? There was no redemption for me. We shared the quiet hum of the city without speaking for a while, and I focused on the smoke as I drew it into my lungs before letting it slowly escape.

'Look, the moonlight on the sheet is attracting moths,' she said. Glancing down, I was unnerved to find a scattering of winged insects settled all around me. They varied in size and shape, the markings on their wings twitching in the blue light. 'Maybe we'll see one to match your shoulder.'

The sight of the moths, here of all places, brought the nausea back stronger than before. 'I doubt it, they're rare in this country.' I hoped she couldn't hear the shake in my voice. Carefully putting out my joint I tucked the rest back in the tin; it wasn't helping.

'It's the moth from that film, *The Silence of the Lambs*, isn't it?' She framed the question casually, but she was probing again, oblivious to the true extent of the horror I lived with on a nightly basis. But then whose fault was that – I'd warned her to stay away from me, but I'd never given her a proper reason to, not really. I kept everything from her, and why? Because I liked having her around. Because I didn't want to see the revulsion on her face when she realised how much death I was responsible for. And because I didn't want to lose her. But that was selfish – she deserved her chance at escape.

'It's a Death's-head Hawkmoth, but I don't have the tat because of a film…'

I thought she'd take the bait and ask me outright, but she didn't – once again she was letting me off the hook and I was perversely disappointed. I wanted her to know.

A Ruby Tiger alighted on Cally's forearm and she stilled, scrutinising it with rapt attention.

'My Dad used to say my twin brother was drawn to trouble like a moth to a flame,' I volunteered.

The insect on Cally's arm flew away and she looked at me, eyebrows raised and eyes bright with curiosity, silently urging me to continue. I downed my vodka lemonade and she immediately refilled my glass.

'We looked pretty much identical, but Baxter was brave and fearless where I was weak and afraid.' It was strange saying his name aloud and I wondered how many years it had been since I'd said it. I followed the hopping and fluttering of the moths with my eyes to avoid Cally's gaze. It felt like my chest was cracking wide open and a writhing, tangled mass of worms were trying to squirm their way out. I couldn't look at her, but I couldn't stop now, she needed to know…

'We were six years old and playing outside. Ash was away at boarding school. We lived in a big old house in the country back then – swimming pool, stables, acres of land – I don't think we really appreciated how lucky we were at the time. What we really wanted was a tree-house or some play equipment – a climbing frame, a slide, something like that – but Dad considered those things eyesores. Anyway, one day Bax got it into his head that he could make us a swing by tying a length of rope from a tree branch. He found what he needed in the stables, picked out a suitable branch in an oak tree and told me to stand below so I could tell him when the rope was dangling the right height from the ground. I wasn't sure; I warned him it wasn't a good idea and I tried to talk him out of it, but not hard enough. Obviously.'

I swallowed more vodka lemonade, barely tasting it.

'Bax had climbed the tree before, we both had, and he made it up the trunk with ease, the cord looped across his chest as if he were an intrepid adventurer. Once he'd reached as high as he could, some twenty foot off the ground, he uncoiled the end of the rope before starting out along the branch. The rope started to unravel, snagging in places, and he struggled with it. And then he spotted a moth. It was just one of those common hawk moths that camouflage themselves against the bark, but Bax knew I'd be interested and he shouted down to me about it and that's when he lost his balance – right then.'

In my peripheral vision I saw Cally cover her mouth with her hand, but I still couldn't look at her, not until she knew it all.

'I watched as he started to fall; arms flailing, rope tangling... he hit his head on another branch on the way down but that wasn't what killed him – he didn't hit the ground either. The rope lassoed around his neck, fracturing his spinal column mid-fall and choking off his airway.

'And I didn't do anything, I just stood there – frozen in shock – watching him hang high above me; watching the life go out of him. I knew he was dying, but I couldn't move. It was only when it was over and he was just swinging there, silently, it was only then that I was able to move again; life rushed back into my limbs; adrenalin I suppose. Even then I didn't try to climb up and untangle the rope, I just ran back to the house screaming for help. But it was too late – I was too late – I'd let him die.'

'No.' Her voice sounded strangled and when I looked up I was appalled to see her face streaked with tears.

'Why are you crying?'

'It wasn't your fault,' she said, swiping at her cheeks.

'Don't give me that bullshit; don't try and make excuses – I didn't even *try* to save him; that's the sort of person I am; a coward; that's who I've always been.

'No!'

'Yes. You just don't want to see it.'

'You were six years old – it was just a tragic accident – there was nothing you could have done. If you'd climbed that tree after him you might have fallen and died, too.'

'Exactly! That's what should have happened! Instead death has shadowed me my whole life, killing off anyone I get close to.'

'You can't really believe that. You realise how crazy you sound?'

'Yeah, and maybe I'm insane, but I'm telling you – that's what happens – I'm cursed – people close to me die.'

'That's ridiculous…'

'For fuck's sake, you aren't listening to me. Do I have to spell it out? BEING AROUND ME TOO LONG WILL GET YOU KILLED!'

She shook her head, her eyes wide, her face silvery in the moonlight as more tears fell.

'Why are you crying? Why are you even here? Did you just get bored with your safe little life in suburbia?

Decide to rebel? Six months roughing it in London? Stripping and slumming it with a loser like me before you fuck off back home—'

She slapped me across the cheek, the snap resounding through the garden, the sting spreading with a soothing warmth. For a while there was silence, only punctuated by the chilling scream of a fox and a police siren in the distance. I turned back to face her, and she looked shocked, as though *I'd* slapped *her*. 'God, I'm sorry,' she said raising her hand to her mouth again.

'I deserved it,' I said, feeling calmer. 'I deserve far worse.'

'You didn't; you don't, you really don't,' she said, rapidly shaking her head.

As I reached out to take her hand she flinched. 'Does it hurt?' I said. Her palm might have been inflamed but the cool moonlight made it hard to be sure.

'Yes,' she said. 'I've never hit anyone before.'

I nodded, still staring at her hand and hating myself for attacking her. I wasn't used to talking about this stuff – it made me feel weak, vulnerable and exposed.

'I don't understand how you can blame yourself for something that was entirely out of your control,' she said quietly.

'My Dad did – *he* blamed me. And my mother never got over it. I tried to make up for everything by being more like Bax – stronger, braver... I got the tattoo to remind me... but maybe I just made things worse.'

'I'm so sorry.'

I shrugged. I didn't want sympathy.

'Your twin... is that...?'

'What?'

'Is that why you avoid your reflection? Is that why there are no mirrors in your flat?' Her intuition was surprising, I could almost hear her mind figuring me out.

'When I see myself, I don't just see me. I don't *want* to see me, but I don't want to keep seeing Bax either, it's too fucking painful.'

'You're not a vampire, then?'

I rolled my eyes, but the smile hovering on her lips made me want to smile in return. I sighed instead. 'You shouldn't be around me – look – I've already driven you to violence.'

'I don't have a home to go back to,' she said.

'No?'

She shook her head but didn't volunteer any more.

'Are you sure? Because every time you mention Wildham you sound like you miss it.'

'I do. But that doesn't mean I can go back.'

I was tempted to ask her why but I knew she wouldn't tell me. 'We shouldn't have come down here, this place—'

She cut me off with a kiss and the sense of relief was immense. How had I not lost her yet? Her fingers fumbled to unbutton my shirt and I hauled her onto my lap so that she was straddling me. I unzipped her dress. She removed my shirt. I lay back to admire her and she gasped.

'God, Bay, what happened?'

Lifting my head, I followed her eye line to the dark bruising on my ribs and set my head back down again. 'Nothing. It doesn't hurt.'

'You've been fighting.'

It wasn't a question and I didn't reply, but I could hear the disappointment she was holding back. Between the tree canopies above, I could pick out a few stars, despite the hazy glow of London's lights. Without a word she leaned down and gently pressed her mouth to my ribs; her lips soft, her hair lightly brushing my skin; her tender forgiveness both soothing and arousing.

Cally rode me like a goddess on horseback; her shoulders thrown back and her pale skin glowing ethereally. She was so beautiful that it hurt my eyes to look at her; as if she was an angel from heaven. I lay there, hypnotised, absorbed in the delicious feel of her body as she worked me inside her. For a while the garden around us receded; the ghosts dispersed and my many sins and secrets melted away. In that brief, perfect moment, it was just her and me, and it was magical.

But afterwards, holding Cally in my arms, the moon stared down at me, and a cold sense of dread crept right back in.

Chapter Forty-seven

Slipping an eye mask on, I pulled the sheet up over me and hugged Bessie, my stuffed bunny, for comfort. I missed Bay. I'd barely seen him since our night in the garden. He'd finally told me about the devastating death of his twin; confessed to a lifetime of grief and guilt so awful I could barely comprehend it. But my knowing made him uncomfortable – he was determined to distance himself from me – and I still had no idea how to help him.

Not to mention that I'd slapped him – which was the last thing I should have done – he'd been punished enough. But of all the rude and hurtful things he'd said to me, that was the worst – because it was true. He was right. Compared to his life, mine *was* safe and suburban. I'd been blessed with an easy ride and I'd wasted it; frittered it away being afraid. In the past four months I'd experienced more exhilarating highs and dreadful lows than I had in the rest of my life put together. Since meeting Bay I could no longer predict what I was going to feel from one moment to the next, and it was strangely addictive. And like most addictions it was poisonous.

Squeezing Bessie I willed myself to go to sleep. It was already 11 a.m. and I had to be up for work in six hours, but I couldn't stop worrying.

It was just as well Bay was avoiding me. I constantly craved his company, but that night, after he opened up to me, the sex had been dangerously intense. The emotional distance we'd so carefully maintained between us was eroding. I now understood why Bay was always pushing people away; with the tragic death of his twin brother and then his mother, he'd got the crazy idea into his head that he was cursed. And here I was, a nuclear time bomb set to destroy him. Tick, tick, tick.

I should leave right now, but where would I go? I couldn't bear to face my parents, not yet, and none of my old friends would even recognise the new me. I'd never felt more alone…

The intercom buzzed and I groaned into my pillow. Who was that? It was almost certainly a delivery for Bay, it might even be Tom. I should just ignore it.

At the sight of the familiar face on the small screen, I wanted to weep. I pressed the button to speak, but I had a lump in my throat and when I opened my mouth no sound came out.

'Cally… is that you…?' Liam's voice rumbled out of the intercom as comforting as an old blanket.

'Hi,' I said at last. 'What are you doing here?'

'I just wanted to see you; to see for myself that you're OK, that's all.'

'Oh.'

'Can I come up?'

Bay's proximity on the other side of the wall made me anxious. 'Umm, I could meet you somewhere instead?'

'I've only got half an hour, can't I just come up? I don't have a hidden agenda, I promise.'

There was no music coming from next door and I figured Bay would almost certainly be asleep at this time of day. Buzzing Liam in, I pulled on a dressing gown and then hovered nervously in the doorway as the lift rose. He ducked as he exited the car, angling his body sideways to accommodate his broad shoulders. I'd forgotten how huge he was. He smiled when he saw me, but paused to admire the view from the landing window.

'Wow, you can see for miles from up here.' His deep voice seemed too loud in the small space and I shifted nervously from foot to foot.

'Come in, I'll make some tea.'

As I closed the door safely behind us, I almost sagged with relief. Filling the kettle I made tea while my ex strolled over to the windows and whistled at the panoramic view.

'There you go,' I said, handing him a mug of milky tea with three sugars – the way he liked it.

'Thanks.' He was silent for a long while, but that was not unusual for Liam. Years ago when we first got together it unnerved me, but it was simply how he was. 'Sorry if I woke you,' he said at last, eyes still trained on the view.

'You didn't, I'd only just got into bed.'

He nodded, thoughtfully. 'Big night?'

'No, not at all I… I work shifts, that's all.' I hoped he wouldn't ask me to elaborate, and he didn't.

'You seem different. Marguerite said you'd changed, but I wanted to see for myself.'

'Oh God, whatever she's told you, it isn't true.'

He turned to me then, his expression reassuring. 'Don't worry, she only said you seemed happier and more… confident.'

'That and my address…'

He smiled. 'Yeah, that too. So, *are* you happy?'

'Yes, I am.'

'Really? Because you look tired and you've lost weight…'

'I've just been working really hard and… and I've started writing a book of sorts and that keeps me up when I should be sleeping…'

'A book? That's great, Cally.'

'Yeah. What about you? How's work?'

'Great actually – I'm restoring and re-landscaping the grounds of Wildham Hall.'

'Wow, that's a big old place, isn't it? Congratulations.'

'That's why I'm in town; I want to find out what I can about the original gardens – I've got an appointment at the British Library.'

'Sounds exciting.'

'Yeah it's… interesting.' He took several long gulps of tea.

'What are you not saying?'

'Nothing. It's just that I… I've met someone.'

'I'm so pleased for you,' I said, my eyes pricking with tears. It was a relief to see Liam so content and quietly optimistic. Perhaps I hadn't broken his heart after all; perhaps our relationship was never meant to last; perhaps, despite the cowardly way I'd gone about it, I'd done the best for Liam by leaving him. 'Do you want to tell me what she's like?'

'I'd rather not – it's early days…' I nodded, privately glad to escape too much detail.

We chatted for a while, and he updated me on various bits of news about the rugby club and our friends. Thinking about them made me feel horribly homesick, but

I was careful to hide it. After all, it wasn't my home, not anymore.

'I think I know why you left,' he said, handing me his empty mug as we neared the door.

'Oh?' Panic stirred in the pit of my stomach.

'I was holding you back.'

'No.'

'Yes – it's OK, I get it; I'm not a particularly ambitious guy, I never have been, and you wanted more. But you only had to ask, Cally; I would have let you go.'

'I'm sorry.'

'It's fine, really; as long as you're happy, that's the main thing.'

As he hugged me goodbye, it was so comforting and familiar I nearly burst in to tears. Quickly withdrawing from his embrace I opened the door. But there, hunched on the window ledge, blocking the light like a malignant shadow, was Bay.

Oh crap. I'd missed him so much. An electric pulse of desire swept through me at his mere presence, culminating in a low thrumming sensation somewhere deep inside me. But this was bad. I didn't want these two men to meet. Bay puffed on a cigarette, his darkly glowing emerald gaze briefly hitting mine before sweeping on to Liam.

Flustered, I stumbled over to the lift and pressed the call button as if Bay wasn't there. The doors slid open immediately, but to my horror Liam stepped towards Bay and offered him his hand to shake.

'Liam,' he said, amiably.

269

Bay slowly unfolded himself, rose to his feet, so that he was closer to Liam in height and took a long, insolent drag on his cigarette, ignoring my ex's hand completely. 'You found her, then?'

Liam let his arm drop to his side as they eyed each other. 'Friend of yours?' he said mildly without looking at me.

'Er, yes, this is Bay, my next-door neighbour,' I said, stepping up beside Liam, my pulse throbbing in my temple as Bay released a cloud of smoke. Liam nodded and started to turn away, but Bay wasn't done.

'What did you do to make her run from you?'

His question stung. Did he really think Liam had hurt me, or did he simply want to know how to get rid of me?

Liam calmly turned back to Bay. 'Why don't you ask her?'

'I'm asking you.'

'Stop it guys, this is childish,' I interrupted. Bay was clearly spoiling for a fight, and although Liam was managing to keep his cool, he wouldn't do so indefinitely. He was bigger and heavier than Bay and could defend himself if necessary, but he was essentially a pacifist at heart. Whereas Bay had a wealth of fighting experience and a death wish. I wasn't sure who would win if these two giants came to blows, but I wasn't about to find out.

As they continued to eyeball each other I stepped between them with my back to Liam. Bay's inherently appealing scent, mingled with turps and tobacco, almost made me swoon. I was temporarily transported back to a fortnight previously, when I'd stood between two men for a very different reason, and heat rose to my face at the memory. I stared up at Bay until he transferred his frighteningly intimidating gaze to mine. It almost made me cower, but I stubbornly maintained eye contact. 'I've told you before; Liam's never hurt me, OK?' As we stared at each other his eyes gradually began to soften. Behind the anger I could see his pain and it made my chest ache. 'Please,' I added.

Bay lifted his cigarette to his lips and abruptly turned back to the window, effectively releasing us, and I gratefully took the opportunity to steer Liam into the lift.

We descended in silence, my head ringing with dissipating tension and relief.

'That guy's in love with you,' Liam said, when we reached the street.

His words made me hot and cold all at once, but I tried to keep my expression neutral. 'Maybe,' I said.

'Do you trust him?'

'Yes, actually, I do.'

'Are you sure?' Liam placed his large hands on my shoulders. 'I need you to be sure…'

'I trust him,' I said firmly. It was the truth.

Bay was gone when I returned to the landing. Bypassing his door I went straight to my bed alone and cried myself to sleep.

Chapter Forty-eight

I woke in a cold sweat, tangled in the sheets and screaming her name. No. Fucking please no; she's not dead, she's not dead, she's not dead – it was just a dream.

Fuck.

My nightmares had come back tenfold, only now Cally was in them too and she had a starring role. Reaching for my fags I tried to light up, but my hands were shaking too badly. I was losing it. I was losing her. I could feel it.

Staying away from her was eating me alive. She said she had no home to go to, but her ex would take her back in a heartbeat, I could see it in his eyes. Seeing her smiling up at him, bare-legged in her dressing gown, had almost killed me. I was ready to beat him to a pulp, but what would that achieve?

Rescuing my watch from the floor I squinted at it. Ten past six – she'd be leaving for work soon and then she'd be dancing naked for a whole load of fucking wankers who didn't deserve to breathe the same air as her. Ah fuck. I hurled my watch across the room and it collided with something in the shadows before clattering to the floor. I couldn't let her do it.

Chased by the visions from my nightmares, I exited my apartment and hammered my fist on her door. She opened it looking startled, wearing a pretty off-the-shoulder dress and clutching a bowl of cereal in one hand. Grabbing her I crushed her to me, her breakfast landing on the doormat as I buried my face in the sweet scent of her hair with a moan.

'Bay? What is it? What's happened?'

'Bad dream,' I croaked. She stroked my back with her hands and I shuddered beneath her touch, my heart-rate thundering in my chest. 'I need to fuck you.'

'What?'

'You heard,' I said, shifting my gaze to hers. She still looked bewildered but there was something else in her eyes too – something hungry. I kissed her and she tasted of black coffee and quiet desperation. Half-sighing, half-whimpering, her body melted into mine, her nipples hardening against my chest. Kicking the bowl out of the way and the door shut behind me, I sucked on her lips and tongue as I manoeuvred her backwards into Sidney's flat.

'Wait,' she said, breathlessly pulling away, her face flushed and pupils dilated. 'I have to go to work.'

'No you don't.' I lifted her up off the floor and she instinctively wrapped her legs around my hips.

'Yes, I do. Can't we do this later?'

'No.' Her eyes closed as I kissed her neck and carried her to the nearest available surface. Setting her down on the dining table, I tugged down the top of her dress and took her nipple in my mouth, while reaching up under the skirt and ripping off her knickers. Gasping, she slid her hands down to my butt, where she squeezed it through my boxers. As I transferred my mouth to her other nipple, I palmed her between her legs and found her ready for me. Rocking into my hand, she ground against my fingers with a groan, and the sound almost made me come. She wanted this as badly as I did. Without hesitation I pulled out my cock, positioned it between her thighs, and thrust up inside her with a grunt. She stared back at me, dark-eyed, lost and hungry – completely at my mercy – as I claimed her body for myself, yet again.

I took her right there on Sidney's clear plastic dinner table, rutting and grinding into her, over and over again, never getting close enough, or deep enough. She collapsed back onto her elbows, her breasts jiggling to our frantic rhythm as I took her harder and faster, her eyes begging me not to stop. As she detonated, splayed out beneath me, she cried my name: 'Oh yes, oh Bay, oh God, Bay…' I'd never heard a more perfect sound, and it tipped me over the edge. But as the aftershocks of our shared explosion ebbed away and our breathing slowed, she began to look angry.

'Get off me,' she said, batting me aside. I still had my boxers around my thighs and almost toppled over as she hopped off the table, straightened her dress and stalked off into the bathroom, slamming the door behind her.

Pulling up my pants I trailed after her, pressing my head to the door. 'Fuck, Cally, did I hurt you?' I quaked at the very idea.

'No,' she snapped, 'but I'm going to be late for my shift.' She turned the taps on and I had to wait for the noise to die down before protesting.

'Don't go. You don't have to go.'

'Of course I do – *it's my job*.' Opening the door she pushed past me and strode into the bedroom. I stood in the doorway as she pulled on a fresh pair of knickers. The thought of anyone else seeing them made me want to throw up.

'I don't want you to go.'

'Why not?' she said, glancing at me in the mirror as she brushed her hair.

'You know why not; don't make me say it.'

'I don't know what you're talking about,' she muttered, picking up her handbag and heading for the front door.

'Wait,' I growled, stepping in front of her, barring her way. 'Did that mean nothing to you? You can come for me like that and then go spread your legs for a bunch of fucking strangers?'

A brief flash of pain flared in her eyes and then her expression tightened with determination. 'Yes. Why, it's never bothered you before?'

'It has... it *does* bother me – I just said I don't want you to go.'

'Tough – it's not up to you. Get out of my way.'

'Why are you being like this?'

'Like what? You warned me to stay away from you, remember? Repeatedly. Go home, Bay.'

She had a point and it hurt like fuck. I had no business trying to keep her for myself. Incapacitated with despair I watched as she walked out and left me there, without looking back.

Chapter Forty-nine

I cried in the taxi on my way to work. It was awful saying those things to Bay; walking out on him like that; pretending I didn't care, when the truth was I cared far, far too much. I was furious with myself for being unable to resist him. His turning up out of the blue like that – half-naked, wild-looking and smelling so good – it was all too much. He'd grabbed hold of me without warning or hesitation; as if I was a life raft and he was drowning; his desperate need igniting my own. I wanted him so badly I couldn't see straight, think clearly, or stop him. He made me feel so goddamn alive.

But if Bay was starting to get jealous and possessive, then things had gone too far between us. One of us had to draw the line. But was I strong enough? Right now it didn't feel like it.

My shift was a struggle. I no longer enjoyed my job; I was exhausted all the time and constantly had to take extra breaks. Pavel fined me for being late, and by the time I'd paid the standard house fee my measly tips had been reduced to almost nothing.

On my return I went and sat in Bay's mother's garden for a while. The excessive heat of the last few weeks was finally gathering in dark clouds and a storm was brewing. As a refreshing breeze picked up I savoured it, along with the relative peace and quiet under the trees. Bay would be waiting for me upstairs, but I had no idea what sort of mood he'd be in. Part of me wanted to hide in my own bed and wallow alone in self-pity; I just didn't feel up to arguing with Bay; defending my actions and seeing his pain. But a bigger part of me longed to admit defeat; crawl into Bay's bed and submit, surrender, let him have his way. And that part of me worried me most of all.

Eventually a scattering of raindrops drove me into the lift and up to the top floor. Bay had left his door on the latch – a clear invitation – although something about it didn't seem quite right. I was quietly sneaking into my own flat when it dawned on me – there was no music leaking out of Bay's place; not even that low, spooky Hans Zimmer stuff.

Maybe his play-list had finished and he was so engrossed in painting, or whatever else he was doing, that he hadn't noticed? Maybe he was asleep? Reluctant to run into him, I hovered in my doorway, barely breathing, straining my ears for any noise at all, but there was only a low, menacing rumble of thunder that made the hairs stand up on the back of my neck.

'Bay?' Haunting flickers of lightning aside, it was completely dark in his flat; even darker than usual. Leaving the front door open wide I used the light from the landing to grope my way over to one of the spotlight rigs trained on the wall. Switching it on I was temporarily blinded, and as I waited for my eyes to adjust, heavy rain lashed at the windows and filled my ears. 'Bay? Are you here?' My own voice was too anxious and too loud. Picking my way over to the empty bed I turned, and that's when I saw them – his bare feet – sticking out from behind the kitchen counter.

Stumbling towards him, my stomach plummeted with dread. He was sprawled on the kitchen floor, shrouded in shadow and not moving. 'Bay?' I switched on the kitchen spotlights, and as they flickered into life the true horror of the situation was revealed in all its Technicolor glory.

He lay face down in a pool of blood and vomit. It might as well have been a lake. I'd never seen so much blood. There was a cut on his head and his skin was deathly pale. Was he dead? 'Oh God no, Bay!' Collapsing to my knees beside him I patted his cheek, relentlessly shouting at him to wake up. But his skin was unnervingly cold and he didn't react. Lowering my ear to his mouth I checked to see if he was breathing, the smell making me want to gag, and then I promptly burst into tears as I felt his shallow breath on my skin. Reaching into his trouser pocket I dragged out his mobile and called for an ambulance. While I waited for it to arrive I squeezed Bay's hand, rambling hysterically to the woman on the other end of the line about there being too much blood and too many drugs, and how I didn't want him to die...

It was some relief when the emergency services arrived and took control. While they checked him over I was instructed to gather together anything he might need for the hospital. Unable to stop shaking I gathered a change of clothes from Bay's wardrobe and toiletries from the bathroom in a daze. By the time I returned to the kitchen, the two paramedics had him strapped to a stretcher with a drip in his arm, but he was still unconscious. One of the two theorised that he had overdosed and passed out, hitting his head on the way down. But she didn't say he would be OK. She swept the prescription drugs from the counter top into a clear plastic bag, leaving behind the empty vodka bottle, Bay's credit card, a rolled bank note and a sprinkling of white dust.

They let me travel with him to the hospital. I held on tight to his blood-stained hand, silently willing him to be OK. On arrival the nurses wheeled him away and a woman asked me questions while I sat in an uncomfortable plastic chair in a waiting room full of strangers. According to his records he didn't have a next of kin, so I told her about Ash, but then regretted it and worried that I'd done the wrong thing. I was only his neighbour after all. At some point I must have fallen asleep, because I woke up with a crick in my neck and dribble on my chin.

'Bailey Madderson? You can see him now,' said the male nurse standing over me.

'What? Is he… is he OK?'

'Yes he's awake now, you can go and see him if you want.' I hugged the poor guy as I thanked him, repeatedly, overwhelmed with relief.

Bay had his eyes closed when I stepped inside the curtained cubicle. There was still a drip in his arm, but the cut on his head was hidden beneath a big bandage and most of the blood on his face had been wiped away. Instead he had the residue of something black around his mouth – charcoal maybe. They'd dressed him in a white patterned hospital gown, not his style at all, and he was covered by a sheet from the waist down. Opening his eyes, he pinned me with his green gaze and I stared back, mute.

'You look about as shit as I feel,' he croaked.

I wanted to hit him for everything he'd put me through, but it was so good to see him alive and as insulting as ever. I threw myself at him, sobbing noisily into his neck while he lay there.

We didn't speak for a long time. Even after I'd calmed down and freshened up in the Ladies', I simply sat by his bed, idly flicking through a magazine while he dozed. I was too angry to speak. Finally it was Bay who broke the silence.

'You can go if you want. I doubt they'll release me until mid-morning at the earliest.'

Setting the magazine aside I crossed my arms. 'That's it? You're dismissing me…? No "thank you"? No "I'm sorry"…?'

'Oh that's why you're hanging around – I did wonder.'

I glared at him, enraged.

'OK, what would you like me to say? "Thank you for saving my miserable life"? "I'm sorry you felt the need to call an ambulance"? What?'

His sarcastic tone couldn't disguise the raw emotion behind his words and my anger receded in a weary sigh. 'Please stop doing this to yourself.'

'What?'

'This,' I said, gesturing limply at him. 'Punishing yourself with drugs and alcohol and God knows what else. It can't have been fun, what you've just been through, so why do it? Why not get help and stop?'

'You can't ask me to change my lifestyle when you won't even consider changing yours.'

'What's that supposed to mean?'

'Stripping. I asked you not to go to work and you just—'

'It's my job, Bay! Jesus, is that what this was about? Are you punishing me because I wouldn't do what you wanted? Because you don't like the idea of other men seeing me take my clothes off?'

'No, I'm merely pointing out that you're being hypocritical—'

'No, you're trying to emotionally blackmail me to get what you want,' I said, rising to my feet. 'This is wrong, I can't do this, I'm done.' Picking up my bag I turned to leave.

'Cally…?'

His voice cracked and it was almost enough to make me turn back. But I couldn't help him; if anything I was making things worse. And anyway, drug addicts have to want to help themselves, isn't that what they say…? Gritting my teeth I walked away, shock and exhaustion numbing my emotions.

But as I was leaving the ward Gibbs and Trudy were just arriving. We all stopped, Trudy smiling uncertainly and Gibbs eye-balling me with silent accusation.

'Hello, Cally,' Trudy said.

'I'm just leaving, OK?' I held up my hands defensively. 'He's all yours.'

'You're running out on him you mean,' Gibbs muttered, a verbal punch to the gut.

'Hey, c'mon, sweetheart, that's not fair,' Trudy gently interjected. 'Cally saved his life by bringing him here, and he's a big boy…'

'If I find out that you're in any way responsible...' Gibbs began, pointing a shaky finger at me.

'OK, just leave it,' Trudy said, physically steering Gibbs past me and into the ward. For a moment I just stood there, motionless and drained, before slowly making my way back to my flat and the gory mess Bay had left behind next door.

Chapter Fifty

I was accustomed to loss. I'd lost a lot of people over the years, starting with my twin aged just six. When I let Bax die, I amputated exactly half of myself, and I'd not been whole since; I never would be, and I was used to that. I could deal. But Cally... Cally... missing her was something else entirely.

She wasn't even dead, in fact she still lived right next door, but it felt like my internal organs had been ripped out through my eye sockets – I was a husk; a ghost; a shadow in excruciating mental, physical and emotional pain. Before her I didn't know what I was missing; didn't know I could be happy; didn't know I could care so much about another person.

She was absolutely right to stay away from me, because I loved her; I'd fallen in love with her, as trite and ridiculous as that might be, and more than anything I wanted to protect her. Since being discharged from the hospital two weeks previously, I'd managed to avoid any direct contact. Instead I'd become a fully paid-up, certifiable member of the stalkers club.

Not that I followed her *everywhere*. Sometimes she snuck out without me hearing while I was listening to 'Something I Can Never Have' by Nine Inch Nails on repeat, or busy adorning canvases with her image, or trying and failing to sleep. But three times a week I dressed incognito and followed her to work; paying entry along with all the other losers and sitting at the back keeping tabs on her from afar. She seemed tired and subdued lately, something I fervently hoped was not my fault, but she never missed a shift. The way she danced at the club was different to the way she'd danced for me – less lively, less soulful, as if her mind was preoccupied and she wasn't really there. Cally was always worth watching, though; she lit up the room and was popular with the staff and the regulars, who all knew her as 'Luna'. Keeping one eye on her and the other on her fans, I silently begged one of them to put a toe out of line so that I could kill them with my bare hands. It would make me feel so much better.

Tonight I might just get my wish; there was a guy sitting eye-fucking her who had caught my attention. He looked wealthy and successful – average height, build and looks, but suited and booted and sporting an expensive-looking gold wristwatch. His smiling, non-threatening gaze was sliding casually all over her as if he was above her charms. But I knew differently. His body was strung tight with tension, his jaw twitching and his hands fisted under the table – he was struggling to refrain from touching her.

Leroy had noticed, too. The twenty-four-stone bouncer looked out for all the girls, it was his job, and Cally was one of his favourite charges. He'd clocked my interest in her from day one and acknowledged it occasionally with an amused raise of his eyebrow, but he'd known me long enough to know that harassing women wasn't my style. If Mr Flashy Rolex made a wrong move, Leroy was sure to swoop in and intervene – I only hoped he'd give me a pop at the bastard afterwards.

But the punter in question managed to restrain himself, and Cally's shift passed without incident – leaving me both relieved for Cally and disappointed for me. When she stepped down for the night and disappeared backstage to change, I followed Mr Rolex outside and took up residence in my usual spot – a shadow by the door, from where I could observe Cally climbing safely into a taxi. Ivor, the doorman, greeted me with the same wry amusement that Leroy conveyed.

'Back again, Bay? What are you, Luna's guardian angel or something?'

'Hardly,' I muttered, retrieving my fags from my pocket. 'More like a wolf baying at the moon.'

'Eh?'

I howled, just once, long and low, to prove my point and Ivor chuckled.

'You're cracked, man, seriously.'

'Yeah, probably,' I lit up. 'Just pretend I'm not here, OK?'

'Yeah, yeah, I know.'

Mr Rolex had stopped across the way to take a leak in a doorway, and I kept one eye on him, wishing he'd hurry up and leave. As I was finishing my fag, Cally emerged through the door, filling my vision. It was torture being so close and not being able to touch her. Smiling, she pecked Ivor on the cheek goodbye. 'I'm just nipping to the shop to grab a pint of milk then I'll be right back,' she said.

'No, Luna, you know the rules…' Ivor warned as she started to walk off in the wrong direction down the alley.

'I know, but I'll just be two minutes, I promise,' she called over her shoulder, hurrying away into the shadows.

'What the fuck?' I muttered, incredulous.

'I know man, but what can I do? These girls never listen to me and I can't leave the door…'

Shit. I cast an eye around for Rolex but couldn't see him. Which way had he gone? 'I've got it,' I said, discarding my fag butt and going after Cally.

Up until this point I was fairly sure she hadn't spotted me at the club; I'd been careful to stay hidden and I was reluctant to blow my cover now, but there was no way I was letting her walk an alleyway alone at 3 a.m. Staying several paces behind, I kept to the shadows, carefully side-stepping bin-bags, takeaway boxes, broken glass and anything else that might give my presence away. The last thing I wanted to do was frighten her. She had almost reached the busy main road when a man suddenly lunged out from behind an industrial-sized bin and grabbed her.

It was so awful and so precisely what I'd feared most that for a second I thought I must be hallucinating. But she yelped through the hand over her mouth as he pushed her roughly up against a wall, and my primal kill instinct kicked into overdrive. Running up I punched him in the side of the face so hard that his grip on Cally loosened immediately; his knees buckling. 'Don't fucking touch her, you fucking son-of-a-bitch!' As he went down I hit him twice more.

'Bay?! What…?' Cally was still pressed against the wall but staring at me with an expression of utter horror – the exact way I'd always imagined her looking once she discovered the real me. Now that it had finally happened, I didn't like it.

'Get in a taxi and go home like you were fucking supposed to, Cally.'

She jumped, stumbling away from me towards the street, shaking like a leaf, and I hated myself for being so blunt. Rolex was groaning and attempting to drag himself up off the tarmac, but she didn't need to see all the bloody damage I'd inflicted, so I kicked him in the gut to keep him down.

Flinching she glanced down at him, eyes enormous. 'W-what are you going to—?'

'*Now*, Cally,' I growled.

I waited while she turned, flagged down a black cab with one trembling arm, climbed in and pulled the door shut behind her. Once she'd been safely whisked away I returned my attention to the piece of shit at my feet. He'd successfully managed to sit up and was now cradling his face in his hands, his watch glinting as it caught the lamplight.

'I think you broke my nose,' he said, stunned.

'I'm only too happy to break something else if you'd like?'

'Fuck off,' he said, spraying blood over his own trousers.

Bending down, I grabbed him round the neck and shoved him back against the wall. He grunted as his head connected with the brickwork, his eyes widening in fear. 'You ever touch a woman like that again and I'll cut your dick off and make you eat it, understand?'

He nodded rapidly in acknowledgement, eyes bulging, and I released his windpipe. Once I'd wiped the blood from my palm on his tailored suit, I adjusted my tie, straightened up and walked back to the club to make damn sure Rolex would be barred from every strip club in London, for life.

Chapter Fifty-one

I woke on my own bed to loud snoring and the weight of an arm wrapped around me – my favourite arm – inked with a forest of trees stretching up to a full, pale moon.

I'd come home alone, but here he was in my flat, on my bed, bare-chested and spooning me from behind. He must have used the spare key to get in, but why? And then it flooded back. One moment I was taking a quick short cut through an alley, and the next moment I was being attacked by a man I vaguely recognised from the club. Clamping his hand over my mouth he'd shoved me against a wall with viciously clear intent. But before I'd even had a chance to process what was happening, there was Bay – a law unto himself – savage, uncompromising, and utterly sublime.

I wasn't a fan of violence. What I'd witnessed in the fight club aside, I had little first-hand experience of fighting, and disapproved of it on principal. But witnessing Bay's particular brand of swift justice up close highlighted the horror I'd have suffered if he hadn't been there to intervene. Yes Bay was unstable, stubborn and secretive and he must have been following me again without my knowledge (how else could he have been there at precisely the right moment?), but I'd never been more grateful to see anyone in my life.

Twisting my head around I looked up into his handsome face, all shadowed with grief and guilt. Finding him collapsed on his kitchen floor and fearing he might die; they were easily the worst minutes of my life so far, and I'd had a few bad moments recently. It had made me furious with him. But since we'd fallen out at the hospital, life had felt empty. I was miserable without him. Somehow, somewhere along the way, I'd fallen for this troubled man; hook, line and sinker. It was deeply unfortunate and I was determined he would never know, but there it was – I loved him.

It was only midday, I was shattered and ought to go back to sleep. But I wasn't sure how long Bay would stick around. He looked unusually peaceful as he snored into my hair – and it was so good lying in his arms, cocooned in his warm scent and the steady rumble of his breathing – I wanted to enjoy it for a while. Lightly tracing the lines of his tattoos I experienced a flashback of the punches I'd seen him throw – lightening quick and sickeningly brutal-sounding. I wanted to check the knuckles of his right hand for damage, but they were hidden under the pillow beneath his head. What had happened after I left? Did he hurt the guy some more? And if so, how badly? At the time he'd looked capable of murder, but I couldn't believe Bay would actually kill someone...

The snoring had ceased. Sensing his penetrating gaze I looked up over my shoulder to meet it, but he was almost unrecognisable. Propping himself up on one elbow Bay stared down at me looking anxious, wary, and heartbreakingly vulnerable.

'Sorry, I didn't mean to fall asleep – I just came to check you got home OK and I didn't want to wake you...' he said.

I stared at him, speechless. Bailey Madderson *never* apologised for anything.

'And I'm sorry I shouted at you like that in the alley; sorry you had to see all that. I'm *not* sorry that I was there – I dread to think what might have happened – but I *am* sorry I was sneaking around following you – I should have been open about it. Also, while I'm at it, I'm sorry for what I said at the hospital and for overdosing and letting you find me like that – it was fucking stupid and not fair to you at all—'

'Stop,' I whispered.

'Basically I'm sorry for all the shit I've put you through—'

'Stop. Talking.'

He opened his mouth to speak again and I silenced him with a kiss. His body was still pressed up against mine and as he hardened against my behind, I ached with desire. But his kiss was different from any before – hesitant, cautious, as if he was afraid to hurt me. It was disconcerting. Obviously we had important things to discuss and issues to face, but right now I was too tired for all that, I simply wanted, needed, Bay to be Bay.

He was still wearing the suit trousers he'd worn to blend in at the club. Reaching down I unzipped his fly and released him, but he was still paralysed with doubt and didn't make a move. Lifting my dress I eased down my knickers and guided him between my legs from behind, and he groaned, deep down in his chest. By flexing my pelvis I massaged back and forth along his length, tasting his growing need on my tongue. When I could stand the teasing sensation no more I broke our kiss and leaned forwards away from him, angling my hips so that he slipped effortlessly inside me; sinking deep into my core, on a long, despairing groan. With his fingers he lightly caressed my body as he took me at a languid, leisurely pace; rolling his hips with a steady rocking motion; stoking and coaxing my climax so adeptly that I felt like I was spellbound or dreaming, or floating outside of myself, safe in his arms. Afterwards we fell back to sleep, him still wrapped around and inside me, as if we were one.

But when I woke again in the evening he was gone and my skin cooled with fear. Was that a goodbye fuck? At the time it had felt natural and easy; almost unbearably so.

As I opened the bedroom door I was greeted by the smell of toast, fried eggs, and bacon.

'You hungry? I'm making breakfast,' he said.

Was there ever a sexier sight than that of the wild and unruly Bay Madderson stood butt naked in my kitchen, holding a spatula? I grinned as I made my way over to the breakfast bar and sat down. 'What are we having?'

'Egg and bacon butties. Unless you'd prefer cereal, in which case you can get out.'

I laughed. 'But I live here!'

'For now,' he muttered, returning his attention to the eggs sizzling in the pan.

'For now,' I conceded.

The butties were delicious – the bacon crisp at the edges and the eggs runny in the middle. Bay mostly ate with his left hand; the knuckles of his right looked raw and inflamed and reminded me of things I'd sooner forget. But we needed to talk about them – I still wanted to protect him from what was to come if I could.

'Last night, after I left…' I began.

'You want to know if I killed him?'

My mouth went dry. 'I wasn't going to say that.'

Bay shrugged. 'Bastard's still breathing.' A wave of relief swept through me, but I tried not to let it show on my face. 'Not that he deserves to be. I spoke to Leroy and he's on their shit list now, so he won't be setting foot inside another strip club in the city.'

'Thank you,' I said. 'For being there; for what you did—'

Bay shook his head and scowled at me. 'Don't do that – don't thank me. "Violence is never the answer", isn't that what they say?'

'Yes, but, I still appreciate it…' We fell into an awkward silence while I tried to work out what I should say. I loved this man; my reluctant hero; my dark knight… could I really push him away?

'I know you don't want a proper relationship with me,' Bay said bluntly, as if reading my mind. 'I totally get it, believe me. I still worry that your hanging out with me will somehow get you killed, even though, like you said; "that's crazy, superstitious bollocks".'

'I believe the word I used was "ridiculous".'

'Same difference. The thing is, could we just go back to how we were before? Just hang out and fuck?'

I set down my coffee, afraid I'd drop it. 'I—'

'I'll stop using,' he went on. 'I've been clean fourteen days already and, aside from a little weed, I managed three months before that. I'm not really an addict – I can stop with the right motivation.'

'I'm not giving up my job, Bay.' My voice sounded amazingly calm as I lied to him. I'd actually given Pavel my notice the night before, but I didn't want Bay to know. I didn't want him to think I was quitting for him; I didn't want to give him hope.

'OK.'

'And you have to promise to stay away from The Electric Fox.'

'Do you promise never to walk down that alleyway again; let the doormen do their job and protect you?'

'Yes.'

He shrugged. 'OK, deal.' He looked so serious. 'So that's it?'

'What?' I said.

'If I behave, we can be friends again?'

'I guess so…'

His whole face transformed into a grin so rare and dazzling it took my breath away. I smiled helplessly back, determined to make Bay smile more often.

'OK, what now?' I said.

'Now I'm taking you next door to shower, paint and fuck you,' he said, a dark glint in his eye. Warm desire pooled low down between my legs. Bay was back.

Chapter Fifty-two

'Can I get you another?' the barmaid said.

'No, I'm good.' I chucked another piece of popcorn towards my mouth, missing completely. 'One's my limit.'

She pulled a *yeah right* face at me and went back to rinsing out glasses while I refocused on my near-empty beer bottle. I didn't give a shit what she thought, that was my rule; my strategy; my coping mechanism – one drink in each bar – that was what got me through. I'd been working my way round Soho since 8 p.m. and I'd been hit on and sworn at more times than I could count, but I was almost there. Soon I'd see her again.

Cally and I spent virtually all our time together now – sleeping either at her place or mine. It was almost certainly unhealthy, living in each other's pockets all the time, but neither of us wanted to admit it. It was September, we had less than a month left together and the clock was ticking. I had no idea what would happen when Cally's contract ran out and Sidney returned, and she refused to discuss it. Another house-sitting job in London appeared to be out of the question, though I couldn't understand why. In all honesty I wanted her to stay on with me. Hell, I'd happily *pay* her to live with me, but she wouldn't consider that either.

The only time we now spent apart was while she was working, and those nights were proving tough. Trying to paint was pointless – I was too anxious and distracted and my desperation ruined the work. I'd never felt more like an addict. The temptation to ring my dealer and request two eight balls with a side-order of pills was immense. But I'd promised.

On Friday evening Felix had dropped by to let me know all my pieces from the exhibition had sold, and that he had a list of people interested in seeing more. So I'd showed him a few of my paintings of Cally – not the nude ones, obviously, those were for my eyes alone – but those of her dancing, eating, brushing her hair, just to see what he'd say. I'd never seen Felix so happy.

'You're in love, Bay,' he'd said, slapping me on the back, 'and it's going to make us rich'.

To which I simply replied: 'I'm already rich…'

But I could no longer paint on the nights that Cally was dancing at the club, so I'd taken to bar-hopping instead; staggering from one hell-hole to another and counting the hours, minutes, seconds until I could reclaim her.

At 2.30 a.m. on Sunday morning I made my way home to meet her, slightly inebriated, admittedly, but having successfully survived another weekend without stalking her, abusing narcotics, or topping myself. When she stepped out of the taxi I was waiting for her and kissed her hard, right there in the street. I kissed her all the way up twelve storeys in the lift before pulling off all our clothes and dragging her straight into the shower. In my addled state I imagined I could smell the club on her, the stench of other men's eyes on her skin, and it made me crazy. Thankfully she let me soap every inch of her beautiful body without a hint of reproach, and I knelt down and worshipped between her legs with my tongue until she climaxed, crying out my name.

By the time Cally returned from dressing next door I'd sobered up somewhat. I had Nine Inch Nails playing and the large canvas I was currently working on laid out on the floor where I could work at it from all angles. She was wearing one of my old hoodies over a pair of leggings and carrying a punnet of nectarines. The sweatshirt was her colour – a washed-out crimson – but it swamped her completely.

'Does your grandmother know you're visiting me, Little Red Riding Hood?' I said, pulling the hood up over her damp hair – she looked cute, rosy-cheeked and good enough to eat.

She laughed. 'I always preferred the wolf in that story anyway,' she said, leaning up on the tips of her toes and kissing me.

But my baggy clothes couldn't disguise the fact that she'd been losing weight. Cally had always been slim but now she was slender – verging on too thin. When I picked her up she felt feather-light and her skin was too tight over her cheekbones, wrists, and knees. I thought at first it was down to all the stress I'd caused her, but now I wasn't so sure. Some days she had little appetite, as if nauseated, though she would never admit to it.

On my bed, Cally settled herself cross-legged as if painting was a spectator sport. She held a nectarine in one hand and a small, sharp-looking knife in the other. Pausing in my work, a loaded brush in my hand, I stared as she carved the fruit into quarters, the juice trickling down the blade and dripping into her lap. Removing the stone she discarded it along with the knife, before reaching out and popping a piece into my mouth whole. The ripe sweetness exploded on my tongue while I watched her bite into another segment. Fluid escaped down her chin before she could catch it with her tongue, but her attempts had me rock-hard in my pants. Why was every single thing this woman did so damn seductive? Vibrating with barely-suppressed need, I waited as she polished off the next two pieces, but when she began to suck the sticky pulp from her fingers it became too much.

Throwing my paint brush aside I dragged her down onto the wet canvas with me and kissed her, the syrupy sweetness tasting even better on her lips. She shrieked and giggled as I peeled off her clothes, the paint sticky on her skin and in her hair. 'Hurt' played out over the loud speakers; Trent's melancholic lyrics underlining my pain as I entered her. With wet, black hand prints, I branded her body; her milky white breasts, hips, and thighs, while thrusting and grinding inside. And with her fingernails she dragged scarlet paint across my naked chest, as if clawing at my heart.

But we never fucked anymore; no matter how rough it got and no matter what we called it – I *made love* to Cally each and every time. She had become everything to me; I'd never been as genuinely, frighteningly happy as I was with her. And when I was inside her, I could swear she felt the same. Yet every exquisite, mind-melting, earth-shattering orgasm was tinged with sorrow, and I couldn't shake the terrifying feeling that, one way or another, I was losing her.

Chapter Fifty-three

He was absolutely dead on time. I'd only been sat in the coffee shop window for a few minutes, when a sleek black BMW with tinted windows pulled up to the kerb and Ashwin Madderson emerged from the back, smoothly buttoning the jacket of his navy three-piece suit. He stood the same way Bay stood; shoulders back and feet firmly spaced and planted, passers-by parting like a sea around him. I should have known that a man as rich and successful as the CEO of The Madderson Corporation, would be punctual.

But I had hoped to have a few moments to myself to prepare for this meeting; I wasn't feeling well, and being apart from Bay only made me feel worse. Having worked out my notice at the club I was free to sit in all-night diners and quietly work on my book while Bay assumed I was off dancing. But deceiving him was taking a toll on my emotions. It didn't bode well for September the twenty-eighth when I would have to move out, leaving him behind forever.

Ash clocked me as he entered, his shiny leather shoes ringing out on the tiled floor as he approached.

'Cally, lovely to see you again.' He towered over me, handsome and intimidating, one hand casually placed in his pocket.

'You, too,' I mumbled, blushing and reverting to shy mode. As he pulled up a chair and sat down beside me, the BMW glided away into the traffic and I tried to collect my thoughts.

'So what's this about? Do you want money?'

'No!' I was as shocked by his assumption as much as his directness. 'As I said in my email, I want to talk about Bay.'

'Why? Does *he* need money?'

'Not at all – why do you assume this is about money?'

'Because it usually is, but OK, if it's not that, what is it?' This wasn't going well. The way Ash was staring at me, I was starting to feel like an insect pinned to a board.

'Did you want a coffee or anything?' I gestured at the counter across the room.

'Not particularly, I'm a little pushed for time, why don't you just spit it out?'

'Actually I'd rather show you,' I said, collecting my bag and standing up. Ash's eyes narrowed with suspicion but he followed me out the door, across the street, and into the up-market gallery opposite without argument. Once we were stood in front of Bay's paintings, Ash gazed at them with a stunned expression, before moving closer to carefully scrutinise each canvas, one by one. Eventually he returned to my side, looking lost in thought.

'This is really Bay's work?'

His name was printed clearly for all to see, but I confirmed it anyway. 'Yes.'

'And the red dots…'

'They've all sold,' I said, pride creeping into my voice. He nodded. 'I—'

'Cally! It's so good to see you again, how are you?' Felix said, appearing at my shoulder and smiling warmly.

We exchanged pleasantries and he gently boasted about all the rave reviews the exhibition had received. 'Bay's not with you this evening?'

'No, I'm afraid not, but let me introduce you to Ashwin Madderson, Bay's brother.' Felix's eyebrows shot up in surprise. 'Ash, this is Felix Sandon, Bay's long-time friend and agent, and the curator of this exhibition.' The two men appraised each other as they shook hands.

'It's an honour to meet you. Your brother's exceptionally talented – you must be very proud.'

Ash was caught off guard. 'Well, yes, I am actually... yes, I am.'

'Wonderful,' Felix said. 'Well if I can help with anything, please just let me know. Cally, always a pleasure.' He bowed to me before moving away.

'You like them, then?' I asked once Felix was out of earshot.

Ash nodded. 'I think I recognise some of these trees...'

'Yes, you probably do... I don't suppose you know who the girl is?' I added on impulse.

'I would guess it's that girl Bay lived with for a while, I can't recall her name; Vanessa... Veronica... something like that. She was a singer in a rock band if I remember rightly.' Jealousy stabbed viciously at me and I mentally chided myself for it. Of course Bay had ex-girlfriends lurking in his past – he was an attractive thirty-six year-old man – and he wasn't mine, not really. I had absolutely no right feeling jealous at all... 'She died about three years ago under suspicious circumstances. I think it was ruled a suicide in the end. Bay was a suspect for a while, but he was never charged so... I guess he didn't do it...'

Ash didn't sound nearly as convinced of his own brother's innocence as he should, and it made me angry. 'You guess?'

My raised voice surprised him. 'I don't really know much about it – I was getting married around that time and the company was involved in a hostile take-over...'

'You mean you weren't there for him,' I said, trying not to shake with indignation.

'I offered my help and he didn't want it,' Ash said stiffly, an edge of warning in his tone. 'Not that I have to defend myself to you, Cally, but if Bay had been charged with anything, I would have been here.'

'OK,' I said, wondering if I should change the subject. 'Why are you trying to take Bay's home away from him?'

Ash sighed heavily and looked down at the floor. He was counting to ten under his breath and I hoped he wouldn't walk out. 'He told you about that, huh?' I nodded. 'Because it's wasted on Bay. Aside from living off the rent, an office block is no use to him. It's prime real estate, right in the heart of the city, worth billions in the right hands...'

'But he doesn't live off the rent – there is no rent.'

'What do you mean?'

'I mean he leases out those offices to charities, and only charges them enough to cover the maintenance.'

'But... that's just stupid,' he said.

'Or incredibly kind and generous.'

'So how does he pay for all the drugs, booze and women?'

'I'm not aware that he has to pay for women,' I said pointedly.

'Sorry, maybe not women, but you know what I mean. He must be getting money from somewhere.'

'Yes – the sale of his paintings I would imagine. That's what I'm trying to tell you – he's not what you think – he's not a lost cause – he's a successful artist, his work sells all over the world.'

'If that's the case I'm genuinely happy for him. But he could live anywhere and do what he does, it doesn't have to be there; and we can easily relocate the charities to more suitable premises.'

'And the garden? The trees? The memorial tree? According to Bay it's all that's left of your Mother's legacy…'

'*We* are my Mother's legacy – me and Bay and my kids. If my Mother were still alive I'm sure she'd agree we were more important than a few trees hidden away in a sentimental garden nobody ever uses.'

'You have kids? I didn't realise, Bay never said.'

'That's because Bay doesn't know.'

My mouth dropped open and I gaped at him.

'Come on, Cally, you know what Bay's lifestyle is like, artist or not, he's a drug addict – I don't want my kids exposed to that sort of thing.'

'But he's a good person. Maybe your kids would be a good incentive for him to stay clean…'

He shook his head. 'Look, I love Bay, I do, and I know he's had it tough, but I have, too; I lost a brother and a mother as well. But ever since she died, Bay's hated me. I don't know if he blames me for her death or—'

'No, he blames *himself* for your mother's death, and he pushes you away because he loves you.'

'That makes no sense.'

'I know. I think even he realises that, but it's how he feels.'

Ash shook his head again. 'So how can I help him when he won't let me?'

'You could start by listening to him – really listening to him – instead of writing him off, bullying him and making him feel like crap all the time.'

'I don't bully him.'

'No? What would you call threatening to take his home away?'

Ash left soon after that. I can't say I was surprised, I'd given him a fairly good grilling and plenty to think about. I hoped that once he'd calmed down he would consider things from Bay's point of view.

Settling in the back of a diner with my laptop, and driven by a hunch, I Googled the lead singer of Bleeding Trees. Her name was Vesper Page; she was both talented and beautiful and only twenty-six when she died. Her stage presence was distinctive – frilly white feminine dresses teamed with black boots, studded leather accessories and heavy eye make-up. There was no doubt in my mind that she was the girl from Bay's paintings. From an image search of the band I also recognised their bass guitarist; a younger-looking Tom, and another piece of the puzzle fell into place. Despite only having produced one album before Vesper's death brought their story to a premature end, the band had a loyal following.

I could easily see why Bay had fallen for Vesper, but knowing him as well as I did, I refused to believe he could be responsible for her death. That he might blame himself for it anyway, would not surprise me. As I packed up my laptop and caught a cab back to Bay, the one question that really bothered me was this:

Was he still in love with her?

Chapter Fifty-four

While she did her hair and make-up in a mirror next door in preparation for her punters, I chewed nicotine gum and searched for a pair of shoes. Why I was bothering to try and give up fags was a mystery – it wouldn't be enough to stop her fucking leaving me when the time came.

Aside from the nights when Cally worked her shifts, we'd barely left my flat in four weeks. One night I took her to see a show, and we'd been out for dinner a couple of times, but mainly we stayed in the flat, wrapped up in each other. Sometimes she watched while I worked out, lifted weights and attacked a punch bag to the brink of collapse. Then she'd lick the sweat from my skin, teasing me with her tongue until I came in her mouth. Other times I would go down on her while she tried to sleep, eat, read, or watch a movie. And I had her everywhere I could; in the shower, across the kitchen counter, up against the windows for all to see; always wanting more. We had just three more nights left together, and two of those she'd be working – it was making me sick to the point where I'd lost weight, too. The anticipation and our near-obsessive desperation was slowly destroying us.

Cally reappeared with mascaraed-eyelashes and crimson lips. 'I'll walk you to the station.'

'You don't have to do that—'

'I'm walking you to the station. Give me your bag, I'll carry it.'

Stepping closer she tipped her face up and pressed a tender kiss to my lips, her eyes locked on mine and instantly soothing the fury inside me. I sighed and she handed me her bag.

'Why's this so heavy, what have you got in here, your laptop? Why are you taking it to work?'

'You never know when inspiration might strike.'

I'd still not read any of Cally's writing, she forbade it, and her laptop was password-protected. 'You just don't trust me not to hack into it while you're out.'

She smiled up at me without replying as we stepped into the lift, the doors sliding shut behind us. Raising my fist I pressed it to where the imprint on the back wall, neatly fitted my knuckles. 'This dent is going to haunt me when you're gone. I wanted to fuck you so badly that day…'

'Why did you hold back?'

I shrugged. 'Maybe deep down I knew it would change me forever.'

Reaching out, Cally pressed the emergency stop button and the lift lurched to a halt. 'Do it now,' she said, her eyes bright.

I didn't need asking twice. As she positioned herself against the back wall of the lift with her legs spread I let her bag slide to the floor, spat out my gum, unbuttoned my fly and took my cock in my hand. I was ready for her – I was always ready for her – and I could tell she was ready for me, too. It was clear from the way her eyes burned as they followed the movement of my hand; it was written in the flush of her skin, the parting of her lips, the increase in her breathing and the tightening of her nipples.

Lifting her skirt I took my sweet time removing her knickers; I liked hearing her beg, and the devil in me wanted her to be late for work. Grazing her thighs with my fingertips I kissed her thoroughly; teasing her and making her whimper. What we did to one another – the effect we had on each other – was punishment in its most pleasurable form. As I pushed my fingers up between her legs she moaned just like that first time, right here in this lift; suspended between our shared world on the twelfth floor and the real world outside. She was so stubborn that night – hell, she was still just as stubborn now.

As she lifted one long, limber leg high up over my shoulder in open invitation, I calmly withdrew my fingers and sucked them – patiently savouring the delicious taste of her while she implored me with her eyes.

'Now, Bay, please.'

My cock jerked at her words and I couldn't refuse. She guided me to her entrance and without hesitation I slammed into her, pinning her to the wall of the lift with one, deep, feral thrust. Her eyes rolled back as she groaned and shuddered with satisfaction, her body clenching around me as if welcoming me home. Grinding into her I circled my hips to be certain she experienced every inch.

'You feel that?'

'Yes.'

'I'm going to fuck you hard, Cally; you're going to feel me here inside you while you dance for them.'

She closed her eyes. 'Yes.'

The lift shook as I took her; ruthlessly drove her to a screaming climax, and filled her with my seed.

'So stubborn,' I muttered into her hair afterwards, holding her in my arms and listening to her heartbeat thump against mine. We didn't speak as I walked her the few short metres to the tube station. What was there to say? I didn't want her to go to the club and she knew it. At least this time she wasn't angry that I'd made her late.

'Try not to drink too much,' she said, as I kissed her goodbye at the barrier. But I didn't reply; I could make no more promises. Helplessly I looked on as an escalator carried her away out of sight.

Emerging back onto the street I chucked my pack of nicotine gum into the nearest bin. I lit up a fag and headed back in the other direction to start my pub crawl.

'Bay!'

Glancing around I spotted my brother and wished I hadn't. 'Fuck off, Ash.'

'Look I'm sorry, OK? I'm here to apologise – I never should've sent that letter – I should have talked to you about it instead.'

'Damn right.' I kept walking but he kept pace with me.

'You have to admit – you're not the easiest person to talk to.'

'Just fuck off, I'm not in the mood for this.'

'Please, Bay, let me buy you a pint, several pints if you like, you're my only brother after all…' It was starting to rain and the apparent sincerity in his voice piqued my interest.

'Whatever.'

We were on our second pint in The Blackfriar when my curiosity finally won out.

'So why are you back, don't you live in the states anymore?'

'I've been overseeing a large acquisition – I won't bore you with the details – but it has been worth the visit. I fly home in the morning.' Setting down his glass he shifted against the bar to face me. It was standing room only on Friday nights, especially wet ones. 'I saw your paintings.'

This was the last thing I'd expected him to say, and I suddenly found I couldn't look at him.

'They're really good, Bay – more than good – I mean I'm obviously not an expert, but even I can see how talented you are. I met your agent and he said the critics were loving your stuff, and Cally said—'

'Cally? You spoke to Cally? When?'

'A week ago when she showed me your work. She asked me to meet her at the gallery, and I'm glad I did 'cause it really opened my eyes. She said some things that made me think.'

'What things?'

'Things about you and me – things I needed to hear. Look, I haven't been fair to you and I'm sorry.'

I shrugged and signalled the barman for another round of drinks by waving a twenty at him.

'I want you to come to LA.'

'What? Why?'

'I want you to meet your nieces.'

I stared at him as he pulled out his wallet, flipped it open and showed me a photograph of two small, dark-haired, green-eyed angels.

'This is Olivia, who has just turned two, and Isobel who's seven months.' My hand shook as I studied the picture. Of course Ash had kids, and of course he'd kept them from me – I was a monster and they were innocence personified. 'You can see our mother in them, don't you think?'

I nodded, swallowing the lump in my throat. 'Why now?' I said, handing the photo back.

'I just think it's about time, don't you? Livy loves to paint, maybe you could teach her…?'

I snorted and took another gulp of beer, but deep down the idea appealed.

'Bay, about that letter…'

'Have it, take it all, I don't care.'

'You *do* care, and rightly so, but listen, we're happy to buy it from you at market price. And we can relocate all the charities that are based there at the moment – find them alternative premises that are still low-rent and fit their purposes. We can even cover all their moving-costs, it's not a problem.'

'And the garden?'

'We keep the garden, but why not open it up to the public? We could make it a place for Londoners to escape the stress of the city and eat their sandwiches. It would enhance people's quality of life, and should increase the value of the surrounding properties. The Isabella Madderson Memorial Garden; what do you think?'

'You've given this some thought.'

He nodded. 'Well…? Should I start getting plans drawn up?'

'Knock yourself out.'

'I'd expected more of a fight.'

'I have other things on my mind.'

'Cally?' he raised his eyebrow.

I scowled at him over the rim of my pint glass as I took another mouthful of lager, but I couldn't deny it.

'Have you told her?' he said.

'What?'

'That you love her.'

I rolled my eyes. Was it that obvious? First Felix and now my brother; did everyone know? 'There's no point – she's leaving next week.'

'Where's she going?'

'I don't know.'

'Abroad?'

'I don't know.'

'How long for?'

'Forever.'

'Even more reason to tell her.'

'I'm pretty sure she already knows, she just doesn't care.'

'If there's one thing I know for sure, it's that that girl cares about you. Why else would she be showing me your paintings behind your back? Maybe she just needs to hear you say it; know you're committed. Women like to be clear on that stuff.'

'What makes you a fucking expert?'

'Hey – I'm just trying to help – she seems like a nice girl, if a little confrontational for my taste…'

I smirked. 'Gave you a hard time did she?'

'She looks so shy and unassuming!'

I laughed and Ash did too, it felt surprisingly good.

Then he looked me in the eye. 'Don't lose her over a misunderstanding.'

*

'Bay, what are you doing here?' Ivor was hunched in the doorway, sheltering from the rain.

'I've come to see C— Luna.'

'Luna…? But she doesn't work here anymore.' I stared at him and he pulled an apologetic face and shrugged. 'She quit a couple of weeks ago…'

'Fuck,' I muttered under my breath.

Chapter Fifty-five

I was staring vacantly at the blank screen of my laptop, when I sensed someone enter the diner and make a beeline for me. At the sight of him my heart lurched painfully in my chest. He looked cold, wet, and angry.

'Why didn't you tell me you'd quit? Why are you hiding from me?'

Raindrops sparkled in his hair as Bay glowered down at me, and the hurt behind his words tugged at my soul.

'I'm sorry,' I said, my voice a whisper.

'Don't tell me you're fucking sorry, just answer me.'

'Hey, I won't have any trouble in here,' the guy behind the counter warned. 'Either calm down and sit down, or take it outside.'

Bay flashed him a look that could kill, but when I reached out and took his hand, the fight went out of him. Pulling out the chair opposite he sat down heavily, shoulders slumped.

'How did you find me?'

'There aren't many places that stay open all night.' Bay eyed my coffee and then ordered one for himself with a bark. When it was brought over Bay took a sip – scalding hot, black, and without sugar. 'Why won't you tell me where you're going next week?'

Withdrawing my hand from his I tucked my laptop safely into my bag without reply. I was afraid my evasion would make him angry again, but what could I say? Certainly not the truth.

'I love you,' he said, his voice unexpectedly loud and blunt, causing other people to turn and look. I spontaneously burst into unladylike tears. 'I know you don't want to hear it, but it's the truth,' he said, passing me a flimsy paper napkin.

Desperately trying to regain my composure, I wiped at my eyes and nose, hating myself for causing a scene and wishing I was somebody else; someone luckier, stronger, braver. Before Bay I was never this emotional; never prone to tears.

'It doesn't change anything, does it?' his voice was dry, his eyes unblinking.

I shook my head and blew my nose and he leaned forwards in his seat, bathing my face in his unrelenting gaze.

'You're afraid of me, is that it...?'

He was throwing me a lifeline; an easy way out and though I was ashamed of myself, I took it. 'Yes,' I said, meeting his eye. 'Were you ever going to tell me about Vesper?'

He blanched, his eyes widening and jaw tightening.

'I can't stay with you, Bay; this was only ever supposed to be temporary – you know that.'

'Yes,' he whispered as if winded, collapsing back into his chair, the light fading from his eyes with a bleak acceptance that was hard to witness.

With a trembling hand I drained the last dregs of my cold coffee while Bay simply sat, slumped and staring at the floor. Despite all my best intentions, I'd ended up breaking the heart of the one person I cared about most.

'We still have a couple of days, right?' his voice was defeated; he wouldn't even look up at me.

I nodded.

'Let's just go home.'

'OK.' Forcing back my tears I paid for our drinks at the counter, pulled on my coat and followed him outside.

We made love for the rest of the night. I lost count of how many times – we simply stayed in Bay's bed and devoured each other for bitterly-sweet hours on end, without arguing or flirting or even talking. It was torture; the sorrow-laden desire in his eyes and his every touch so intuitive, reverent and resigned. I wept each time I came, I couldn't seem to help it, but Bay kissed the tears from my eyes without commenting on their hypocrisy; without pushing for an explanation or laying any blame. He held me like he loved me, pathetic tears and all.

As day dawned, the city woke and Bay finally grew weary and spent. While he slept I studied him; listening to the steady pulse of his heart, breathing in great lungfuls of his scent and trying to memorise every line, curve and detail of his handsome face. How could he possibly believe I was afraid of him? I trusted him completely. I would never love anyone as intensely or as deeply as I loved him – he was my everything, my all.

It was time to go.

Chapter Fifty-six

Before I was properly conscious, before I'd even opened my eyes, I knew she was gone. She was no longer in my bed, that much was obvious, but somehow I knew that she wasn't anywhere in the flat or next door either. Cally had finally left me – packed up and vanished two days prematurely. I didn't want to believe it at first. I kept my eyes squeezed shut and told myself it wasn't true, but after a while the silence screamed her absence.

When there was no reply at the door to Sidney's flat, I let myself in with the spare key. The place was immaculate – she hadn't left in a hurry – she must have been packed for days. There was no note and I couldn't decide if I was disappointed or relieved. In the bathroom, catching a faint whiff of her perfume, I hated her – hated the sadistic bitch for doing this to me – making me fall in love with her and then leaving a fucking great hole in my existence – as if my life wasn't riddled with enough holes already. The mirror above the sink shattered in a cobweb effect where my fist connected with it, crimson splashes of blood decorating the clean white ceramic of Sidney's suite. But I couldn't feel it. I doubted I'd ever feel anything ever again.

*

A voice called my name and I blinked and shivered. The lights of late-night London shone like stars beneath my feet, under a black sky heavy with cloud. It was drizzling, and as the wind gusted around me the moisture

317

on my skin felt sharp as ice. How long had I been sat up here on the edge? I vaguely remembered climbing the stairs to the roof, but I usually only made this journey once a year on April first; the anniversary of Vesper's death. She was down there somewhere waiting for me; calling to me. But it was September. I was clearly fucked.

The wind snatched the fag from my hand and it dropped away into space, quickly swallowed up by the gloom. With stiff fingers I picked up the open vodka bottle beside me to take another swig, but then I heard my name being called again and hesitated. Was that was a bloke's voice…?

'Bay! Here you are! What the hell are you doing up here? It's bloody freezing.'

Shifting slightly to look over my shoulder I recognised Tom approaching me across the roof, dressed in his delivery uniform, a package under one arm. 'How did *you* get in?'

'The door to the street wasn't shut properly – lucky it's only me.'

Shrugging, I knocked back vodka, savouring the burn.

'I tried your door and then Cally's and then I noticed the cold draft coming from up here…'

The mere mention of her name made me wince.

'Great view,' Tom said, gingerly lowering himself to the roof edge beside me.

Once he was seated he crossed his arms for warmth and gazed around, casually swinging his feet back and forth above the void below, as if he hadn't a care in the world. Couldn't a guy contemplate suicide in peace?

'Where is Cally tonight anyway?' he said turning to me.

My hand automatically strayed to my chest as if I'd been stabbed. 'She's gone.'

'Gone wh—'

'I don't know where, she's just fucked off!' I snapped.

'OK… and you're sitting up here getting wasted because…?'

I looked at him, incredulous. 'Isn't it obvious? Because she's calling me. She's down there calling to me, can't you hear it?'

'Who, Cally?'

'No! Not fucking Cally – Vesper. This is where she did it, she jumped from here and that's where I found her; down there; impaled in the trees, blood everywhere…'

Tom looked uncharacteristically solemn as he looked at me. 'Vesper's not down there, Bay, and she's definitely not calling you.'

'I drove her to it.'

Tom shook his head. 'You're not to blame for her death. I don't know what happened between you two; why you fell out or whatever, but Vesper… she'd suffered with depression all her life. She'd done it before – tried to do it in all sorts of different ways – before you even knew her. Each time she somehow sweet-talked the hospital into discharging her, but she never stuck to her follow-up appointments, or her medication. I think it was only ever a matter of time before she succeeded.'

'She'd tried before…?'

'Yeah – you remember all those leather cuffs and bracelets she always wore on her wrists? That was to hide the scars. She'd tried other ways, too...' Tom shook his head to dispel the memories.

This new information stunned me into silence. How had I not known that Vesper suffered with depression? Why had no-one ever mentioned it? If I'd known I could have been so much more careful. Covering my eyes with my hand I groaned.

'Look, what I'm trying to say is, Vesper wouldn't want you to throw yourself off this building – she loved you. And I'm pretty sure Cally does too, man.'

I sighed heavily, exhausted from the sheer weight of guilt on my back. 'No.'

'Yes. Seriously man, tell me you're not going to let a woman like that get away?'

'Don't you think she's better off without a bastard like me?'

'First off; you're not half as bad ass as you like to think you are...'

I glared at him and he laughed, holding his hands up in mock surrender.

'Don't push me off, OK, I could be wrong, but you've been a good friend to me over the years; sticking up for me with Dad, bailing me out when I got arrested... and you've got to admit, getting us that record deal was pretty amazing...'

Shaking my head I gazed out towards the horizon. 'I just had the right contacts, you guys did all the work.'

'Whatever; my point is, you're not all bad, OK? And secondly; Cally's crazy about you – I saw that for myself up close and personal – you can't fake passion like that.' An image of the two of them together reared up in my head, making me grimace. Tom rushed on. 'What I mean is, the woman clearly loves you, but maybe she isn't sure you feel the same? Maybe she's just testing you – maybe she hoped you'd fight for her – after all it's not like the great Bay Madderson to walk away from a fight is it?'

'For fuck's sake,' I muttered. 'She knows how I feel – I told her and it didn't make any difference – she still left.'

'So then track her down and *show* her, and then if she still won't take you back, well, at least you tried, right?'

'Mmm… maybe,' I lifted the bottle to my lips again. Tom put a hand out to stop me and then quickly withdrew it when I glared at him.

'You might want to sober up and let that crap clear your system before you go after her – you stink.'

'Clear off you little shit.' I rounded on him and he laughed, carefully shuffling backwards, away from the roof edge.

But I didn't take another drink. The kid was right; I never gave up this easily when I wanted something; I was stubborn to a fault and too selfish to be a martyr. Why not find her and show her I was serious – give her one last chance to reject me again? After all, it couldn't possibly hurt any worse than it already did.

Tom followed me through the fire exit and back down to the warm, dry emptiness of the floor below. Without Cally it no longer felt like home. While Tom roughly dried his hair with a towel and complained about the damp seat of his trousers, I signed for the parcel of pigment he'd brought and filled the kettle. He clocked the battered state of my knuckles but wisely refrained from commenting.

'So, how are you going to find her?' he asked cheerfully, steaming mug of coffee in hand and eyes bright with excitement.

'Good question,' I grunted.

Chapter Fifty-seven

It was peculiar being back in Wildham. Everything looked exactly the same; the green verges, clipped hedges and tidy front gardens; all so very welcoming and familiar, but shrunken somehow; as if I was viewing it from a distance. The sensation made me feel dizzy. Head down, hair flying, and a rucksack on my back, I walked quickly across town from the train station, dragging my suitcase behind me.

Reaching the town square I started to feel faint and perched on a bench to catch my breath. The seat was damp with drizzle. People of all ages mooched in and out between the shops, many of them wearing brightly-coloured waterproof jackets, or clutching umbrellas and pausing to greet one another, regardless of the weather. I'd missed Wildham so much – had been looking forward to seeing it again – but now that I was here I couldn't summon any feelings of joy or relief, only grief.

'Cally!' a familiar voice called out to me through the rain. 'You're back!' Silently I berated myself for stopping to rest; of all the people I could have bumped into…

'Hey, Liam,' I said, squinting up at him. 'I'm just visiting, actually – Marguerite…' I hadn't yet thought up a plausible excuse for being here and my sentence tailed off.

Glancing down at the suitcase at my feet, my ex looked unconvinced. 'Don't you see enough of her in London?'

I smiled and looked down at my hands, at a loss for more lies. 'How are you?'

'Good thanks – busy. How about you? Are you feeling OK? You look a little…'

'I'm great! Really. I'm really good,' I forced a smile, my cheeks straining, my teeth gritted together holding back everything I was keeping from him.

He stared at me for a long moment and then shook his head. 'Take care, Cally,' he muttered as he walked away.

It was after two when I reached Marguerite's one-bed flat above the card shop. I hadn't really expected her to be home on a Saturday afternoon, but she was, and I all but collapsed in her hallway as she greeted me with surprise.

The time had come and I told her everything – about the doctor's diagnosis at the hospital, about my reasons for running away, about all the fun I'd been having over the past six months, and about Bay. It was strange to finally admit it; how he made me feel; how hard I'd fallen for him and how devastating it was to leave him behind. My words poured out in an almighty torrent, as if they couldn't wait to leave my ailing body, punctuated only by occasional hugs and endless cups of tea.

Marguerite took my news surprisingly well under the circumstances. She was upset, obviously, and chastised me for not confiding in her sooner; I'd "handled it all appallingly badly" in her opinion. But in due course my steadfast best friend insisted that I must stay with her and declared that "everything will be OK". True or not, it was exactly what I wanted to hear.

Now I was hunched over her coffee table in the early hours of Sunday morning, trying to compose a letter. I'd been listening to Lana Del Rey's 'Summertime Sadness' through headphones for hours and I was exhausted, but couldn't sleep. My body clock was a complete mess – I'd grown used to being up all night and sleeping during the day like a bat, or more accurately, like Bay. The camp bed Marguerite had kindly set up for me in her bedroom was narrow and uncomfortable – not to mention that she snored like a sow with blocked sinuses. But honestly I had too much on my mind to sleep.

My doctor, relieved to hear from me at last, had pulled some strings and got me booked in for urgent tests, first thing Monday morning. He wanted to assess the spread of the disease so that treatment could finally begin. The next few months were going to be hell, but I was too emotionally drained to feel scared – I just wanted to get on with it. Now that I was no longer in denial, my brain tormented me with thoughts of all the things I was losing by dying early – the places I'd never visit, the friends I'd never make, the books I'd never write, and the children I'd never have. In our six years together, Liam and I had never discussed having kids, and I'd not given it much thought, but knowing I would *never* have them was crushing.

These stark realisations had been queuing up in the shadows of my mind for months, just waiting for an opportunity to bombard me. But even these gloomy ruminations were preferable to thoughts of Bay and the time I would lose with him.

Missing him was a physical, all-consuming, soul-destroying *thing*, more potent than I could ever have prepared for. We had grown far, far too close – I could see that now – the fact that we had no future, that I'd kept secrets, refused to admit I loved him, and ultimately walked away from him, made no difference at all – he had become a part of me. Knowing him had altered me so irrevocably that I was no longer whole without him. And that made me anxious. Did he feel the same? Where was he now? What was he doing? Was he safe or was he slowly sabotaging himself with a cocktail of drugs and alcohol?

Ash had returned to LA and I didn't have contact numbers for any of Bay's friends. Should I call the tattoo parlour and ask Gibbs or Trudy to check on him? I'd already Googled the number, but if Bay was coping alright without me, their intruding concern would simply add insult to injury. Maybe I should give him the benefit of the doubt – Bay would get over me in time...

The same thoughts, fears, and arguments chased around my head in a relentlessly loop, so I was trying to focus on something productive instead: composing a letter of explanation to my parents.

Of course it was a cowardly way of doing things; I ought to break the news in person, but I simply didn't have the time or energy for a trip to Spain. I hoped a hand-written letter might be less jarring than a phone call or email; hopefully I could downplay matters, reduce any sense of urgency and manage their expectations. Plus the snail mail would give me time to wrap my head around my test results before they inevitably arrived; I had no doubt that Mum and Dad would be straight on the first plane over here to kick up a fuss – and when they did, I'd be glad to see them.

Abandoning my pen on the blank white page, I moved over to the living room window, drew back the curtains and peered up at the sky. But it was a dark, cloudy night; spots of fine drizzle flecking the glass, and all celestial bodies hidden from view. One glimpse of the moon was all I'd wanted; to reassure myself that I hadn't just dreamt the last six months; to feel closer to Bay; to convince myself that he was alright. But the rain only fell harder – the night as dank and as bleak as my heart.

Chapter Fifty-eight

'SIDNEY!'

'Jesus! Bay.' Sidney clutched his chest with both hands. 'You nearly gave me a frigging heart attack!' He had a key in the door and two large, wheeled suitcases stationed either side of him. 'What are you doing lurking there like that? Were you lying in wait for me or something? Some welcome home! You shouldn't have – really.'

'Welcome back,' I said grudgingly.

'Aren't you usually asleep at this time of day? Hey, are you alright? You look even worse than usual…'

'Shut up for a second, will you? I need the name and address of the house-sitters you hired.'

'Why? What's happened? Oh lord, what have they done?' He paled as he spoke, hurriedly unlocking the door and pushing his way inside.

'Nothing – everything's fine – I just need to talk to them.' But Sidney wasn't listening, he was too busy casting an eye over his house-plants and then counting his beloved fish – making kissing sounds at them through the side of the tank. 'Sidney…?'

'Yes, righto,' he said distractedly, checking both the bedrooms and then wandering into the bathroom. 'Holy hell, what happened in here?'

'Oh, shit I forgot about that – don't worry it was me – I'll get it fixed.'

'What'd you do, pick a fight with yourself?' Sidney said, backing away from the gory mess of blood and broken mirror and glancing down at my right hand.

'Something like that – I'll get it sorted, OK? I really need that information, Sidney.'

'Alright, alright, keep your hair on. I've just got here; I've just spent twelve hours travelling halfway round the planet and I'm jet-lagged. I could really do with a cup of tea, a chocolate digestive and a hot bath...'

'*Now*, Sidney,' I growled.

He sighed huffily and returned to the landing to wheel his suitcases inside. I watched with barely-contained impatience as he closed the door, carefully laid one case flat on the floor and unzipped it. 'Oh, it's not in this one – it must be in the other one...' When he finally extracted a slim folder of information I snatched it out of his hand and quickly flicked through it as I made my way back next door. 'You're welcome!' Sidney called after me.

*

Marguerite looked exactly as I remembered – a small, curly-haired sprite with a stick up her arse and eyes that said "what the hell are you doing in my office?" so that she didn't actually have to say the words out loud Pursing her lips she raised an eyebrow at me as I towered over her desk.

'Just tell me where she is.'

'She doesn't want to see you, Bay.'

'I won't hurt her – I just want to talk to her – I give you my word.'

'That wasn't... that isn't...'

'What?'

'It's not like that.'

'What's that supposed to mean? What is it like?'

'You love her, don't you?' She sounded more sympathetic than I'd expected and her question caught me off guard. Unwilling to admit my feelings to her and unable to deny them, I simply glared. But the answer must have been written all over my face because Marguerite slumped in her chair with a sigh, dropping her defences along with her perfect posture. 'She's trying to protect you.'

'From what?'

'From more pain,' she said flatly. My gut twisted with unease. It was disconcerting seeing a woman as thorny and intractable as Marguerite look so defeated.

I snorted. 'That's ridiculous.'

'Is it?'

'I don't need protecting by anyone – especially not by you.'

'You don't think she can hurt you?'

'She's already hurt me,' I snapped, the truth ringing painfully in my ears.

She nodded thoughtfully. 'Cally wants to do this alone; she wouldn't even let me stay with her today... but... I told myself that if you turned up...'

'Just tell me where she's hiding. I'm not leaving this office until—'

'She's sick,' she interrupted. 'She's at the hospital getting more tests done, but... you need to prepare yourself, Bay. She might be dying.' Her voice cracked on the last word, tears welling in her eyes and I stood there, swaying slightly, overcome with horror as my darkest fears were confirmed. Deep down I'd suspected she might be ill for weeks – I hadn't wanted to believe it. But dying...? My legs gave way and I sank heavily into a chair, my head in my hands, my heart breaking. Not again. This couldn't be happening again. Would it never fucking end? Death had been stalking me my whole life, stealing everyone closest to me; my twin, my parents, Vesper... as if punishing me for something. And now Cally...?

'Which hospital?' I croaked.

Chapter Fifty-nine

He stood defensively in the doorway to my hospital room; feet planted, hands shoved in pockets and scowling – his dark eyes shimmering with unshed tears. At the sight of him my pulse soared, my blood rushed in my ears and my heart tightened in my chest. God I'd missed him. We'd been apart forty-eight agonisingly-long hours, and I'd never known misery like it. But here he was in Wildham. Bay had found me. Secretly, selfishly, I'd hoped he would.

But he looked angry, and rightly so. I swallowed several times before I was able to speak. 'I was sick before I met you, so don't even think about trying to blame yourself for this. It isn't your fault.'

'You should have told me,' he growled, making the hairs stand up on the back of my neck. Prowling towards the bed, gaze fixed on mine, he looked more lupine than ever in his dishevelled, unshaven state. 'You could have been getting treatment all this time, instead of fucking about with me.'

'But I was happy fucking about with you.' As he loomed over me I shifted against the pillows at my back. 'I've felt more alive in the past six months than I ever did in the thirty years before that.'

'You still should have told me,' he said, his jaw rigid with hurt.

Instinctively I reached out and took his left fist and the familiar feel of him sent a shock-wave of emotion through me. 'I didn't want you involved in all this.'

'But I *am* involved – I'm involved heart, body and fucking soul,' he said, his confrontational tone morphing into despair.

Traitorous tears leaked out of my eyes. 'I'm sorry – I never meant for that to happen – I never wanted to add to all your pain.'

'What pain? I was doing just fine and dandy before you came along.' His smile was more of a grimace and didn't reach his eyes.

'You know that's not true – you're still grieving for your last girlfriend...'

He frowned.

'Vesper,' I clarified. 'You didn't kill her; I know that because I know *you* – you're a good person. And yet you blame yourself for her death. You're still in love with her, aren't you...?' Comprehension dawned on his face as he stared at me. Here I was asking him the one question I didn't want to know the answer to, in a last, feeble effort to push him away, while my entire being was screaming at me to grab hold of him and never let him go.

'No... Vesper wasn't my girlfriend; she was my sister; my half-sister in fact.'

I blinked at Bay in surprise and he finally broke the intense eye-contact between us and sat down on the edge of my bed, huffing out a long breath. He kept hold of my hand and tightly laced his fingers through mine. 'Tell me,' I said.

'Haven't we got more pressing things to talk about?'

'I want to know.'

He sighed again, resigned. 'When Dad died I found these photographs hidden away in an envelope – nineteen of them. They were all of the same girl; one for each year of her life as she grew up. It didn't take me long to figure out that Dad had cheated on my mum sometime after Baxter died, and that the woman he had an affair with, Valerie Page, had been sending him pictures of their daughter, Vesper, ever since.'

'I'm sorry.' I squeezed his hand in sympathy and he returned the gesture. 'Do you think your mother knew?'

He shrugged. 'I don't think so, I don't think Ash does either, but I was curious to meet my sister. She was easy enough to track down through Facebook – she was living in London and the lead singer in a rock band, so I befriended her and her band mates.'

'Like Tom,' I murmured.

'Yeah, Tom played bass for the band – Bleeding Trees – they were actually really good...' He tailed off.

'So... how did Vesper feel about having a half-brother?'

'That's where I really fucked up. She had no fucking clue,' he said bluntly. 'I always intended to tell her eventually. I just wanted to get to know her first, see what she was really like, before I dropped the bombshell. She'd never known who her father was and didn't seem to care, but she was great y'know – she was fun and we had loads in common. We hung out, got high, and when she needed a place to stay I let her crash at mine. That was when I should have told her – right then – I had no idea that she might develop feelings for me; it never crossed my fucking mind.' Bay rubbed irritably at his jaw with his free hand as the last pieces of the puzzle finally fell into place.

'She fell in love with you.'

Bay nodded. 'It was awful. One minute we were getting wasted and the next she was trying to kiss me, and it was like some nightmarishly bad trip. I pushed her away and blurted out the truth, just like that, in the worst fucking way imaginable – told her she was my sister and that she couldn't possibly feel that way about me because that would be sick and twisted. I was a complete fucking bastard. And then, to top it all off, having rejected and humiliated her, I just fucked off out and left her all alone…'

'And that's when she…'

Bay swallowed and nodded again, still avoiding my eye. 'I found her in the garden – she'd jumped off the roof and landed in the trees – a broken branch went right through her…'

'I'm so sorry,' I whispered.

'I didn't know she'd tried to do it before; I never knew she had a history of it; if I'd known…' he tailed off bleakly. 'I'll always blame myself. I handled things badly. I didn't know her very long, but I really cared about her.' He turned to me at last, his expression weary. 'But, you are the only person I've ever loved like this, Cally. I can't even explain how much I love you…'

'Don't,' I said, fresh tears springing to my eyes. 'I love you, too.'

He raised a sceptical pierced eyebrow. 'Even after everything I've just said?'

'Yes. Of course. You know I do.'

His eyes bored into mine as if he desperately needed to believe what he'd surely known, on some level, all along.

'But you have to stop punishing yourself,' I said. 'You'd never intentionally hurt someone you cared about, and, ultimately, you're not responsible for other people's actions. You have to let go of your guilt or it's going to destroy you.'

'What's the point – losing you would destroy me anyway.'

Pain lanced through me and I closed my eyes, hating myself all over again. How could I have dragged him into this?

'Tell me what we're dealing with.'

'You don't know?'

'Marguerite said it was cancer and that it might be terminal, but I want to hear it from you.'

Looking down at our joined hands I traced the worn cuff of the battered leather jacket he was wearing. 'Back in March I went to my doctor because I was having some irregular bleeding. I thought it might be something to do with the pill I was on, but after giving me a physical and taking blood and urine samples, she referred me here for more tests. An ultrasound showed a tumour in my womb so they did a biopsy and sent off for the results. On April first, the gynaecologist told me it was cancer. No joke.'

Bay's hand tightened around mine.

'He said I'd need more tests before they could begin treatment to determine the stage and see how far it had spread. But I didn't keep the appointment – I ran away to London instead. I know it was stupid and reckless, but I

336

was frightened. You have to understand, my life before I met you was no life at all. It was safe, quiet and boring – I ate, slept, worked in a call centre… I never went anywhere or did anything. The thought of enduring months of chemotherapy and dying before I'd even lived was unbearable…'

'So… you don't *know* that it's terminal – you're just jumping to conclusions.'

'OK, but even if it doesn't kill me, I'll have to have a hysterectomy – I won't be able to have children, Bay. *Ever*.' My voice broke and my vision blurred with tears and I kept my head down; I couldn't face him. I had no idea if Bay ever wanted to be a father, but he needed to know it was never going to happen with me.

'Cally, Look at me.' His voice was gruff with emotion. I shook my head but he lifted my chin with the fingertips of his other hand. The expression in his eyes as they met mine was so loving, so sincere, that it only made me feel worse. 'I'm sticking with you through this, OK? There's still hope.'

I shook my head again. 'I'm going to be sick for months; I'm going to lose all my hair…'

'So what? I'm not going anywhere – you're always saying how lovely Wildham is, and with Ash developing The Tower I need a new place to live.'

'But I don't want you to see me like that.'

'Tough shit.'

Despite everything, he made me smile. Reaching over beside the bed he passed me a box of tissues. Unwilling to lose the physical connection between us, I dried my eyes and blew my nose one-handed. The clinical gown the nurse had insisted I wear made me feel distinctly unattractive, condemned, entirely at the mercy of strangers. But the familiar weight of Bay's hand in mine was profoundly comforting. 'You really like Wildham?'

'Cobbled town square, two pubs and a garden centre, what's not to love?'

I snorted, more pleased than I wanted to admit. 'Actually, a man was shot dead at the garden centre a week ago by a hitman for the Russian mafia.'

Bay's mouth dropped open. 'You're kidding.'

'Nope. Marguerite just told me.'

'How the hell did that happen?'

'It's a long story – I'll tell you later.'

Bay looked back at our linked hands. 'So what happens now? More tests?'

'Yes. They've already given me a pelvic exam and taken more samples. I think they're going to give me another ultrasound next.' I gestured at the sonography equipment lurking in the corner of the room. 'I hope it's soon because I'm not supposed to empty my bladder until after the scan and I'm bursting for a pee.' Bay smirked but didn't comment. 'Then I've got to have another biopsy, and a CT scan, MRI, PET... I don't know; a whole load of acronyms...' Bay released my fingers to rub his face with both hands. 'You look exhausted, have you had any sleep?'

He shook his head. 'My bed feels all wrong without you.'

I swallowed, determined not to cry any more. 'Lie down here,' I said, shuffling sideways and patting the bed next to me.

'I don't want to hurt you.'

'You won't – I'm not suddenly made of glass.'

With a glance towards the door, Bay shrugged out of his jacket, kicked off his trainers and lay down beside me. Drawing me close into his body, he enveloped me in his distinctive smoky scent, suffusing my body with warmth from head to toe.

For two days I'd thought I'd lost him – that I'd never experience being held by Bay, like this, again. A whimper of relief escaped my lips as I pressed my face into his chest and he hugged me tighter. We lay like that for a while, not talking. By focusing on the steady, soothing beat of Bay's heart I tuned out the busy sounds and smells of the hospital – the bustle of other patients and nurses, the ringing and beeping of phones and equipment, the stench of disinfectant and illness.

It seemed miraculous that the man I loved was really here and willing to journey through Hell with me, despite the losses he'd already endured, and even knowing I had no future to offer him; only pain. If he wasn't so obnoxious he'd be a saint. But the idea of dying and leaving him all alone still worried me.

'You should tell Ash about Vesper,' I said.

'Yeah, maybe.' His breath was warm in my hair.

'She was his sister, too. I know you're afraid of losing him – I know you think you're cursed, but it's not true. He's your brother... let him in; let him help you.'

'He told me what you did. You went behind my back and showed him my work.' I held my breath wondering if he was angry. 'I have nieces. He wants me to fly out to LA and meet them.'

Drawing back my head I smiled up at him. 'That's wonderful – are you going?'

'Yeah, once you're well again – you can come with me.' He smiled and kissed me lightly on the mouth.

'Bay—'

'C'mon, if a free trip to LA isn't an incentive to get better, I don't know what is.'

His smiles were so rare and precious that I was reluctant to lose this one by being stubbornly pragmatic. And I loved the idea of the two of us flying off to America together – it was a vision far more appealing than reality. Instead of arguing I kissed him back, but slower this time, and we lost ourselves in each other; revelling in our togetherness, no matter how temporary it might be.

Chapter Sixty

The doctor did a double-take as he swept into the room – he wasn't expecting to see two people on the bed. A short, compact sort of man with a receding hairline, he donned a neatly-knotted, expensive-looking, cerulean-blue tie beneath his clean white coat. Giving me an obvious look of disapproval, he cleared his throat while I disentangled myself from Cally's embrace and climbed off the bed. It might have irked me if I wasn't so afraid of him or, more accurately, afraid of what he was about to find lurking inside Cally's body.

'Hello, Calluna, I'm Doctor Whitlow, I've come to do your sonogram.'

'Hi,' she said quietly.

'If you'd like to wait outside, there are some seats further down the corridor...' With the terror ringing in my ears it took me a second to realise he was addressing me.

'I'm staying,' I said, squeezing Cally's hand tighter.

'I'm sorry but—'

'Please, let him stay,' Cally said. 'I want him to stay, please...?'

'You're sure?' he said sternly.

Cally nodded and Whitlow conceded without further argument. As he wheeled the ultrasound equipment closer to the bed and faffed about setting it up, I just stood there ineffectually. He asked Cally to raise her gown to expose her stomach, and my chest ached. Her lovely tummy – smooth, soft and creamy, punctuated by the delicate whorl of her belly button and a small freckle near her ribcage – so familiar; so perfect. It seemed inconceivable that such a beautiful body could be harbouring such a dark, ugly secret.

'I'm going to apply some lubricating gel now; I'm afraid it will feel rather cold,' he warned. As the doctor applied the probe to Cally's skin I couldn't watch – it was too scary; too bitterly ironic. Most couples had ultrasounds for happy reasons; in order to see their baby for the first time, not to stare death in the face. I turned back to Cally and her bright eyes latched onto mine, instantly steadying me. Whatever the results, however long she had left, we would spend it together, just her and me. I would be strong enough for both of us, no matter what.

Whitlow was quiet as he worked – gently manipulating the probe, scanning, tapping at buttons on the machine – seemingly oblivious to the intense anxiety that filled the room like a toxic smog. At least he had the screen angled away from us; the horror hidden from view. Holding on to Cally's hand, I stared into her wide Prussian-blue gaze and gently stroked her hair; focusing on how good it was to be near her and resolutely blocking out the screaming in my skull.

Eventually, after what felt like an hour but was probably less than half that time, the doctor cleared his throat.

'OK, I don't know quite how to tell you this…' Cally and I wrenched our eyes away from each other to look at him, her fingernails digging into my hand. 'I've identified the remains of the original tumour, and I can't find any evidence of any others. So that's good news.'

'Remains?' Cally's voice was hoarse.

'Yes. It seems that the original mass in the wall of your womb, instead of growing as we would have expected, has actually shrunk in size and all but... disintegrated.'

We gawped at him, speechless, like two of Sidney's fish.

'Obviously we'll need to do more tests to confirm and to make sure the cancer hasn't spread to anywhere else, but the signs are looking good.'

'But... the nausea, the weight loss... why...? How...?' Cally began.

'Good questions,' Whitlow said with a smile. 'I think it may have something to do with the fact that you are pregnant. Approximately twelve weeks I'd say.'

I couldn't breathe or swallow, let alone speak. I gaped in shock, trying to register what was being said and failing entirely.

'What...?' Cally breathed. I glanced at her and her face was as white as the sheet beneath her, eyes wide with alarm.

The doctor calmly rotated the monitor screen around towards us. 'It's widely known that pregnancy hormones – oestrogen, progesterone and so on – have various beneficial effects on some women and can actually improve their health,' he said, making further adjustments to the machine. 'Some pregnant women experience relief from diseases such as psoriasis and rheumatoid arthritis. It seems that in your case, getting pregnant may have shrunk your tumour.' As he reapplied the probe to Cally's stomach the screen flickered into life and a shape emerged out of the grainy shadows; a recognisable shape; a foetus.

Cally clapped her other hand over her mouth and began to shake. I suspected she was crying but I couldn't move, couldn't take my eyes off the image on the screen; a head with a prominent little nose, a rounded stomach and jerky little limbs kicking with life – my child.

'I think you should sit down – you look like you might keel over.'

Again it took me a moment to realise the doctor was talking to me, but he was right, my legs had turned to jelly and I felt light-headed; completely stoned. With one hand I dragged a chair closer to the bed, while Cally clung on to my other, and then collapsed heavily into it.

'You're the father, I take it?' Whitlow said.

In a daze I turned to Cally for confirmation and she nodded, tears cascading down over her cheeks. I passed her the box of tissues and she extracted one with trembling fingers and wiped ineffectually at her face. 'Sorry, I'm sorry,' she muttered and I reflexively drew her hand to my mouth and kissed her fingers, still at a loss for words.

'It's quite alright,' he said. 'This must be a shock for you – it's a lot to take in.'

'Is… is the baby OK?' Cally whispered.

'As far as I can tell at this stage, yes, everything looks perfectly normal and healthy.'

We exchanged a look, Cally and me. Her nose was running and tears dripped off her chin, but her mouth curved up into a tremulous smile which seemed to make my heart lurch into life in my chest and start beating again. Was this really happening? Was she going to live? Were we really going to be parents? God I loved her...

'There's just one more thing that I need to tell you and then I'll give you some time alone,' Whitlow said.

Mentally bracing ourselves, we turned back to the doctor in unison. He re-adjusted the probe and the image on the screen shifted, disappeared and then reappeared in reverse. For a long moment he looked at us expectantly while we gazed blankly back.

'Twins,' he said at last. 'You're expecting twins.'

Epilogue

Carefully I pick my way along the frosty pavement with my head down and my chin tucked into my scarf; my breath condensing in the wool. As I hurry from one patch of lamplight to the next, my mind is back in the doctor's office; his words swirling around my head on repeat.

I was on my own to receive the news this time; Bay wasn't there to hold my hand as he was when the radiologist announced my pregnancy three and a half years ago. But I only have myself to blame. Nowadays our relationship is based on trust and honesty rather than secrets and lies, but old habits die hard. To protect Bay, I kept this particular appointment from him and attended it alone.

Inserting my key in the front door I hear shrieks and squeals coming from inside, making me smile. Hanging my scarf, coat, and bag in the hall, I take a deep breath before pushing open the door to the living room.

Despite the Victorian splendour of our London home, the reception rooms are reminiscent of Bay's old apartment with its high ceilings, exposed brickwork and bare floorboards. But his vast, wall-mounted oil paintings lend a rich sumptuousness to the rooms, and I've furnished them with colourful furniture to provide a family-friendly atmosphere.

With a roar, Bay rises up from the middle of the floor; a small, pyjama-clad boy dangling from each tattooed arm. Ryan and Reece giggle hysterically, clinging like monkeys as Bay – aka the Big Bad Wolf – stalks around the rug barefoot, growling and pretending to shake them off. Their obvious happiness makes my heart swell almost painfully in my chest.

'Mummy's home!' Reece spots me first, detaching himself from his dad and barrelling head first into my shoulder as I crouch to catch him in a hug. His twin is never far behind, and I hold them both close, savouring their soft, milky warmth as they chatter about their day.

It's good to be home.

After only a couple of minutes they are off again – Ryan chasing Reece across the room and under the dining room table; a den full of cushions and toy cars. As I straighten up, Bay draws me into his arms and kisses me. He smells of wood smoke and baby shampoo and tastes of chocolate ice-cream.

'Mmm, you boys have had your tea, I take it?'

He smirks. 'We saved you some dessert. Where are all your bags? Don't tell me you spent all afternoon shopping and didn't buy anything.'

'I did get something, but I'll show you later.'

'That sounds promising.' He nuzzles my earlobe but before I can respond there's an almighty crash. We part to find one of the dining room chairs pushed over on its side and the twins looking startled and sheepish.

'He did it!' Reece says defensively while Ryan hides behind a cushion.

'OK, bedtime,' Bay says, righting the chair and chasing the boys towards the stairs. 'Whose turn is it to choose a story?'

As the stampede of feet recedes upstairs I collect up various toys that lie strewn across the floor, deposit them in a toy chest and draw the curtains against the icy night. In the kitchen I start off the dishwasher, wipe down the breakfast table and then pour two glasses of wine. Taking one with me I leave through the back door and pick my way across the moonlit garden to where two out-buildings nestle side by side in the shadow of an oak tree.

What with being a mum, working part-time as a choreographer, and having a book published, I've never been busier. My 'Guide to Late-night London' is selling in airports and bookshops across the globe. A personal, and often tongue-in-cheek, take on the city, it reads more like a blog than a guidebook, but if the Amazon reviews are anything to go by, people appreciate my informal style. Mel, my publisher, is pushing me to write more books on different cities around the world, something I'm keen to do if I live long enough.

But I've not yet found time to utilise my beautiful dance studio. The single-storey brick-built building was habitable enough when we bought it, but Bay has had extras installed: a fully sprung floor, a mirrored wall, a barre, frosted windows, a surround-sound music system, a changing room, and even separate secure access to the street behind. The project was his gift to me – as if his companionship, twin sons, and a whopping great multi-million pound home weren't enough. My intention is to teach; to run a variety of dance classes and workshops and bring the space to life, but in the meantime it sits waiting in readiness.

By-passing my studio completely I let myself into Bay's instead, curious as ever to see what he's been working on. The converted garage retains a raw industrial feel, but the same comforting aromas that I always associate with Bay surround me as I warm my hands in front of the wood burner. Switching on a lamp and pressing play on his music system, I'm pleased when the languid strains of Portishead emanate out into the space. On the daybed in the centre of the room I sit down to view his latest canvas – a riot of colour, texture and movement that will almost certainly resolve into a picture of the boys at play.

Bay's portraits always have an abstract quality and an edginess to them – a sense of his mood or that of the subject, or both. But thankfully his work has lost the disturbing melancholic darkness that used to haunt it. The faces he paints are almost photographic in their accuracy, and his professional services are permanently in demand. Felix has endless lists of patrons eager to commission Bay to immortalise them on canvas; he need only name his price. But Bay is Bay; it isn't about the money. The sale of his office block to The Madderson Corporation has left us more than provided for, and he'll only ever paint people he likes.

With the dawn of fatherhood, Bay has finally been lured into the daylight. He still, on occasion, stays up all night and then sleeps the morning away like in the old days, but it's rare, as he hates missing out on time with me and the boys. Bay's new wild and uncompromising passion is simply being a family man.

'If I have to read 'The Three Little Pigs' one more time, I'm gonna start smoking again,' Bay says, ducking into the studio and closing the door behind him. Despite the chilly conditions he's barefoot, with a glass of wine in one hand and a baby monitor slung at his hip like a gun in a holster.

I smile. 'Did they go down OK?'

'Yeah, they're pretty knackered; they've had a busy day tearing around the park.'

A low murmur of nonsensical chatter drifts out of the monitor and Bay unclips it and sets it down on a cluttered table top. Crouching down he opens the door of the stove and chucks in two extra logs. They hiss and flare as they catch light, and I gravitate closer. Straightening up, Bay pulls me into his arms and I hold him tight, resting my head in the hollow between his jaw and his shoulder, closing my eyes and inhaling his scent through his T-shirt. We stay like this for a long time, just holding each other.

'I have a confession to make,' I say at last.

'Mmm?'

'Those tests I had at the hospital, to check for my cancer...?' Bay stills beneath my cheek, his heart-rate accelerating in his chest. 'I went back today and got the results.'

'Without me?'

I glance up at him and the anger in his eyes can't mask his fear. 'I'm sorry; I didn't want to ruin your birthday.'

'I don't give a fuck about my birthday, you know that.' He takes a step back away from me. 'You should have told me.'

'I'm telling you now,' I say gently.

Setting down his drink he rubs his face with both hands. The boys have stopped chuntering and fallen asleep, and in the gap between two songs, the silence is loaded. 'Tell me.'

'I'm still in complete remission.' Bay closes his eyes, his features slackening with relief. 'They couldn't find any tumours or any trace of the cancer; not even in the blood work. I don't have any more appointments booked. In fact, unless I start experiencing symptoms, I don't have to go back for re-testing for three whole years.'

'Thank fuck.' Bay tugs me back into his embrace, squeezing me, his voice gruff. 'You're really in the clear?'

'There's no guarantee, but the signs couldn't be any better.'

He kisses me on the mouth and I can taste his fear receding, mingling with the wine and morphing into desire. My hands slip underneath his shirt seeking the warmth of his body and he lifts and drags it off over his head. With my eyes I devour the hard planes and taut muscle of his chest, while my fingers trace across his skin and linger on the letters inked over his heart that spell out my name. Seeing it there still brings tears to my eyes, as does the tattoo of the boys' names at the pulse point of his right wrist.

'I'd be lost without you. You saved me,' he says, taking me in his arms, the heat of his body rousing my nerve-endings. I sigh and he runs the tip of his tongue down my neck, his breath making me shiver.

'It's you that saved me. If you hadn't got me pregnant when you did...'

'Don't...' he growls in warning, the low vibration of his voice making me ache.

'I'm sorry I went back to the hospital without telling you.'

'Forget it. Best birthday present I ever had.'

'Does that mean you don't want the gift I've got for you?' I tilt my head back and smile up at him.

He grins wolfishly, almost blinding me with happiness. 'I'll take whatever you can throw at me, Cally, you know that.'

Reaching into the top of my dress, I pluck a folded sheet of paper out of my bra and offer it to him. 'Sorry it's not wrapped.'

His eyes narrow, a curious smile hovering on his lips before he snatches it from my fingers, opens it and scans the text.

'Four tickets to LA!' I say with glee. 'I thought it was about time we took a holiday. I've cleared it with the doctor, and Ash of course. Him, Marcie and the girls, they're expecting us next week – they can't wait to see the twins.'

'Fuck, you are devious,' Bay mutters before kissing me again, harder this time and with intent. Letting the booking confirmation drop to the floor, he grabs my bottom and pulls me roughly up against him, the solid length of his erection digging into my lower belly. 'I love you,' he mumbles against my lips.

'I love you, too,' I breathe, as he eases me backwards onto the bed and slowly lifts my dress.

THE END

Grace Lowrie

Having worked as a collage artist, sculptor, prop maker and garden designer, Grace has always been creative, but she is a romantic introvert at heart and writing was, and is, her first love.

A lover of rock music, art nouveau design, blue cheese and grumpy ginger tomcats, Grace is also an avid reader of fiction – preferring coffee and a sinister undercurrent, over tea and chick lit. When not making prop costumes or hanging out with her favourite nephews, she continues to write stories from her Hertfordshire home.

Safe with Me

An emotional and evocative story about the deepest bonds
of friendship.

Abandoned as children, Kat and Jamie were inseparable
growing up in foster care. But their bond couldn't protect
them forever.

From a troubled upbringing to working in a London
greasy spoon, Kat's life has never been easy. On the
surface Jamie s living the high-life, but appearances can
be deceiving.

When they unexpectedly reunite, their feelings become
too intense to ignore. But as secrets come back to haunt
them, are they destined to be separated once more?

Proudly published by Accent Press

www.accentpress.co.uk